See what critics a
of Readers Fav
Barbara Oliverio:

"Scintillating and refreshingly original….there is more to this romcom than meets the eye as Oliverio cannily entwines the joys of cooking and love with the sustenance found in the sanctuary of family."

Bookviral.com

"…all the ingredients for the perfect romcom…fascinating characters who spring from the page with their energy… interesting settings that are clearly depicted for us… lots of fun, dollops of anguish, and a well thought out and executed plot."

Readers Favorite

"…a wealth of fantastic and hilarious characters…"

Novelgrounds

"This was a good first book from the author, and to top it off we got some authentic recipes provided in the back."

Mrs. B's Books

"…just the thing to take my mind off the wet, windy, wintry weather raging outside my windows last weekend."

BondiBookGirl

"Great debut. Barbara Oliverio thrills readers with a recipe of humor and a crisp storyline…I loved it, loved it."

Chicklitpad.com

"Reading about the cruise made me want to take another one (it's been 8 years). The fun, formals and frivolity of a cruise are well-portrayed in this charming book."

Window on the World

"Overall, Barbara Oliverio has again delivered a fun, easy-going and thoroughly enjoyable romantic comedy; I can't wait to see what she comes up with next!"

"A Spoonful of Happy Endings"

Passports and
PLUM BLOSSOMS

Passports and Plum Blossoms:
An International Romantic Comedy

Published by Scolapasta Press, Ltd.™
Denver, CO
719.339.6689

Library of Congress Control Number: 2015914635

Oliverio, Barbara
Passports and Plum Blossoms:
An International Romantic Comedy
Barbara Oliverio

ISBN 978-1-517208677

       1. Romance
       2. Comic Fiction
       3. Humor

This book is printed in the United States of America

Passports and
PLUM BLOSSOMS

An International
Romantic Comedy

BARBARA OLIVERIO

DEDICATION

For all the little girls who sit on their step reading about faraway places and dreaming about going there – I was you. See, you'll get there.

And for Darby. You'll be in my heart, always

ACKNOWLEDGMENTS

My overwhelming thanks go, as always to my late parents who gave me my life, my Roman Catholic faith, and my blue-collar work ethic. Thank you to my big brother John who always has been and always will be my champion and who understands that to be an Oliverio means that the truth never gets in the way of a good story. Thank you to my extended family. Thank you to all the readers of my first two books who believe in my ability as a storyteller and want to read more PG-rated books featuring characters that can be witty and current without compromising their values.

Xie Xie (thank you) to the wonderful tour guides in Xi'an and Beijing who helped Darby and me navigate the beauty and wonder of those cities and to all of the strangers in Singapore and China who loaned bits and pieces of themselves to some of the scenes in this book. (Yes, we did sit family-style with an international mix of people to eat chili crab, but no, there was no flying sauce.) Most of the historical and geographical information in this book is accurate; my apologies for bending any minor facts to fit the story.

Thank you to the great crews at the coffee shops and sandwich shops in the Denver area who patiently refill my iced tea cups as I sit in the back booths madly typing away on those days that I need to leave my own home office when I am writing my books.

Thank you to the powerful team that turns my scribbles into real live books: Susan Hindman and Val Gyorgy for awesome editing and cover design, and the rock stars that are Polly Letofsky, Andrea Costantine and Gail Nelson. To be an independent publisher is to appreciate the intricate workings of the entire process and the necessity of a good team.

I couldn't do what I do without occasionally bending the ear of some great people as I bounce title, plot and other ideas: Thank you Nancy, Krista , Maryanne, Christine, Margaret and other folks that I may have buttonholed all along the way. (Carolyn Clingman and your Book Club – you rock!)

Finally, the lion's share of acknowledgement must go to my favorite traveling companion, the man who understands that binge watching the Hallmark Channel is research, the man who doesn't bat an eye when I come home smelling like men's cologne from the department store because I'm trying to define a character, the man who understands that I'm not talking to myself but that I'm testing dialogue out loud, the man who patiently packs and unpacks book materials into my car and assists at my table at my book events — my own leading man, Darby.

CHAPTER ONE

"More champagne?"

"Just leave the bottle."

The well-trained waiter barely hesitated as he unwrapped the white linen from the bottle of bubbly and set it on the impeccable tablecloth in front of me, but I did detect a slight smirk as he turned to walk toward the bar to retrieve another bottle and continue his journey around the room.

The four pairs of eyes surrounding my table were not as careful in concealing their judgment.

"What?" I challenged as I refilled my flute.

"Nothing," said one of my tablemates, Elizabeth, the non-confrontational type who couldn't even be drawn into a discussion earlier of whether the vinaigrette or the honey mustard was the better choice for dressing. She quickly turned to her husband. "John, I see Wallace over there. Shall we go say hello?"

They were up and moving across the floor, swallowed in the group of laughing wedding guests as the dance band played yet another reception favorite.

"And you two?" I faced my brother and sister-in-law. "Shouldn't you be sliding electrically or something?"

"Annalise," Nicky began, in that older brother tone, which was ironic considering I was the older by a staggering two years.

"Don't start with me," I waved him off. "Even you have to admit this is the cherry on the cake's icing. Coming to *this* wedding of *this* couple, only to hear that *this* bride has just been offered a position with *that* company. It's just too much, Nicky!"

The echoes of this perfect storm of chaos were still abuzz in my ears.

"Ladies and gentlemen," the adoring groom had begun moments before as he pulled his beloved to the microphone after the traditional toasts, champagne flutes in hand. He looked dashing in his mourning coat. Tails, of course. She in a creamy, off-the-shoulder, intricately embroidered gown that called to mind Jackie Onassis or Princess Kate.

"Ladies and gentleman," he had repeated. "I am so proud to call this beautiful woman my wife. But this amazing lady continues to astound me. During the planning of this wedding, she managed to not only interview for but land a job with one of the top marketing firms in Denver. Please raise your glasses to the youngest director of marketing at the BCB agency!"

The room burst into applause.

Except for me. The only other person who had been a candidate for that marketing position.

"We didn't know he'd make that announcement, sweetie," said Nicky's wife, Amanda, as she pulled my thoughts back to the moment. "Look, no one else knows that she beat you out for the job."

"Oh, I'm sure it will get around," I said and clumsily leaned my chin onto my fist with my elbow propped on the table. I was not one to drink much, so my one glass of champagne had quickly gone to my head.

"Let's just take that before you hurt yourself," Nicky said as he gently pulled the champagne bottle from my hand and replaced it with a wedding cookie.

"What's this?" I frowned.

"You know that Nonni would tell you to eat something and then everything will be better."

I couldn't help but giggle. Our late grandmother had been old-school Italian and believed that any problem could be solved with a heaping plate of pasta. My good mood passed quickly, though.

"Nicky—" I began, but just then our parents returned from their circuit of table visits and began chattering.

"Well, isn't this a nice wedding!" my mother said as she sat importantly. "The ceremony was beautiful, even if it is in a mountain resort hotel instead of a church."

"Marie," said my father as he dabbed perspiration from his brow, "the bride's people are not our people. You know that if it had been Annalise's wedding—"

He stopped, glancing at me, realizing his error.

"What, Pop? Another reminder that I'm still single?"

"No, darling, it's not that …" He looked to my mother for assistance.

"Annalise …" My mother's tone was practical rather than soothing. "You know your father was just pointing out a simple fact and not trying to hurt your feelings. If and when it's your turn, it will be your turn and that's that."

If? Thanks for the vote of confidence, Ma.

"Well. I guess there has to be at least one single girl to try to catch the bouquet," I quipped.

"Speaking of which, I think they're getting ready to do that now," Amanda said. "The wedding planner is gathering people together. Gosh, she's pretty enough to be a model."

I glanced over at the wedding planner, who managed to look stunning in her professional navy suit with her sleek blond hair caught up in a smart chignon.

"Her husband manages this resort," Nicky said, pointing to the tall man with tousled brown hair and sapphire eyes who was consulting with the captain of the dining room crew.

"I hear they met when she managed an event on a cruise ship where he was the director," Ma said.

Great, I thought, even the event planner at this wedding managed to have a fairy-tale romance!

"I'm not going out there to try to catch that particular bouquet," I crossed my arms and pouted, my own hazel eyes blazing.

"Gypsy." My father put his arms around my shoulders and gathered me to him, using the pet name that only he was allowed to use. "My sweet Gypsy. If you don't want to, you don't have to. It's not important."

I looked into his hazel eyes that mirrored mine and decided, what the heck, it's just a silly wedding custom. Sliding back my chair, I smoothed down my olive green lace cocktail dress to join the other laughing singletons.

"One … two … three!" the bride laughed and hiked the bouquet over her shoulder. As if it were aimed, it passed directly over my outstretched hands to the woman behind me who had barely even reached for it.

Yep. I should have known that would happen. Even though she hadn't planned it, this woman had unwittingly taken everything I wanted. Including my boyfriend, whom she had lured, snatched away, and, just today, married.

CHAPTER TWO

"Annalise, are you up here?"

The voice of my best friend, Rory, echoed as she climbed the stairs to search for me in my childhood bedroom at my parents' house.

"Where else would I go?"

For days following the wedding, I had made very few forays any further than my room. My mother had managed to get me cleaned up enough to attend Sunday Mass—no one stays home from Mass in Maria Fontana's house—but otherwise I had a very limited circuit within the house that included my bedroom, the bathroom, and the kitchen for supplies of comfort food. My very traditional mother also insisted that I eat dinner with the family every night, but the minute I could escape, I slumped back upstairs, my bunny slippers making a sad flapping noise with every step.

Rory bounced into the room, then immediately halted when she saw me. The scene was obviously a lot worse than what she expected.

"Annalise?" Her tone was hushed, as if she had entered a hospital room.

"Huh?" I answered without looking at her, one of my arms wrapped around a tub of Rocky Road ice cream while I used a Double Stuf Oreo as a very effective and edible scoop. Cookie crumbs decorated my cheeks, and I'm pretty sure there were even some embedded deep in my hair, which at that moment did not shine with its usual natural deep chestnut glow. My outfit for the day (week?) consisted of a pair of Nicky's old Batman pajama bottoms, decidedly saggy at the behind, topped with a tattered hooded sorority sweatshirt generally reserved for yard work or house painting.

When she didn't respond, I looked up and saw her face, which was aghast at my appearance.

"So, did my mother summon you from New York to try to talk some sense into me?" I asked, crunching extra loudly. After college graduation, Rory pursued her journalism studies with a fellowship at Columbia University in Manhattan, and followed that with working at the trendy *It's Fashion!* magazine where she was currently an associate editor. At the same time, I had landed an opportunity in the marketing department of a multinational corporation whose US headquarters happened to be in the Mile High City. We managed to keep our childhood friendship alive and shared our experiences—large and small—via phone, text, Skype, and as many visits across the country as possible.

Rory hesitated but opted for the honest approach.

"She did call me, but honestly, you've been so out of touch recently that her call came only about a split second after I had already booked a flight home."

Moving the detritus from the foot of my bed, she plopped down cross-legged and waited. Many years of friendship had taught her that if she pushed, I would just crawl into an uncommunicative shell, so it was just best to wait for me to speak.

I put my ice cream tub on my nightstand, wiped my hands on my sweatshirt, leaned back, and burst into tears. Rory jumped over to my side and hugged me.

She let me cry until my tears slowed, then said finally, "All right now, use your words."

"I … he … she …" I began helplessly.

Rory rocked me and said, "Well. That's a start, I guess. Pronouns are always good."

I sniffed loudly.

"C'mon, Annalise, let's have it." Rory searched in vain for a tissue box on my nightstand and finally leaned over to find the roll of toilet paper that I had been using to mop up tears for the past several days. I pulled off a length and blew my nose.

"Well, you know how I was totally over the fact that Dylan and I broke up and that he was with Martie Williamson?"

She was silent.

"What?" I dared her to contradict me.

"Um. So you're finally admitting you are over that?"

"Didn't I have to be, being as how they were … oh, I don't know … GETTING MARRIED?"

She rolled her eyes.

"Well … Annalise, sure, you might have been able to tell other people that, but you forget that I've known you since we were in kindergarten in Sister Frances's class. I've seen you more than once blink those big eyes innocently while you were lying your behind off. You weren't over him as quickly as you told people."

I blew my nose and unsuccessfully began, "Well …"

"Well, nothing. Come on, admit it. You two may have broken up quite a while ago, but when she moved here three months later and you found out that they were dating, you weren't exactly calm about it."

I picked at my comforter and didn't reply.

"Then when they got engaged, you didn't take that too well either, did you?"

"Hey, I have never said anything bad about her!"

Rory's eyes scrunched as she crossed her arms.

"What?" I challenged.

"Uh. You once said that the way she chooses to wear her hairstyle is as if God had not created taste."

"That doesn't sound like me!"

Rory hit me with my stuffed Mickey Mouse.

"It sounds exactly like you because it WAS you!"

"Hey!" I grabbed the doll and hugged it to me. "Don't take it out on Mickey."

Rory continued, "I'm not judging you. Actually, that was a pretty funny comment you came up with. I'm just saying you may like to think you got over him quickly, but you really didn't. What I don't understand is why you took a chance on bringing all that up again by going to the wedding."

I hugged Mickey closer and wiped an encroaching tear from my eye with his ear.

"I don't know. My parents have been friends with his parents forever and they invited the whole family and it would have been a whole thing if I wouldn't have shown up. I mean, we broke up so long ago, you know?"

"Yep," she conceded. "It would have looked strange, I guess. I'm just sorry I wasn't in town to, I don't know, go along to make snide remarks about the bridesmaids' dresses or something."

She reached over to the nearly empty bag of cookies, retrieved two and handed me one. We crunched as we pondered for a moment.

"That really wasn't the problem, Rory," I said finally. "It was the fact that he announced that he was so proud of the fact his fabulous bride had this new job. You know, the one I had applied for and was, I thought, the final candidate for? I know, I know, he probably didn't know she beat me out of it, but it felt like it. There she was, freakin' superwoman, living my life. Well, my life with a worse haircut."

Rory stared at my hair pointedly. My 'do was decidedly bedraggled since I had pulled my long tresses up into a lazy washerwoman topknot from which random pieces hung lankily into my face.

"Oh, you know what I mean." I waved her off. "My hair is usually cuter than this."

"Well, I would say that YOU are usually cuter. Have you seen yourself in a mirror?"

"Hello?" I threw one of the other stuffed animals that I had surrounded myself with at her. "I'm going through a tragedy here. A little sympathy, please?"

I could feel tears starting again.

The unwitting teddy bear sailed back toward me.

"Look, I've got all sorts of sympathy for you, but it's not the end of the world. Don't you think you've wallowed enough?"

I stared at her.

"What? You've been here exactly a nanosecond and you think I've 'wallowed' to use your word 'enough'?"

She sat on the edge of the bed and ran her fingers through her own russet hair prettily.

"Yes. And I stand by my statement. C'mon, Annalise, would you really have wanted to stay with him?"

"Well, no …"

"So it doesn't matter who he ended up with, right?"

"Well, yes …"

"And didn't you tell me after the final job interview that you weren't really sure you wanted that job anyway?"

"Well, maybe …"

"So. Maybe this was all for the best."

Humph. She really ticked me off when she was right.

And she had a point. Sure, I didn't enjoy hearing that I didn't get that job, and I REALLY didn't like hearing that I didn't get it in exactly the way I heard it, but when you get right down to it, I only wanted it because I had been out of work for so long and had been on so many interviews that it was more a matter of taking the first offer that came along.

Six months ago, my whole department had been laid off, and I had been pounding the pavement looking for a job ever since. In high tech, marketing is always the first department to be let go and the last one to be staffed back. To top things off, my roommate in our trendy Highlands bachelor-girl apartment moved out without notice. I wasn't able to find a new roommate in time to renew the lease, but luckily, I was able move back in with my parents in the suburbs. All in all,

I felt like I was moving backward in life, not forward. While I was job hunting, I even worked part-time as a waitress at the same restaurant where I had worked so many summers during college. What next? Go back to high school?

So … was that marketing position actually my dream job, or was it just an escape plan?

"I hate it when you are right, Rory."

"Then you must always hate me," she punched me in the shoulder.

I wanted to cry but smiled tentatively. My family had been very supportive, but I guess I just needed some extra perspective from my best friend.

"So, what do we do now?" she began in that tone she always adopted when she was in planning mode.

"We?"

"Annalise, we're best friends, right? What else would you expect—oh, come on, I thought you were done crying!"

"You made me cry, you goof, because you are so YOU!"

She smiled. "Wouldn't be any other way. Okay, let's get organized here. First order of business I'd say is definitely a shower for you, Miss Stinky. While you clean yourself up, I'll get rid of those disgusting clothes and clean up this pigsty."

CHAPTER THREE

"Well, who is this pretty girl?"

My mother's sweet tone was one she usually reserved for children and the elderly.

"Did you forget what I looked like so soon, Ma?"

My words may have been clipped, but I crossed the kitchen and hugged her from the side as she stirred a giant pot of aromatic spaghetti sauce on the stovetop.

"Mmm. Meatballs or sausage?" I queried.

"Both," she answered as she slipped a few onto a plate for Rory and me. "I'm making sauce to take to your father for the Knights of Columbus social night tonight."

Rory wasted no time moving around the kitchen retrieving the necessary items for us to make ourselves sandwiches with the savory meatballs. She was as comfortable in our kitchen as one of Ma's own children.

"She looks pretty good all cleaned up, doesn't she, Mama Fontana?" she said, tossing me packets of cheese and roasted peppers from the refrigerator as I sliced bread from the breadbox.

My mother wiped her hands on her apron and came to sit beside me, pushing my overgrown bangs behind my ears.

"I'm glad to see you looking more like yourself, sweetheart. But what is this outfit you have on?"

Rory had managed to discard my sloppy hoodie and pajama pants while I showered, but when I tried to find something to wear, even after only a few days on my calorie-laden diet, everything in my closet was, er, a little snug. I was in yoga pants and a mismatched tunic that, frankly, was not draped as loosely as it should have been. My long, wavy hair was squeaky clean, but I had done nothing more than pull it into a quick braid that hung down the middle of my back.

"Too many Oreos, I guess," I shrugged as I sliced meatballs and sausage onto the bread, garnished them with liberal triangles of cheese, and topped it all off not only with peppers but several rounds of salami for good measure.

"Are you sure it was just the Oreos?" Rory asked, as she gracefully folded exactly one meatball and two roasted pepper slices into a slice of bread to make half a sandwich.

"What?" I said around a huge bite. She remained silent, but glanced at the tribute to Italian foods I had fabricated, which was at that moment dripping down my hand, forcing me to lick my wrist in a most indelicate manner.

"What?" I repeated with a bit more force.

Realization dawned.

"Oh, no, you're not going to deny me a sandwich, are you?"

"Sandwich, no," she paused. "Entire meal for a family of four, yes."

I tried to appeal to my Italian mother, the one person I could count on who wouldn't deny me the right to eat, but she had disappeared into the pantry to retrieve a cardboard box in which to place the giant pot for transport in the car.

"Look, Rory, you're not going to food-shame me into thinking I need to be a size zero. You know I'm a curvy girl." I pointed to my hips, inherited from my southern Mediterranean ancestors.

"Curvy is one thing, Annalise. But working on cardiopulmonary disease is another." She shook her head and continued. "You've obviously been eating your emotions and have piled a little extra weight onto your delightfully curvy frame very quickly. I'm just saying you need to slow it down, that's all."

I looked down into my hands and saw how difficult it was to keep together the monstrosity I had concocted. It was worthy of a challenge on the *Man v. Food* show. She was right. If I continued on the path I'd started after the wedding, I would be a candidate for a heart attack before I turned thirty. I know my Nonni and my mother would encourage me to eat, but even they were prudent women who knew that balance was the key in life.

Fine. I was just about to deconstruct my masterpiece when my mother walked back into the kitchen to sit at the table with us.

"Ma, want to share part of this with me?"

I pushed the plate toward her. A curvy woman who was not afraid of food, she rearranged the ingredients of my hoagie on a piece of bread, claiming one meatball, half the cheese, and some of the salami to make her own sandwich—I guess I did have a lot there—and joined us in our companionable snack.

"So, my girls, what are you planning to do after you eat?"

"Well, my room is clean."

"Thank goodness," my mother said as she crossed herself. "I was afraid I was going to have to send the bomb squad in there soon."

"Thank Rory, you mean," I pointed to my friend. "She managed to get it all done while I was in the shower."

"It wasn't too difficult," Rory shrugged. "I just divided things into 'laundry' and 'trash,' then applied a little elbow grease with the vacuum and cleaning products."

Rory had always been a one-woman whirlwind. I had stepped out of the shower, and my room was meticulous. It seemed lighter by half.

Hey … wait a minute.

"Rory, what was that third bag?"

"It was giveaway. Anyone want some fruit salad?" She moved to the refrigerator with an innocent air.

Giveaway!

"Who gave you permission to give anything of mine away?" I put my hands on my recently expanded hips.

Rory took her time returning to the table with fruit salad, bowls, spoons, and a serving implement.

"Rory, delaying your answer won't make me forget the question. What's in that third bag?"

"Only things that a normal adult would have discarded long ago—oh, sorry, I used the word 'adult' there."

"Ma!"

My mother took delight in witnessing the familiar give-and-take that had been part of her life since I first brought home the scrawny, freckled redhead from school. Rory had seemed shy at first, but she could absolutely hold her own in our rambunctious, extended family.

"Leave me out of this, Annalise. I'm sure I would agree with her."

I leaned back and crossed my arms, but Rory patted my knee with a loving gesture.

"Calm down," she said. "Sheesh! All I did was round up all the stuffed animals and random gifts from Dylan. I thought perhaps you might want to have a fresh perspective? Was I so wrong?"

I uncrossed my arms. She was right—once again. If I was going to put Dylan behind me I really needed to rid myself of any reminders of that time of my life.

"You're right. As a matter of fact, after we eat, let's take them down and donate them today."

"Atta girl!" my mother said. "Take them to the church. The youth group is collecting things for their annual garage sale. Won't that make you feel better to know that you're helping them make money for their pilgrimage? Remember how you girls loved that trip when you were in high school?"

Rory and I smiled at one another. That weeklong trip to the biannual World Youth Conference in our senior year was one of the highlights of our school years. We still kept in contact with some of the people we'd met from all over the world.

"I forget where the trip is this year," I said.

"I think it will be in Yugoslavia," said my mother.

"Wow! I loved our trip to Canada, but don't get me wrong, I really wish we could have gone a bit further afield."

She hugged me. "Well, you girls have your whole lives to travel. Just keep those passports up-to-date. Right now, how about taking those donations to the church? And while you're at it, let's pack these meatballs and sausage and take them to the Knights of Columbus hall for your father."

It was short work to pack the delicious results of my mother's cooking into the trunk of the car. We tossed my bag of donations in the back seat to drop off on the way back. As we backed out of the driveway of our modest home, my mother ran onto the porch, waving a piece of paper.

"Girls! On your way back, could you stop at the grocery store and at the hardware store for a few things?"

"No problem, Ma," I grinned as I dashed up the porch stairs for the list.

When we finally got on the road, Rory glanced at me. "What are you laughing about, happy face?"

"Oh … just thinking that no matter how old we will get, this will be us—dashing around, running errands for Ma."

"Having adventures?"

"If that's what you call going to the Home Depot for"—I consulted the list—"a new mop head."

"Ah, but adventure is in the eye of the adventurer," said Rory.

"Easy for you to say. You live in Manhattan, the busiest city in the world."

"You could always move out there and join me."

"What are you saying? You're never coming back to Denver?"

She shrugged and glanced at me from the corner of her eye.

"I don't know, Annalise, I kind of like it there. I bet you would like living there, too."

I paused to think about it. I certainly liked visiting there. It's not that I had never thought about moving away from Denver, it's just that I thought the opportunity had never presented itself.

Hmm.

Job hunt in Manhattan? Could I do it?

"What do you think?" Rory turned toward me. "We were roommates all through university and didn't kill each other. I'm sure we could make it work again."

"I'm not worried about that. I just never thought about it, that's all."

"Well think about it. I think it would be great. At least come out and stay with me for a while and check out job opportunities. I know my apartment is a squeeze, but one more can't hurt."

Rory shared a brownstone in Brooklyn with two other young women who I knew must be good roommates to meet her standards.

"How would Lisa and Rachel feel about you just asking me to move in for a while?"

She waved me off.

"They'd love it. We were just talking about the fact that having someone else to share the rent would help all of our pocketbooks. You know they like you. My room is big enough for another bed."

"But is your closet big enough for my clothes?" Of the two of us, Rory was definitely the fashionista.

"I'm sure I could make room for your knockoffs," she teased.

"Knockoffs! Just because I don't have access to Lisa's discounts!"

Rory became serious and turned toward me.

"I think it would be awesome, Annalise. You have great credentials, and I really think you need to broaden your horizons outside this city."

Hmm. It didn't sound so bad. Maybe I did need a change of venue to change my perspective.

"I think I need to broaden something beside my hips obviously," I said drily.

"Oh, you know I think you look gorgeous no matter what. But we do agree that you need to watch your health, right?"

"I know, I know," I nodded.

We pulled into the Knights' parking lot at the same moment my father was walking out the front door. If he was shocked to see me outside the house, he hid it well.

"Hello, my girls," he grabbed us each into one arm in a bear hug. "Good to see you, Rory. I'm especially happy to see YOU outside the house, my Gypsy girl." He gave me an extra hug.

"Thrilled to see us or the pot of meatballs and sausage you know we have for your social?"

He gave us each a quick buss on the cheek before reaching into the trunk to pull out the giant pot of my mother's delicious sauce.

"I'll admit, the guys are looking forward to hoagies for tonight's card game, but something has come up that might interest you, Annalise."

Oh sure. He had probably twisted the arm of a buddy and convinced him he needed a girl Friday and that I was just the right person to fill the bill. Ever since I had been laid off, Pop had "hired" me to do an odd job or two in his insurance office, but he truly didn't have enough work to keep me busy for very long. He was trying hard to get me a job, bless his heart.

"What's up, Pop? Envelope stuffing? Data entry?"

Not that either was beneath me. My parents had taught my brother and me the value of all forms of work.

"Oh, I think you're going to like this opportunity," he said over his shoulder.

We followed him in, greeting some of his brother Knights along the way who were preparing the hall for the evening's activities. Finally we reached the kitchen, and my father heaved the pot onto the counter, turned to me, and placed his hands on my shoulders.

"Gypsy girl, I've made arrangements for you to go to China!"

CHAPTER FOUR

"China? Pop, if you're tired of me living at home, I'll move out, but, seriously, you don't need to send me all the way across the world!"

What on earth was he thinking?

China?

What would I do there? I didn't speak the language—what was it? Mandarin? Cantonese? I didn't even know. And where exactly was he thinking of sending me? The country was jillions of miles in area. My head was whirling. Surely he was joking. I love my father, but his sense of humor has always been peculiar, to say the least! That had to be it. He had said it as a joke and had some real project in mind for me, like a marketing project for a Chinese restaurant. Wasn't one of his Knight brothers the owner of a Chinese restaurant?

"Oh, Pop, you are so funny." I hopped up to sit on the counter, and Rory hopped up next to me. "What is it really?"

"Hold on," he patted my knee. "I need to tell Frank how to set up the side tables in the social hall. I'll be right back."

He bustled off, and Rory and I stared at each other. She began to say out loud the things I was thinking, but I cut her off, shaking my head.

"He's just joking, Rory. This is just his crazy way of telling me he has an opportunity for me to work in the china and glassware department at Kohl's or something."

"I don't know," she shook her head. "He's pretty quirky, but he looked serious there."

We swung our legs back and forth in unison, silently contemplating what Pop had in mind.

"You know ..." Rory started.

"Stop it," I shook my head. "I'm not even going to speculate on what he's thinking until he gets back."

"Okay," she said and switched topics slightly. "I think it's sweet that your dad has been looking for opportunities for you."

"That's my pop. He's always been willing to let me make my way, but he's always had my back. I know that people don't understand the whole Italian Catholic 'family comes first' theory, but that's how we roll."

"Oh, I know. I've got the Irish Catholic version going on at my house, remember?"

We smiled at one another knowingly. As best friends, we had been in and out of each other's homes enough over the decades and appreciated our families' values.

Pop returned to the kitchen with two paper cups brimming with icy cold drinks.

"Here you go," he handed one to each of us. Without tasting, we knew they were Shirley Temples, the nonalcoholic treats we had been allowed ever since we were tiny. It brought back fond memories of many Saturday dances when the adults socialized while we children played together in the corner of the Knights' hall.

"Thanks, Pop." I grinned as I pulled the cherry from the drink and dangled it into my upturned mouth. "You know that we do drink alcohol now, right?"

He shook his finger. "Not while you're driving around town running errands for your Mama, thank you very much."

"Yessir," Rory and I chorused.

"Now," he clapped his hands together, "let me tell you about this trip to China."

I stopped slurping and became attentive.

"I was on the phone with your Aunt Lilliana," he said, referring to his oldest sister. Auntie Lil was the oldest of the eight children in my father's family and had never married. She had been a career girl, serving as a secretary to the superintendent of schools a few counties over until her retirement. Auntie Lil had never moved out of our grandparents' two-story home in Pueblo, Colorado, preferring to stay with Nonni Anna and Poppy Sam until their deaths. Her siblings and the assorted adult grandchildren and cousins wanted Auntie Lil to move into a smart little condo closer to the rest of us in Denver. She held her ground, though, and I loved visiting her because it seemed as if the house was a slice of time preserved and intact.

Lately, Auntie Lil had been slowing down ever so slightly, after being hospitalized for a minor heart incident. My father and his siblings had begun keeping an even closer watch on her, much to her dismay.

"Is something wrong?" My face must have shown my worry.

"No, no," my father assured me. "Nothing is wrong at all. But here's the thing. Your aunt has decided that she wants to take a trip."

"Auntie goes on trips with her New Life group all the time, Pop," I said. She was active in a ministry at her parish dedicated to the needs of single, widowed, and divorced senior citizens. They sponsored activities every weekend, from concert trips and luncheons to pilgrimages to churches outside the area. They were amazingly busy for people "of a certain age."

"Well, this time she wants to go a bit further than St. Louis," he said referring to the last New Life bus trip. "She found a group that is going on a trip to China!"

"Wow! That's awesome, Pop, but what's it got to do with me?"

"Well, she and I discussed the fact that going that far away with her recent health problems might not be a good idea."

Rory and I glanced slyly at one another. We knew that when he said "discussed," he meant that he talked while she tried with great patience to listen before doing what she wanted. Even though he was the youngest of the siblings, being the only son he maintained a big brother mentality in the hierarchy. Huh. Same as my younger brother Nicky and his continual advice for me.

"Are you listening to me, Annalise?"

Oops. I must have drifted off.

"Sorry, Pop," I grinned. "So … you and Auntie Lil … 'discussed' … her trip."

"Right. And we think it would be good for her to have a companion who would have her best interests at heart traveling along with her, and we think you might be the perfect person to do that."

What! Were we living in a Jane Austen novel? Sending the niece along as a traveling companion?

"Pop." I wanted to be as delicate as possible. "You can't be serious. I can't imagine that Auntie Lil actually wants a companion, first of all."

"No," he bobbed his head energetically, "she was the one who brought up the idea!"

Hmm. I doubted that.

"Come on, Pop. I can't believe Auntie Lil—my Auntie Lil, who has been whitewater rafting, who has climbed Mt. Evans, and, oh, I don't know, could probably outrun our marathon runner Rory here—"

"Hey!" Rory stopped slurping her Shirley Temple.

"Ssh. I'm trying to make a point," I waved her off. "Anyway, Auntie Lil is not a wilting flower. I can't see her requesting a 'companion.'"

I hopped off the counter and started to pace. I stopped and whirled around.

"Or did she come up with that idea as some sort of compromise because you were insisting that she not go at all! Ha! That was it. You and the rest of the aunts didn't want her to go, so she came up with this to keep you off her back."

"Annalise Margaret!"

Uh-oh. My father had used my full name. He was a genial bear of a man, but my brother and I had always known not to push him into "two-naming" us.

"Your aunt is traveling across the world to a country where she doesn't speak the language," he began calmly. "Even though she'll be with a tour group, she won't be with anyone she knows. This isn't with New Life. This is a tour she found out about in the *Catholic Register*, and none of her friends are really interested in going. Plus, it hasn't been that long since she was in the hospital, so we feel—yes, even SHE feels—it would be good to have someone with her from Denver and back."

My father was really good at speaking in bullet points. It was one of the reasons he was such a successful insurance salesman, actually. He could lay out logical reasons like nobody's business.

"Finally, we think it would be good for you to go on this trip. You're between jobs, and frankly you need a project to kick-start your life."

I looked to Rory for help.

She shrugged. "I don't know, Annalise, it sounds like a great opportunity, if you ask me."

Traitor.

"But, Rory, we just talked about me moving out to Manhattan to stay with you and job hunt."

"Manhattan will still be there after you get back," she said with practicality. "This is an opportunity to travel the world."

I bit my lip.

"But Pop," I said finally, "who is footing the bill for this little jaunt? I don't have any money, as you might know since I moved back into my childhood bedroom and am depending on tips from my glamorous part-time job waiting tables to contribute to the household finances."

"Your aunt wants to treat this as a job for you and consider your pay as the cost of the ticket and incidentals."

"No! That's too much! I can't take advantage of her like that."

"She is going to take a paid companion whether it's you or someone else, so why not you?"

"A paid vacation? Come on."

"If it makes you feel better, you can write a book about your trip," Pop suggested. "You can call it 'Travels with My Aunt' or something."

"Graham Greene already did that back in the forties," I said absentmindedly. "Remember? The protagonist in that book got involved in all sorts of crime and high jinks."

"Well, with your Auntie Lil, that probably won't be too far from the truth for you either," teased Rory.

"Ha."

"Look, sweetheart, I have a lot to do here, so we need to postpone this discussion until I get home tonight." He took my hands in his and looked into my eyes. "I would never make you do anything you didn't want to do, but I think this is a great opportunity for you. And it would be doing something nice for your aunt."

He hustled us out of the kitchen and returned to his tasks, and we made our way to the parking lot to continue ours. As we walked toward the car, Nicky pulled up in his car. We stopped to say hello.

"Hey, bro, what are you doing here so early?"

He was also in the Knights organization, having joined the minute he was eligible. Pop had been very proud to be one of the three-generation families until Poppy Sam died.

"I'm setting up the sound system."

"DJ? Isn't this a guys-only event? Who's dancing?"

"Just for the announcements and things," he gave me a punch in the shoulder. "It's really good to see you out of your room. I just dropped Amanda off with Ma. Rory, you came in town in time for a night of chick flicks."

"Sounds good to me," Rory said. "Although with your Ma, that means at least one Dean Martin movie."

"Of course."

"So," he said, leaning back on the hood of his car, "are you ready for your trip with Auntie Lil?"

"And just how did you know about this before me?"

"I just told you, I stopped at Ma's," he grinned. "You don't think she told me?"

Of course she did. Because why should I be the first to hear of a project that would involve me?

"What do you think, Nick? Doesn't this all seem a little *Downton Abbey* to you?"

"Well, Auntie Lil certainly is as imposing as the Dowager," he said, referring to the grand character portrayed by Maggie Smith in one of my favorite PBS series. "But you have to admit Lil is a lot more spry. You know you'd have a lot of fun traveling with her."

"That's true," added Rory. "Auntie Lil has always been a kick. This isn't going to be a trip where you have to assist her in and out of restaurants and things."

"No, probably just the opposite," teased Nicky.

"Har-har," I nudged his calf with my toe.

I pondered for a moment and then countered with an idea.

"What about visas and shots and things?"

"No special shots," Nicky shook his head. "You will need a visa, but if we start the paperwork for that, all you have to do is send it with your passport through to the Chinese Embassy, and it takes about a week—"

He stopped when he realized that he'd said too much.

"Wait ..." My eyes became slits. "You guys have all talked about this already, haven't you?" I kicked him again, harder.

"Ow!"

He put his hands on my shoulders.

"Honestly, Pop called me to use my legal skills to do research for Auntie Lil after they originally spoke about her going on the trip. But I didn't know anything about them asking you to join her before this morning. And stop trying to 'read me,' Annalise. You and I both know you don't have that superpower."

I continued staring into his eyes. He hadn't passed the bar yet, but he was an aspiring lawyer. My ongoing joke was that if I could tell if he was bending the truth—which I've been able to do ever since we were kids—then a judge and jury certainly could.

"You don't know that," I sniffed as I removed his hands from my shoulders and moved to lean on my car next to Rory. She was watching this scene play out as she had done so often before.

"Aaaanyway," he continued his previous line of discussion, "the paperwork is minimal. It's not like you need to request vacation from a job. And Auntie Lil is going to pay you."

He had inherited that ability to lay out bullet points from Pop, all right. A talent handy for a lawyer.

I felt Nicky's and Rory's eyes staring at me.

"I can't come up with any other reasons to not do this. As a matter of fact, it sounds like fun."

"Great!" Rory clapped her hands.

"Awesome!" agreed Nicky.

My father came outside at that moment to wipe his brow from his hard work and, seeing the three of us apparently loitering, put his hands on hips.

"I think we need you inside, Nicholas Samuel. And Annalise Margaret and Rory Elizabeth—"

"Oh, Pop," I went to him to give him a tight hug and a kiss, "don't be mad at him. He and Rory were just making me see the benefits of this trip with Auntie Lil. I think I'll go, okay?"

A broad grin spread across his face.

"Wonderful! We'll have her over for dinner Sunday to make the plans."

"Sunday?" said Rory. "We need to plan starting now!"

She grabbed me by the arm and pushed me into the car. We backed out of the lot, laughing and waving to my father and brother, then turned to one another.

"Wow!" said Rory, "I bet when you woke up this morning, you never thought you'd be planning a trip across the world?"

"Nope," I said, sobering. "I didn't even think I'd be planning this trip across town."

CHAPTER FIVE

"You cut your hair?" Rory's voice rose in so many decibels that I had to pull the phone away from my ear quickly in order to avoid permanent damage to my eardrums. I could hear the next questions clearly even at arm's length:

"When? Why? How? Where?"

"Rory … Rory …" I returned the phone to the side of my head and attempted to catch her attention. Completing preparations for my trip while she was so many miles away had been a difficult proposition since we always loved to bounce ideas off one another. This last decision of mine without her there was certainly a big one.

"Rory!" I finally caught her. "I decided that it would just be so much easier to manage on the trip, that's all. I didn't think it would be a big deal."

"No big deal?" Her voice was incredulous. "Annalise, your hair has been the envy of everyone we've known forever."

"C'mon, Rory, you exaggerate just a bit."

But she was not too far off. I had been voted "Girl with the Prettiest Hair" in high school. It was a dubious honor, but I suppose it beat out "Girl Who Could Whistle Loudest." Hey, we attended a small school, and the senior class had traditions that had carried down for decades.

My chestnut locks had fallen down to about the middle of my back for years, and I was lucky enough that they were shiny and thick. There were a lot of times that I toyed with the idea of chopping them off, but I never had the courage.

"I don't know, Rory, I guess I just needed a change."

"How could you just throw this information out casually during the course of a phone call? How could you not Face-Time me with it the moment after you did it?" she demanded.

"Because I knew I would get this reaction, basically."

"I'm hanging up and FaceTiming you immediately." The line cut off.

I waited patiently for the ring, then held my phone up and struck an ingénue pose.

"What do you think?" I asked.

My new 'do was a choppy bob, layered through the sides and back and flicked out at the chin. The bangs flipped to the side and were flirty and fun.

She paused, and for a moment I thought she didn't like it.

"Rory ... What do you think?"

"It is so cute!"

Whew. One of the things about being best friends was the brutal honesty that we each shared, with no filter.

"But, seriously, Annalise, I've been trying to get you to just get bangs for a million years and you wouldn't even consider it, and here you go and chop all of your hair off."

"I know, I know. But it wasn't an easy decision. You know, not everyone can pull off hair as short as yours."

Rory's own auburn hair was an edgy head-hugging crop that never looked the same two days in a row and that she liked to call "controlled chaos." And face it, no matter how adorable her hair was, it was difficult for me to take hairstyle advice from someone who got their hair cut by elderly Mr. Randazzo at the same barbershop that my dad frequented.

"You look awesome, girlfriend," she pronounced.

"Thank you."

"So," she switched topics only slightly, "with your new hair and having lost all the Oreo-and-ice-cream weight, do you feel like you are ready to go on Friday?"

I couldn't believe our departure date had arrived already.

"T minus 2 days and counting," I affirmed. "Auntie Lil and I are ready to go, but to be honest with you, I'm not so sure that my mom is ready for me to leave."

"Your mom will worry until the minute you're in the air, then the whole time you're gone, and won't stop worrying until you walk back through the airport arrival gate."

"Oh don't I know that. It's her job as a mom. I wouldn't know what to do if she were different, though."

"Are you packed?"

"I have everything laid out and just need to put it in my bags. I am packing very lightly and making sure everything coordinates. My theme is black, white, and gray. I have two pairs of pants, a reversible sleeveless dress, and short and long-sleeve T-shirts in white and black plus some incidentals—you know, scarves and things."

I picked up each item as I mentioned them to her.

"Hmm. Where did you get that idea?" she teased.

"Okay, fashionista, I admit it was from your magazine article on 'Packing for a Trip in a Capsule.' But it does make sense, and it's a lot less to drag around. Don't get too excited, though. Auntie Lil made the same recommendation, and—no offense—she doesn't read your magazine."

"She's always been ahead of the times, hasn't she?"

"I have always like raiding her closet," I admitted. "She has the best in vintage. And it's all because she has kept everything she's ever bought in such good shape."

"Isn't that the truth?" Rory paused. "I am jealous of you."

"Because I can find awesome kitten heel pumps in Auntie Lil's closet?"

"Well, that, and because not only is this trip going to be amazing, but spending time with her will be so much fun. I can't think of anyone her age that is so cool or that I would want to travel with."

"I know what you mean. I know I'm supposed to be her paid 'companion,' but this is really just an excuse for a great vacation. Hold on a second, I hear Ma yelling for me up the stairs. I'm sure she's found another amazing travel necessity or read another horrifying tidbit about the air quality in China that she needs to share with me."

I muted the phone and walked out of my room to lean over the oak railing on the stairs.

"Annalise!" my mother shouted again. "I was at the camping store and found something you absolutely must take with you."

Camping? Did my mother forget that we were booked in nothing but 4-star hotels for the duration of our trip? Wearily, I took Rory off mute.

"Rory, I need to address this issue and call you back. Ma found something at the camping goods store that apparently I cannot travel without."

"Camping? You? You won't even camp here much less in a foreign country. Your idea of roughing it is a hotel without room service."

"Very funny. But whatever it is, she's very excited about it. I'll call you back."

I took a deep breath and went downstairs to see what my mother could possibly have discovered.

"Okay," she began and pulled me over to the dining room table where a veritable cornucopia of purchases were laid out.

"Okay," I began, "why were you even in the camping store—"

She cut me off with a wave of her hand.

"Sit, sit, sit. Let me show you what I found. First, here's a nice small flashlight."

"Because … they don't have electricity there?" I took the slim light that was smaller than my thumb from her and flicked it on and off.

"No, dear, because the article said you should have one just in case."

"Whoa, whoa, whoa. Back up. Another article? I thought you had already read every one that existed."

My mother was a great one for reading articles. If they were on the web, she forwarded them. If they were in print, she copied them and sent them. In either case, she usually made plans based on recommendations given by the author.

We were generally supportive of her, although I was really happy that I was away at school when she read the article on the magical benefits of quinoa. I did notice that Pop's quota of "business dinners" at restaurants spiked for a week or so during that time period. Ever since we had started planning for this trip, she had become the expert on travel to Asia. I had to admit that she'd discovered some interesting tips, but as usual, she was bordering on overinforming.

"Well, this article actually had more tips about hygiene."

"If it is about drinking water, I already know, Ma. I am not going to drink or brush my teeth with any water that isn't bottled, and I'll be sure not to accidentally open my mouth in the shower, either."

"Good, good, but this one focused on the other end."

"Ma! Please!"

"Only in China, dear, you'll be fine in Singapore. The facilities are more Western there. But you need to be prepared in any case."

She piled several rolls of travel-size toilet tissue, packages of hygienic wipes, and travel bottles of hand sanitizer of different brands into my arms.

"Thank you, Ma, I'll be sure to weigh down the luggage with this extra paraphernalia. If you remember, another of the articles you read advised to keep luggage as light as possible." I tried to keep the sarcasm out of my voice.

She tut-tutted in that way only a mother could.

"Well, you'll thank me for this," she said, handing me a small pink tube roughly the length and twice the diameter of a roll of quarters. What could this contain?

"What on earth?" I turned it over and read the label. "She-Whiz, the female device for—"

CHAPTER SIX

No matter how many times I've flown, I have never gotten used to the lengthy trek through TSA. We patiently snaked our way through the first queue—amazingly long for 5:30 a.m.—and made it through to the inevitable shedding of shoes, belts, and other random accessories. One of these days, I thought, I'm just going to travel in pajamas and slippers and avoid a lot of this.

"This would be so much simpler if we just traveled in our pajamas and slippers, wouldn't?" muttered the man in line ahead of me.

"That's just what I was thinking!" I smiled and nodded to him.

We finally made it through, redressed, reassembled, re-combombulated, and boarded the underground train to the concourse. The doors closed a split second before a very attractive man darted across the platform and missed making it onto the train. My mind wandered—what if that was the love of my life and we missed our chance at meeting because he wore shoes that were difficult to lace up and cost him that extra second he needed to make this train? How many missed opportunities could be chalked up to delays in the security area?

"What on earth are you thinking about?" asked Auntie Lil, bouncing back and forth as we dangled from the grips that hung from the ceiling of the train. "You look so far away."

I put forth my theory.

"More likely, he would have been someone who would have stepped on your toe and not apologized," she shook her head ruefully.

"Auntie Lil, you are being too pragmatic for this early in the morning!"

She broke into a smile, and her face—wreathed in the kind of gorgeous wrinkles that one earns from a life well lived and well loved—betrayed her true romantic self. The twinkle in her hazel eyes spoke of her own girlish dreams and escapades.

"Maybe I just need a cup of coffee before I can be too philosophical, dear."

"I think we can take care of that. Our flight doesn't leave for an hour and a half."

The train jolted to a stop, and we joined the rest of the passengers ascending the escalator to the concourse.

Moments later, we were relaxing in a small bakery cafe with steaming cups of tea and coffee and pastries alongside for good measure. We reviewed our itinerary.

"Two days in Singapore on our own, then we fly into China and join your tour group in Xian for a day, then on to Beijing for the remainder of the time," I said. "And the schedule looks jam-packed. Tell me again how you hooked up with these people if they aren't your regular group of traveling buddies?"

"I just saw the ad in the *Catholic Register* and thought it looked like a great trip for the money. No one else from St. Anthony's wanted to go, but I didn't want that to stop me. I've always wanted to see the Great Wall and the Forbidden City and the Terracotta Soldiers, and I'm not getting younger, you know."

"Ha!" I nudged her. "You'll be traveling for another ten or fifteen years before you even think about slowing down."

"If my siblings have any say, they'll chain me to a rocking chair someday soon."

"Oh, Pop and the other aunties are just worriers." I shook my head. "Personally, I think I want to be you when I grow up."

"Well, the first thing to do is not 'grow up' then."

"What?"

"I mean just what I said. Don't grow up. Sure, you'll get older and you'll need to work at a job and hopefully you'll get married, but that doesn't mean you have to be too stable."

"But Auntie Lil, you're one of the must stable people I know! You worked so hard at your job before you retired, and you took care of Nonni and Poppy."

"Sure. I've always been serious about my responsibilities, but you know I've never taken life seriously. We're put here to enjoy all that we're given, sweetheart, and to use our gifts and talents as best we can. No one ever said we had to be glum while we did it."

I pondered that for a moment. One of the reasons I loved Auntie Lil was for her adventuresome spirit. Definitely no one could ever accuse her of being glum. Sure, she was careful with money, but her motto is that there is a time to save and a time to spend. This trip was an example of a time to spend, all right. Everything was costing double with me along.

"Thanks again for taking me with you, Auntie Lil. I'm sure you weren't thinking that your bargain trip would be compromised by having to pay for a 'companion.'"

"Look," she took my hand into hers. "Now that we're not around your father, we can drop the 'companion' business. Good lord, it made me feel like an elderly frump out of a Jane Austen novel every time he said it."

"That's what I said!"

"No, dear," she shook her head, "I know my brother. He would have worn me down to a nub with his objections to this journey unless I agreed to have someone travel with me. Do you realize his first recommendation was that HE come along?"

"Noo!"

She lowered her head and covered her face with both hands.

"Auntie Lil, I can't imagine!"

She raised her face. "Oh, I can. It would have been endless rounds of 'Lilliana, do you need to sit down, dear?' or 'Don't you think that's a bit spicy for you?'"

"Or 'Lilliana, really, another glass of wine?'" I imitated my father's gravelly voice.

We broke into laughter.

"Oh, he means well," she said.

"I know, I know. He just feels that he is so—"

"Responsible for us all?"

"Right."

"Well, he's the only boy in the family," Lil said. "And your Nonni and Poppy drilled that into him, you know, that he was the brother and had to take care of all of us sisters."

"Even though you were all so much older. That's so funny."

"It's just our way. You know it's that way with you and Nicky, even though you are the older one."

"What! He's the prince of the house!" I cried.

"Sure. But think about it for a minute."

She was right, darn it. Even though my mother babied him more than I thought was necessary while we were growing up, both of my parents never let him forget that he would have responsibilities when he grew up. Nicky was a pretty sturdy kind of guy—funny and sweet—but definitely a responsible person.

"Nicky is just like Pop isn't he?"

"Is that so bad Annalise? Your father and I may disagree on whether I need a 'companion' on this trip or not, but I'd rather have him looking after me than not."

"I think he worries more about you because you're the sister that isn't married. The other aunties have husbands to take care of them."

I looked across the table at my beautiful aunt. I had seen pictures of her when she was my age. She was a stunner. Even in black and white, her eyes were bright and sparkly and her wide smile accented her high cheekbones. In all the photos, her haircut was a variation of the way she wore it in her high school graduation picture, a shoulder-length style reminiscent of one that Lauren Bacall wore, flowing from the side and ending just above her shoulders.

"Auntie Lil, why did you never get married?" I had never asked the question before and hoped I wouldn't upset her. "Is it because you felt you needed to stay home to take care of Nonni and Poppy?"

She sighed and ran her fingers through her hair, now gone completely white and cut in that short, aggressive hairstyle that older women adopt because it's easy to care for. She looked off to the side.

"I'm sorry." Great. I started the trip by offending her.

She turned back toward me and her eyes glistened.

"No, sweetheart, it's fine. I let people think that. Oh, I let people think whatever they want. But do you want the truth?"

"Oh, Auntie Lil, I didn't mean to upset you before we started our journey! No, no, no."

I reached for a napkin from the dispenser to hand her, but, ever classy, she pulled a neatly pressed handkerchief from her bag to dab her eyes.

"No. It's okay. You can hear this." She smiled and began.

"After I graduated from high school, I was planning to go to secretarial school. During the summer before classes started, I was dating several nice young men."

"Auntie Lil!"

"Don't raise your eyebrows. Back in the day, 'dating' meant going to the movies or going on picnics or skating. We usually did things like that in groups of couples. I don't know what young people do today."

"Well, Auntie Lil, I can't speak for other girls, but that's still what 'dating' means to me and my girlfriends. If guys expect anything more, then they're sadly mistaken. It's just that we date one guy at a time and don't have multiple guys calling on us."

"If you don't mind my saying so, maybe if you didn't put all your eggs in one basket, it wouldn't hurt so much when you parted company with one of them."

Ouch. That was a subtle jab at my recent depression over losing Dylan.

"But—"

"Annalise," she shook her head. "All I'm saying is you might date more than one fellow at a time to compare and narrow down until you find the one. It's more efficient."

"Right," I said ruefully. "Efficiency. That's what dating is all about. But we're not talking about me, right now."

"Anyway, as I was saying, I was dating several nice young men, but then I met someone who was obviously different."

Her eyes shone again.

"His name was Antonio. He came here from Italy with his uncle to help run the family restaurant. He was so handsome—tall, with black hair and flashing eyes and a smile that could melt your heart. He didn't speak English, and his uncle asked if I could teach him, because he knew that I was fluent in Italian."

"Auntie Lil! Why, that's the stuff of romantic novels."

"Oh, it was, sweetie, it was. At first, we just spent time together with me teaching him English in the corner of the restaurant after it closed, but soon we started talking about more than Italian lessons, and he would come over to our house to get to know the family. One day, he asked me to come for the lessons at a later time. Before it was time for me to get there, apparently he had strung beautiful lights all around the garden and even inside the main part of the restaurant.

She paused and took a deep breath.

"We think that he turned the lights on and somehow, somewhere there was a short and it blew. He was ... he was ..."

"Electrocuted?" I could barely get the word out myself.

She nodded.

"And the restaurant burned down around him?"

She nodded again and stared straight ahead.

"Oh, Auntie Lil." I moved next to her and hugged her. We stayed in silence for a few moments.

"His uncle thinks ... thought ... that Antonio was going to propose that night. He had purchased a ruby ring. They found the ring in the rubble."

She looked down at her hand.

I always thought the chunky piece of gold with the cloudy red stone that she constantly wore was a family heirloom. Now I knew differently.

I had so many questions!

CHAPTER SEVEN

"Is that why Pop worries about you so much?"

"He wasn't old enough to know anything about it." She shook her head. "The older sisters knew that Antonio and I kept company, but I never told any of them how serious we were becoming. I think your Poppy knew, because Antonio would surely have asked permission to marry me, but we never talked about it after the accident. It was different times, dear."

Wow. My Auntie Lil was WAY stronger than I even knew.

"Then what happened?"

"What do you mean? You know what happened. I went to secretarial school, became a secretary, and—"

"No, no, no. With his family, with you and other boy-friends."

She tilted her head and gave me a sweet smile.

"Life happened, dear. His uncle sold the property and went back to Italy. The building was torn down. It's actually the spot where that Discount Tire is on Fifth Street now. I suspect there aren't too many people left who remember the fire."

"But Auntie Lil. You? Boyfriends?"

"He was the love of my life, Annalise. Eventually I dated. There were other nice men, but no one measured up to Antonio. And after a certain age, I just decided that maybe it wasn't for me to get married. Not all people get married, you know."

"But ... no children ..."

"In a family as large as ours, when you're the oldest you generally end up helping raise the younger ones, so I had my share of raising children. And I have all my wonderful nephews and nieces. At this point, I have any number of great-nephews, great-nieces. You know I love spoiling you and giving you back to your parents."

I sighed.

"Oh, I know what you're thinking," she smiled. "But I haven't missed out. This has been my life journey, and it has been a wonderful one!"

I hugged her.

"And, Annalise, don't you worry. You'll find a nice young man."

"Me? How did this get to be about me?"

"I know how much time you wasted worrying about this Dylan."

I loved the way she dismissed him as "this Dylan" as if he were a character in a bad soap. Well. Come to think of it, maybe he was.

"Oh, Auntie Lil," I waved her off. "That chapter of my life really was over a long time ago. I really think those emotions

life forever. All that was left was a whiff of his delicious cologne.

I stood like a goof for a minute, then remembered to
complete my original task.

As I walked back to my aunt with my sad little pack of
gum and her peppermints, I suddenly remembered where I
had seen his face before. He was the man who had missed
the train earlier! Great. I guess I had now become the girl
who LITERALLY always just misses meeting the man of my
dreams.

"You know, you're supposed to be keeping me out of trouble," mocked Auntie Lil. "You were gone so long, I thought I
needed to send out a search party."

I shared the details of my brief encounter.

"How exciting!" she said. "You need to put that in your
travel journal!"

We had agreed to each keep a journal of our trip to make
it easier to recount our tales to the family when we got back
home.

"Oh. Sure. That's all I would need. I can just imagine the
responses. Let's see: Ma would ask me why I wasn't more careful because the stranger could have been a pickpocket. Nicky
would revert back to junior high and make kiss noises. Pop
would ask me why I wasn't by your side constantly."

"Absolutely. You've pegged the reactions to a tee," Auntie
Lil laughed. "Now we had better move to our gate or we'll
miss our flight. Wouldn't that be a story to tell!"

By the time we got to our gate, the first groups had boarded—premium first class, business class, and those with children and who needed assistance. We were the next group
called.

"Welcome!" said the chipper flight attendant as we entered the jet and she reviewed our tickets. "Please take a right toward your seats."

"Of course, take a right," Auntie Lil said over her shoulder as we moved along. "To the left is definitely out of our league."

I peeked toward where she indicated.

Yikes!

I had seen seats in first class before, but those in premium first class were a whole other animal. Each seat was its own individual pod. Each pod could be stretched out into a lounge chair or even into a bed. Passengers who had already settled in were slipping off their shoes and slipping on special cozy socks provided by the airline. As a flight attendant provided champagne or other cocktails, they put their carry-on goods in one of the stowaway areas built into their pods. Large TV screens were built in at the far end of each pod and could be moved forward for the passenger's comfort.

All I could think was "Wow!"

As we settled into our comfortable, yet definitely less posh economy seats, I commented to Auntie Lil, "Those seats aren't even full! Why don't we sneak into one of them?"

"One of the benefits of that seating is that you can board when you wish, dear. I'm sure they're all spoken for. And I'm pretty sure they'd check our tickets before they'd let us up there."

"You're right," I grinned. "It's fun to dream though, right?"

"I'm happy to be right here with you," she patted my knee.

I gave her a hug. After all, I didn't want to seem ungrateful for the fact that she was paying my way on this journey.

"These seats are great," I said. "I like the fact that it's just the window and aisle and no middle, so it's just the two of us here!"

She smiled and we buckled in for the lengthy flight.

CHAPTER EIGHT

Auntie Lil stared at me.

"Is it possible for you to sit still?"

"Seriously? How can I, Auntie Lil?"

She looked at me and burst into laughter. "You are extra fidgety and we've only just left Denver."

I guess she was right. From the moment the seat belt sign went off, I had stood up and sat down several times to retrieve and replace items from my carry-on bag in the overhead compartment. I moved my iPad from the seat pocket in front of me to my lap and back again, buckled and unbuckled my belt, donned then removed my sweater. I couldn't help it! This was the most exciting journey I had ever embarked upon.

"How can you sit there so calm and collected, Auntie Lil?"

She turned and wordlessly peered at me over the top of her stylish reading glasses.

"But, Auntie, we're going all the way across the world. Don't you have even one butterfly?"

"I know, but I'm not going to accomplish anything by dancing around like a jumping bean." She turned back to studying the in-flight magazine.

Humph.

I turned to my other side to see who was sitting there. After all, this person would be my traveling neighbor for the next half day. A trim young woman who looked to be my age was filing pages in a small accordion file. I took in her neatly shorn strawberry-blonde hair and comfortable navy tunic and slacks, and determined that she must be some sort of saleswoman on her way to San Francisco for business. She finished her task and looked my way. Fearful that I was caught staring, I tried unsuccessfully to glance back at my iPad.

"Too late," she said with a smile. "I caught you!"

I turned back with a sheepish grin.

"Sorry if I disturbed you. I was just getting a feel for who my neighbors are."

"No problem," she said. "I fully understand. I had already taken a moment to steal a glance at you and your … mother?"

"Aunt"

"Aunt," she concluded and stretched her hand across the aisle. "Welcome to the neighborhood."

"Thanks. I'm Annalise Fontana, and this is my Aunt Lil, well actually Lilliana."

"Glad to meet you Annalise. I'm Sister Mary Grace Connolly."

"You're a nun! But you aren't in a habit."

"Our order is not veiled, but we do wear a uniform of sorts." She pointed to her outfit. I noticed then that she wore a modest crucifix around her neck.

"We're a teaching order. I'm returning from where I teach in Salida to our convent in San Francisco," she said, indicating the brief stop on our flight.

"Is that home for you?"

"Oh, no. I grew up in Michigan. But when I felt the call, I knew that I wanted to be in the Sisters of Grace. That required me to move to San Francisco."

She went on to explain her teaching order and the particular faith journey that led her there. She looked to be my age, possibly younger, and spoke with such confidence about how she felt the call to religious life and how she moved away from home so easily and now was not even living in the convent where she took her vows. Talk about brave.

"Sister," I finally said. "Were you ever doubtful that you'd made the right choice?"

Her smile reached all the way to her bright green eyes. "No, I discerned my path early on. I sense that you might worry about your decisions. Is that true?"

I laughed. "Oh, you don't know the half of it." I explained my recent descent from the status of gainfully employed with prospects of a long-term relationship to woefully single and left to picking up odds and ends for jobs.

"But you're on this trip now? That's a good thing."

By this time, Auntie Lil had abandoned her reading and joined our conversation.

"She's doing me a great favor by keeping me company on this trip to China, Sister."

"Ha!" I rolled my eyes. "You don't know Auntie Lil. She could go around the world three times on her own. She's doing ME a favor by taking me."

"Well. Then you are both doing each other a favor, right?"

Auntie Lil and I looked at each other with smiles and a hug.

"You're right, Sister," I said. "So what grade do you teach?"

"I have second graders at St. Mark's. It's a small class, only about twenty students."

"I don't know. Twenty seems like a lot of kids to manage to me," I said.

"You'd get used to it. Plus, I'm the oldest of seven, so I have a little experience with a lot of children."

"Just like Auntie Lil!" I cried, turning to my aunt.

"You get used to crowd management when you're the oldest, don't you, Sister?" Auntie Lil smiled.

"Exactly. As a matter of fact, my next-oldest brother is meeting me at the airport in San Francisco. We'll have a little time for a visit while he drives me to the mother house."

"Does he live in San Francisco?"

"He works in a high-tech company in the Bay Area," she nodded. "My father was very happy that he moved there after I did."

"Sound like anyone we know?" I grinned to Auntie Lil, then responded to Sister Mary Grace. "We have experience with fathers protecting their daughters—and sisters, for that matter."

We laughed companionably and continued our conversation for the next two hours, until the flight attendant indicated that we were nearing time to land.

"My goodness!" I said. "I've monopolized your time the whole flight."

"Not to worry," she said. "I've really enjoyed our conversation."

The flight attendant returned to the loudspeaker.

"Ladies and gentlemen. For those of you continuing this flight to Singapore, we have an announcement. There will be a change of airplanes. This plane will need to go out of service at San Francisco. Please do not be alarmed. You will be perfectly safe as we land."

Murmurs shot throughout the aircraft as passengers attempted to figure out what could possibly cause this change.

"What do you think of that, Auntie Lil?"

"Pretty interesting, I'd say."

The flight attendant continued her announcement with even more interesting news.

"In addition, we will need to add time to our layover until the new aircraft arrives. Instead of two hours, we will have a layover of ten hours."

The murmurs rose to a fevered pitch. Passenger reaction ranged from concern to outrage.

"We apologize for any inconvenience. When we land we will have customer service agents available to handle any emergency situations. In addition, each passenger will be issued a restaurant voucher to be used for a meal during the wait. Your baggage will be unloaded and held in a corral and reloaded so that you will not need to recheck."

"Wow! This really is a way to start a trip! How will this put us behind schedule, Auntie Lil?"

She checked our itinerary.

"Well. This puts us in Singapore late, obviously, but it won't cause any problems since we don't have any organized trips there. It just means we cut some of our touring short before we catch the flight to China."

"It's a good thing we're both up for any adventure, right Auntie?" I said.

"Right-o, sweetie. What shall we do with this unexpected time in San Francisco?" She rubbed her hands together.

"If you don't mind a bit of advice," Sister Mary Grace broke in.

"Absolutely! We'll be glad to take it," I nodded.

"Well, my brother only needs to drop me off at the convent, then I'm sure he would be happy to play tour guide for you ladies for a few hours. If you're up for it, that is."

"We couldn't impose on him without his prior knowledge!" I cried.

"Oh, he's my younger brother. He has to do what I say," she joked and waved the thought off with her hand.

Auntie Lil and I looked at each other.

"She's right, Annalise. You know every older sister has the right to play that card."

"I know we joke about that, but seriously …" I looked into Sister Mary Grace's eyes. She was absolutely serious about the offer. "Well … If you're sure …"

"Don't even think about it. I'm just sorry I won't be able to go along with you!"

It was settled by the time we landed. Sister Mary Grace went ahead of us to meet her brother at baggage claim while Auntie Lil and I waited at the customer service desk to receive our meal vouchers and instructions for returning to the plane so as not to miss our flight.

"What are you ladies going to do with your time?" asked the desk attendant, who somehow managed to maintain her composure as passengers with varying degrees of calm lined up before her.

"We're not sure yet," I shrugged. "But whatever it is, I'm thinking it will be fun."

"That's the spirit!" she said as she made a small notation on our voucher. "Have dinner at this restaurant, and tell them I sent you. They're based in Denver, but the one here is really great. And get the tiramisu!"

I looked down at what she had written as we walked away.

"Nonna's Italian Restaurant? Sounds good. Plus I'm always in for some good tiramisu. Have you ever been to San Francisco, Auntie Lil?" I asked.

"Many years ago," she answered, "but I'm sure there are so many new things to see and do now."

We reached baggage claim, and I searched the carousel area for Sister Mary Grace. When I caught sight of her bright strawberry-blonde curls, she was in a spirited conversation with a man whose ponytailed hair was a perfect color match for her own. She saw us, pointed, and waved us toward them. He turned, and his face split into a friendly grin. He was tall and lanky, dressed in jeans topped with a forest-green fleece vest casually fitted over a coordinating checked oxford. His eyes matched her grass-green ones.

"This is my brother, Breccan," Sister Mary Grace said, "but we call him Breck. And Breck, this is Annalise and Miss Fontana."

"Breccan is a very apt name," said Auntie Lil.

I looked at her, puzzled.

"It's from the Irish for 'freckled,'" she explained. Breck's freckles were indeed evident across his cheeks and nose.

"Never try to beat my aunt in a game of Trivia," I laughed.

"I guess I won't," he grinned back. "Pleased to meet you, Annalise, and you, Miss Fontana."

"Oh, no, I'm Auntie Lil." She ignored his outstretched hand ready for a handshake and pulled him in for a hug.

"Auntie Lil it is, then."

Breck turned to his sister.

"Okay, sis, now explain to me exactly what is happening here?"

"Well, as soon as my bag appears, you are going to drive me to the convent as planned, then you'll take these ladies on a tour of the city while they wait for their flight."

She went on to explain the reason for our extended layover, and he nodded through the story.

"That is, if it's not a bother to you," I cut in.

He turned to me.

"Well … I did have some very important plans to attend to."

My heart sank.

"I'm kidding," he smiled. "The rest of my day was going to consist of cleaning my apartment, which I am only too happy to delay, and maybe catching a movie. I'd be delighted to change all of that to show you the town."

I looked up at him and could see that he was sincere.

Well. I guess there could be worse things to do while waiting for a plane than spending time with a charming man!

CHAPTER NINE

The four of us were chatting happily as we made our way to the parking garage when it dawned on me that I needed to make a very important phone call.

"What is it?" Auntie Lil asked as I quickly pulled my phone from my bag and hit speed dial.

"You know that Ma is timing this trip to the second and will be waiting for my call when we reach Singapore. I need to let her know about this delay—hi, Ma." I broke off as my mother answered breathlessly.

"Annalise! What's wrong?"

"What makes you think something's wrong, Ma?" I walked away from our group so that I could have this conversation in private. "We just landed for our layover in San Francisco."

"A mother knows these things, young lady. So what is it?"

I took a deep breath and explained the flight delay to her.

"Hmm, so what will you do for so many hours? Is there somewhere you can relax and somewhere to eat?"

Trust my mother to think of food.

"We're actually leaving the airport to tour the city for a while."

I let her know about our impromptu tour guide and held my breath in anticipation of her response. She did not disappoint.

"A stranger! You girls can't trust a stranger!"

Girls?

"Ma, Auntie Lil is twenty years older than you, and I'm an adult, too, remember. Besides, this is the brother of a nun."

Maybe playing the nun card would help.

It didn't.

"Just because she has taken vows doesn't mean he has. You don't know anything about him."

I knew my mother well enough to let her blow off steam for a moment or two, then she would calm down. I turned to the group and raised my finger to indicate one more moment, then turned back while I listened. Finally, Ma took a breath and stopped.

"Oh, Annalise, I'm sorry. I trust you to make good decisions. After all, you're going all the way across the world."

"Thank you."

"You just be careful."

"We will."

"I love you. Call me when you get back on the plane."

"We will."

"And make sure you eat!"

"Of course," I giggled.

I returned my phone to my bag, straightened my shoulders, and returned to the group. Being the daughter of loving, protective parents is not a job for sissies.

"Okay," I said as we continued on our way to the parking lot.

"How's your mother?" asked Auntie Lil.

"Ma is Ma," I said.

"No further explanation necessary," she laughed.

"Do you ladies have any idea about where you would like to visit in this brief time?" Breck asked as he loaded his sister's bag into the back of a rugged jeep. He noted our dubious expressions as we took in the car that seemed more suited to backcountry touring than city touring.

"Oh, don't worry. We'll not go off-roading today," he assured us. "That is, unless you want to?"

"Oh, stop it, Breck!" his sister swatted him in a familiar sisterly way on his shoulder. "You know they will want to see the city. Besides, these women are from Colorado. They can go off-roading every day if they want to."

Auntie Lil and I both burst into laughter.

"What?" The siblings looked at us in confusion.

"Oh, you obviously have just met Annalise," said Auntie Lil. "She is a city girl through and through."

"Seriously?" Breck looked confused. "But you live in Colorado, the home of hikers, bikers, skiers—"

"Readers, cooks, dancers, singers," I continued. "You know, we're all different people out there."

"All those mountains and you don't climb one?" asked Sister Mary Grace.

"She wouldn't climb one unless there was a mall at the top of it," said Auntie Lil as we piled into Breck's jeep and pulled away.

"Hmm. Well then, we will keep our touring on the light side of active today. But we might need to work on changing that activity level at some point," said Breck as he caught my eye in the rearview mirror and winked.

A shiver ran through me. Was he flirting with me? Stop it, Annalise. He was a nice, amiable man who was just doing his sister a favor. He probably had a tall, stunning mountain biker of a girlfriend who did commercials for Kashi granola bars.

"Well, a visit to San Francisco isn't complete without a trip to Ghirardelli Square for chocolate, so you'll have to include that," began Sister Mary Grace. "I know you can get the famous chocolate candy all over the country now, but there is something fun about having a sundae at the shop."

"I'm always in for chocolate," Auntie Lil nodded. "Before that, though, I would like to see a few things if we have time."

"Name it," said Breck.

"I'd like to see Lombard Street," she requested as she imitated the twists and turns of the iconic street with her hand.

"That's not very far from the convent, so that can be our first stop," said Breck. "Then what?"

"Wait. Let me make a list." I pulled my iPhone out of my bag and opened my note-taking app.

"Are you always this organized?" asked Breck.

"Uh … yeah." My fingers flew as I created an outline. I looked up. "What? Is there a problem with that?"

He grinned in the mirror.

"No, no. But you look so determined. Relax."

She turned to Breck.

"Be good and represent the family well, Breccan Michael," she said with a hug.

"Yes, ma'am." He saluted with a smile as she shouldered her bag and walked through the gate. We watched until she walked through the front door, then he turned to us, clapped his hands together, and said, "Alrighty then! Let's go off on our adventure!"

The one-block section of Lombard Street with its eight hairpin turns was indeed a few short moments from the convent, and we parked at the top of it to get a good view from top to bottom.

"I can't imagine living on that street and having to drive on it every day," I shaded my eyes and took in the row houses on either side. Auntie Lil took a short stroll to snap a few pictures of the flower beds.

"Me neither," said Breck, "but I have always wanted to see if I could take my skateboard from top to bottom."

"You're a skateboarder?"

"Of course, dude!" He struck a skater boy pose. "My shaggy-haired friends and I were at the skate park every day during the summers back home when I was a kid."

I pictured him in baggy shorts and shirt flapping through the skate park's twists and turns, his red curls flying.

"I bet you were a regular Tony Hawk," I said, referring to the most famous competitive skateboarder of the previous 20 years.

"I wish! I guess we all thought we were. When I went to college, my boarding time got cut severely."

"Where did you go to school?" I asked.

"Gonzaga," he said.

"You're a Gonzaga man," my aunt said approvingly, rejoining us. She had a soft spot in her heart for the private Catholic college in Washington state.

"Yes, ma'am. I loved it there."

Fleece-clad, ponytailed Breck certainly looked like he belonged in Spokane.

"What brought you here after graduation?"

"A job offer. I'm a web designer, and I had a great opportunity with one of the best firms in the Bay Area. It didn't hurt that Maggie was here."

"Maggie?"

"You just met her. My sister. Oh, I forgot. Sister Mary Grace. She's been a nun for a while, but it's hard to remember that she isn't my big sis Maggie."

We nodded in understanding. My great-uncle—Lil's uncle—was a priest, and we had to struggle to remember to call him "Father Fontana" rather than "Uncle Sal."

"So, ladies, what now?"

"Well, Breck, if you don't mind ..." began Auntie Lil.

He grinned.

"Hop in, because I think I can read your thoughts."

"What?" I wasn't catching on.

We got back into the jeep, and he drove us as fast as he dared around the turns from the top to the bottom of Lombard Street.

CHAPTER TEN

Fresh from laughing our way down the switchback street, we embarked on the next part of our tour.

"Let's see," I said, consulting my brief list, "what's next? Chocolate, cable cars, or bridge?"

Breck and Auntie Lil barely glanced at each other and said in unison: "Chocolate!"

"No argument here," I grinned.

Breck proved to be an excellent tour guide on the way to Fisherman's Wharf, the famous site of the famous chocolatier, pointing out places of interest along the way.

"You know a lot about your adopted city, Breck," said Auntie Lil.

"Well, I'm a restless guy," he answered. "When I first moved here, I didn't know very many people other than Maggie, so I just went out exploring when I had any time off and she was busy. I didn't have a car, so I walked a lot. You'd be surprised how much of a city you discover on foot."

He looked at me pointedly.

Subtle.

"A-GAIN," I felt it necessary to reiterate, "just because I don't climb MOUNtains doesn't mean I don't WALK."

"I didn't say anything about you," he smiled.

"Annalise, can't you see he's trying to goad you!" Auntie Lil laughed. "And he's doing a good job of it!"

Humph. What was it about this russet-haired man that got to me?

Maybe it was because he reminded me of Rory who had that same red head and freckles. Oh no! I forgot to let Rory know what was up. I glanced at my watch. She would probably have expected a call during our layover. This extended layover would be big news. I pulled out my phone and texted her.

Stuck in San Fran for extended layover.
Auntie L and I on massive adventure.

Her response was immediate.

OMG!! Call me with details.

Can't. Tour guide is part of adventure.

Seriously? Tall, handsome stranger?

I glanced up at Breck in the front seat chatting with Auntie Lil about the Great Fire of 1908. I smiled as I typed.

Hmm. Kinda.

WHAT!!! I need photo and details immediately.

In due time.

Send ASAP.

"What are you doing back there?" asked Auntie Lil. "There's a lot of beeping."

"Oh, just texting Rory about our slight delay."

"And me?" Breck asked. "You haven't left me out, right? Who is this Rory? Is he the jealous type?"

"SHE is my best friend, and, yes I did mention you vaguely." I closed my texting app so he couldn't accidentally see my last text. What a flirt!

We were at a stoplight, and he grabbed my phone and took a flattering photo of himself.

"Hey!" I grabbed it back.

"Just wanted you to have a picture to send her."

"Oh, as if," I reverted to high school slang, but I surreptitiously texted the selfie to Rory nonetheless.

Her response was immediate.

"Very nice! Who is he?
What does he do? How did
you meet? Very exciting!"

I could barely keep from laughing as I responded.

"Rory! This is a longer discussion than warrants a text! When I get a private minute, I'll call you, but until then, chill out."

"Don't forget."

I looked up to see that the car had stopped and Breck and Auntie Lil were waiting for me.

"Let's go, then," I tucked my phone into my bag and jumped out of the jeep.

I knew that Ghirardelli Square was a revamped industrial site, but I wasn't aware that it was the first such project in the United States. It takes up an entire city block and is filled with shops and restaurants.

We took a brochure from the information desk and began to casually stroll through the area, stopping every now and then to duck into a shop that caught our fancy. Finally, we reached the flagship shop, the Ghirardelli Chocolate Shop.

"If we're going to have an early dinner, do we really want to have sundaes?" I wondered aloud, but quickly amended my statement. "What am I saying! We're on vacation. This isn't a rehearsal for being in San Francisco—it's actually being here."

"Hey! I like that!" Breck smiled. "I'm going to adopt that as my personal motto."

"Feel free," I said. "You'll have to give credit to Auntie Lil, though. She's the one who taught it to me."

He turned and looped an arm through Auntie Lil's on one side and mine on the other as we entered the shop with a purpose.

"Onward!"

We managed to keep ourselves to one banana split to share, and we were truly enjoying it when my phone rang insistently. I saw that it was Rory and sighed. I guessed I needed to fill her in on what was going on before she sent a detective to spy on us.

"Hey, Rory," I said as I walked away from the table, leaving Auntie Lil and Breck in a spirited discussion of Gonzaga basketball.

"So spill the beans on what is going on."

"I'm not sure what was going on with the plane or why we needed to leave it, but we needed to wait for another one. I, for one, am happy they would rather be safe about the situation. Very prudent, if you ask me."

"And ...?"

"And? Oh ..." I continued, knowing that Rory wasn't really interested in the aviation particulars. "They gave us each restaurant vouchers. Very generous."

"Restaurant vouchers. Very nice. And ...?" Her impatience was beginning to bubble up.

"And what, Rory?"

"Ooooh. You know, you are very lucky I'm not there to punch you. You are so exasperating. You know I want to know about the hunky tour guide. How on earth did THAT happen?"

I burst into laughter and told her the story of how we met Breck's sister and what followed.

"Wow."

"Wow? That's all you got?" My forehead wrinkled.

"Well, I think it's definitely a 'meet cute' kind of situation worthy of a Sunday afternoon movie. I'm thinking it through, that's all. If he's in San Francisco, that's not really that far from Denver, and—"

"And nothing, Rory. You know as well as I do that long distance doesn't work. Besides, since when have you treated life like a bad Reese Witherspoon movie?"

"Just giving you grief, my dear," she said, and I knew she sported an impish grin on her face whether I could see her or not. "Relax. This just sounds like a fun afternoon spent with a definitely adorable guy. We don't need to shop for china patterns just yet."

"Exactly. Besides he couldn't be less my type."

"Explain, please."

"First of all, outdoorsy."

"Ha! What do you mean 'first of all'? With you, I would think that is the number one deal breaker."

Hmph. To hear her comments and Auntie Lil's, you'd think I never ventured forth from my house unless I was shaded by giant umbrellas and carried to my luxury automobile.

"Annalise? Are you still there? Say something."

"Am I really that princess-like?" I asked, fearful of the answer that my straightforward friend would provide.

She laughed heartily.

"No, you goof, but it's just fun to tease you about it. Heavens, you know my idea of a good time certainly isn't climbing Pikes Peak."

"But you ski and snowboard. And I sit in the lodge and read and wait by the warm fire."

"So? Everyone's different. Besides, I don't LIVE to ski and snowboard like some of our friends."

"You're right," I offered. "In any case, along with being so outdoorsy, this guy seems kind of aimless in that skater boy kind of way."

"Didn't you tell me he had a job as a web designer?"

"Oh, Rory, you know high-tech job descriptions. That could be anything."

"Okay, but I still haven't heard anything to rule him out, again other than geography."

I felt that the conversation was getting too intense, so I needed to draw it back a little.

"Well, Rory, he'd be perfect, but you know I just couldn't be with a … redhead!"

"Why I oughtta …!" she laughed, and I pictured her ruffling her own red curls. You'd be lucky to have an adorable ginger-haired man."

We laughed together.

"Oh Rory, I wish you were on this trip."

"I know. But I know Auntie Lil is a hoot and a great traveling companion."

"Definitely. And remember, this trip isn't about finding romance for me. It's about keeping her company."

"Sure, sure, but a little romance on the side couldn't hurt, whether it's a tall redhead or some other man."

"Rory! No redheads, blonds, or even brunets!"

But after we finished our call, my mind flashed to the handsome, dark-haired stranger I'd encountered in the bookstore. I shook my head as I returned to the table. Thanks a lot, Rory, for putting ridiculous romantic thoughts into my head.

"How is the irrepressible Rory?" asked Auntie Lil as I slid back into our booth.

"Fine, fine," I replied absently, noting that our communal banana split dish was scraped clean. Oh well. You snooze you lose, as my brother would say.

"You should meet Annalise's friend," Auntie Lil said to Breck. "The most adorable girl. Very energetic. Say … her hair is a perfect color match for yours!"

"Really?" he drawled as he leaned back in his seat. "I like her already."

Hey! Wait a minute! Rory wasn't even here, and already I felt in danger of losing a guy to her. How many times in college when we were out did guys chat me up just to get to her?

Or, when we were together, how often was I in a conversation with a promising candidate only to notice that his eye was focused somewhere over my shoulder in her vicinity?

Oh, Annalise, I chuckled to myself finally. Rory was never the type to steal a boyfriend. And besides, I had no claim on Ponytail Pete here other than as a tour guide. I really did have to work on my habit of overthinking things!

"Well, you would. Everyone does. The bigger question is whether she would like YOU." I hid a smile.

"Ouch!"

Gotcha! Take that, ego!

"Of course she would like him, Annalise! He's adorable," put in Auntie Lil.

Breck grinned and put his arm around her.

Thanks a lot, Auntie. Humph. Wasn't it time to shift the conversation?

"Annnnyway …" I started, "enough chitchat about a non-existent meeting! What's next on our agenda? We only have so much time before we have to get back to the airport, remember?"

"You're right, kiddo." Breck ushered us out of the booth.

"Let's find a cable car to ride," suggested Auntie Lil.

"We can actually leave the car parked where it is and walk a few blocks to do that," Breck nodded.

When we left the shop, the weather was breezy and bright. Just the right atmosphere for a stroll on the streets of San Francisco. As we reach the nearest cable car stop, a car was arriving, and we hopped on. It was nearly full, so we opted to stand and lean out the window as it continued on its route.

When the iconic bell rang, Auntie Lil grinned like a kindergartener, and I knew what was coming next.

"Here it comes," I nudged Breck.

"What?" he asked.

"Wait and see." I inclined my head toward my sassy aunt a split second before her crystal-clear voice began:

"I left my hearrrrt ... in San Frannnn-cisco!"

I knew it! She would never have been able to resist singing the unofficial anthem of the city by the bay! I looked around at the other passengers as she continued. Some pretended to ignore her, but a good portion of them listened with smiles on their faces or even joined in. I turned to Breck, who was belting out the song!

I took a second to take a mental snapshot of the moment. My aunt had a way of making the ordinary so very extraordinary. She's the most amazing woman, and I am so blessed that I had the opportunity to join her on this trip! Breck caught my eye and leaned over.

"Hey! Why aren't you singing? Don't you know the song?"

"Of course!" I joined in.

By the time we finished the tune, all the passengers were laughing and singing. Folks waved and nodded as they exited. Since we were going round-trip, we met an entirely new group of people on the way back to Fisherman's Wharf.

At our stop, we hopped off and jauntily returned to Breck's jeep.

"So, ladies," Breck said as he checked his watch, "early dinner?"

"I know we just had ice cream, but dinner sounds fabulous!" Auntie Lil agreed.

I checked the address for the recommended restaurant, and we were on our way.

CHAPTER ELEVEN

We left Breck's car with the valet and pushed open the heavy oak doors to the quaint eatery located on a quiet side street. Immediately, we felt as if we had entered a rustic Tuscan farmhouse kitchen. Small tables were grouped with mismatched chairs. Wonderful smells wafted toward us as we neared the hostess stand.

"Reservations?" asked the pert hostess.

"We don't have reservations, but can you fit us in?" Breck asked with a charming smile.

"Hmm." The hostess wrinkled her forehead slightly. "I'm not sure …"

"We were hoping to get in. Sarah at the airline recommended you highly. She said this was a sister restaurant to one we have in Denver and has the best tiramisu." I pulled out our restaurant voucher and pointed out the handwritten note on the back.

The hostess smiled.

"You're from Denver? The original Nonna's restaurant is there! Have you eaten there?"

I debated on fudging the truth, but I knew that ethically that was so wrong.

"Not yet. But we're looking forward to going there when we get back!"

The hostess burst into laughter. She grabbed three menus.

"Follow me. There's a corner that might be right. It's a small table for two, but we'll make it work."

Almost as swiftly as we were seated, our server appeared.

"Welcome to Nonna's. I'm Gina. Let me tell you our specials."

We soon ordered our food and beverages and were enjoying the crusty bread and olive oil that the server had placed before us.

"I can't tell you how much we've appreciated your time today," Auntie Lil said to Breck.

"It really was my pleasure. I am always happy to share my adopted city."

"You told us you are a web designer, but you didn't really explain your job," continued Auntie Lil. "If you are a designer, are you an artist?"

"Not at all, although Maggie and I do have a baby sister who is a painter who I occasionally consult with on the artistic side of my job. I am on the back end of the operation, the end that programs how the website interacts with the world."

"This was something you studied at Gonzaga?"

"I double-majored in computer science and in web design specializing in e-commerce, then did an internship at a web design firm."

So it seemed that this shaggy-looking fellow was rather well educated! From his devil-may-care attitude, I would have taken him for a typical high-tech cowboy: all flash and no substance. I guess there's a reason that people say not to judge a book by its cover.

He turned to me.

"What is your line of work—that is, when you aren't jet-setting?"

"I'm hardly a jet-setter!" I said. "Up until a few months ago, I was a marketing manager—for a technology company, as a matter of fact—until they decided to outsource."

"Ah, victim of a RIF?" he nodded knowingly, using the abbreviation for "reduction in force," a common term for "layoff."

"Exactly. You know that marketing is the first to go in high tech. And while I've been job hunting, I have been waiting tables and doing other odd jobs."

"My Annalise is a very resourceful gal," Auntie Lil gave me a hug.

"Are you looking to get back into high-tech marketing?" Breck asked.

I paused. The answer should have been an easy "yes," but I wasn't so sure. I loved my last job, but did I love it because of the job or because of the company? Sure I was let go, but that was a business decision from the parent corporation. Our small company was a tight-knit organization, and I had really believed in the software that we produced. Would I feel the same way about another company and its products?

The company where I had most recently interviewed and lost the position to my former boyfriend's bride was an example of that. They were a good organization, well respected in the industry, and the salary they had offered was enticing. I didn't feel, however, that their products were necessarily the best in their market. I wasn't sure I could promote a product that I didn't personally believe in.

"Hmm," I finally said. "That depends."

"On what?"

I looked over at this near stranger. A naturally reticent person, I wasn't sure I needed to open up to someone I had just met hours earlier. But his bright-green eyes and up-turned, freckle-sprinkled nose gave him the air of someone who could be trusted. He munched patiently on a crust of bread as he waited for my answer.

"Well ... I feel strongly about not promoting products that I don't personally believe in. Does that make sense?"

"Totally," he nodded. "When I was given the choice of internships, I could have done one with a huge, prestigious company or a smaller one. The smaller one was more in line with my ... moral compass, let's say, so it was an easy choice. And the company I work for now is the same way."

"Your parents must be proud," Auntie Lil said.

He grinned "Well, I have to admit that they had their doubts at times that I'd settle down from my skater boy ways, but I've never strayed too far from the path they encouraged."

"I imagine your sister is proud as well," Auntie Lil continued.

"My sister the Sister? Well, she's my hero. Of all my siblings, I feel closest to Maggie. If I could find a woman as cool as she is, I'd marry her in a minute."

"Marriage! I can't believe someone who gives off the air of bachelorhood like you do thinks about marriage!" I laughed.

"Well ..." he drawled, "it would take a rare woman to catch me. And I am a catch, you have to admit."

We all laughed as he flexed his biceps.

Our server returned to our table at that moment with our mouthwatering meals, and we prepared to enjoy our dinner.

I glanced at Breck as he and Auntie Lil debated the merits of his linguine in clam sauce versus her penne arrabbiata. Instinctively I knew he was a catch. For me? No. But he would make some woman a good husband. I could only pray that I would find my version of this charming man.

Leaning back as our plates were cleared from the table, we deliberated about dessert. Gina resolved the discussion handily.

"The tiramisu is awesome. You folks should definitely have it."

"Tiramisu all around, then," nodded Auntie Lil. "No diets on vacation!"

"You ladies don't need to worry about dieting, surely!" said Breck.

"Well, aren't you a flatterer," said Auntie Lil, whose figure, like mine, leaned toward the curvy side.

"No," he shook his head, "just telling the truth."

"I believe in all things in moderation and treats when necessary," he continued as three delicious slices of dessert appeared at our table. "And this tiramisu looks absolutely necessary."

We wasted no time in devouring the creamy confection, then enjoyed a leisurely coffee before departing the restaurant.

Hopping into Breck's jeep, we headed toward the airport. My phone rang insistently. This time it was my father.

"Annalise, are you in the air yet?"

"On the way to the airport, Pop. And if we were in the air, I couldn't answer the phone, don't you think?"

My usually logical father ignored my correction of his nonsensical question.

"Well, you call me when you are on the plane. How is your aunt? What have you been doing? Have you eaten?"

"Pop, Pop," I laughed. "We're fine. We have eaten—a lot, as a matter of fact. We actually ate a very nice Italian meal."

"And the boy who has been your guide?"

"Not a boy, Pop," I sighed.

Auntie Lil reached back to grab my phone.

"Samuel Joseph," she said in her best eldest sister voice, "we are both fine. We're eating. Our tour guide is a delightful young man, just as we predicted. He is a Gonzaga graduate. He has neither stolen our wallets nor taken us against our will to some sort of pyramid scheme presentation. Now, please give both of us credit. We will phone you when we are on the airplane."

She punched the "off" button and handed it back to me decisively.

"Oh sure," I tilted my head and smirked, "he'll listen to you."

"I doubt that he listened. As a matter of fact, I'm sure he's sputtering on the other end right now. I simply refused to continue the conversation, and he knows better than to attempt to revive it. Now, Breck, did you say we had time to drive toward the bridge?"

"I'm afraid to say no!" he grinned. "We'll take a slight detour that will get you a view of the bridge and then get you to the airport about five minutes before the time I promised."

And he did.

As he dropped us at the curb—we had insisted that he not take more time out of his day to park and escort us inside—we exchanged hugs, phone numbers, and all other contact information.

"Breccan, you are a delightful young man and a wonderful tour guide!" Auntie Lil proclaimed.

"It truly was my pleasure," he said.

"Please come visit us in Denver," she insisted. "Let us repay the favor and give you a tour of the Mile High City."

"That sounds like a plan to me." He turned to me. "Do you think we can get you up on the slopes if I come?"

"Sorry to disappoint, Breck, but I doubt I'll turn into a skier anytime soon. I promise that I'll find you some ski buddies, though."

As I said that, I pictured my own best pal. Hmm. Maybe auburn-haired Rory would be a good match for this redheaded outdoor adventurer.

"It's a deal then," he clapped his hands together. "And you ladies call us anytime you're in town. Maybe next time we'll skateboard down Lombard Street."

"Maybe!" Auntie Lil said—and I believed her!

We waved as he drove off and turned to enter the airport.

"Well! What an adventure!" Auntie Lil said.

"Right. Who knew?" I replied.

"Now, how do we get back to the original adventure?" she asked.

I looked at our instructions, and we followed them through TSA—once again, shoes off, liquids in bins, etc.—to the designated "holding pen" for our luggage. Once we were matched with our luggage and it was sent to our new plane, we traveled to our gate to await boarding.

Within an hour, we were on our way again to Singapore.

CHAPTER TWELVE

"Ladies and gentlemen, we are making our final descent into Singapore. Please complete the customs documents …"

I clasped Auntie Lil's hand, and we smiled brightly at each other as the flight attendant completed her instructions for our entry into the country nearly a day after leaving Denver. We had passed the time on this leg of the journey reading, chatting, dozing, and eating. My across-the-aisle neighbor did not speak English, but we managed to nod and smile occasionally during the trip.

"Aren't you tired?" Auntie Lil asked. "You didn't sleep as much as I did."

"Couldn't sleep, Auntie! Plus, I started watching that movie near the end of the flight and felt like I needed to finish it."

"It was based on a true story, Annalise. You knew the ending."

"I just like to finish what I start," I shrugged.

She smiled at me and patted my hand.

"Two peas in a pod. That's us! I saw you scribbling away as well. Were you writing in your journal?"

"Oh, sort of," I shrugged. "I decided to keep it as if I were writing letters to someone, like Rory, rather than just writing the facts. It makes it more interesting."

"Hmm. That sounds good."

As the jet touched down, I leaned across Auntie Lil to get a better view of the sun-drenched city-state that we would be visiting for the next few days. The bright blue sky painted with fluffy white clouds reminded me a lot of Denver, but I knew that since we were so close to the equator, the heat factor would be significantly higher than back home.

Once we exited into the terminal of the bustling Changi Airport, we were delighted at how effortless it was to negotiate customs and claim our baggage. We made our way to the taxi stand outside.

"My first international stamp!" I exclaimed as I pointed out the faint stamp on a page in my passport.

"Didn't you get stamped when you went to World Youth Day?" Auntie Lil asked.

"Well … yes. Maybe I should have said 'my first international stamp that wasn't from a country I could drive to.'"

Our taxi driver, Murukan, was a pleasant man who negotiated the twenty-minute trip to our hotel in short order, giving us travel advice along the way.

"Do you like spicy food?" he asked over his shoulder.

"We sure do!" I nodded enthusiastically.

"Then don't leave Singapore without having chili crab. It is our national food, and you will be happy you had it." His eyes crinkled into a smile in the mirror.

"It's a good thing Pop isn't here," I turned to Auntie Lil who nodded in acknowledgement of my father's aversion to seafood.

Even though Auntie Lil was a dedicated researcher of her destination before any journey, she leaned forward to ask Murukan what his favorite part of the city was.

"Do you like to travel a bit off the beaten path, young miss?"

"That is always the best part of a journey," I said.

"Are you going to Little India?" he asked.

"Of course," Auntie Lil answered.

"When you get there, you need to go down to the very end of Kerbau Road to the Lucky Charm music shop. The owner sells beautiful handmade instruments—sitars and such—and will let you test them out and give you a history lesson about them."

"That sounds fantastic!"

"I agree," Auntie Lil nodded.

"Tell them I sent you," Murukan insisted. "They won't attempt to sell you anything, please trust me, missus. Of course, if you do decide to purchase, that is up to you."

We pulled into the curved entryway to our hotel, and Murukan jumped from the car to retrieve our luggage. In a moment, a bellman loaded our bags on a cart and escorted us into the entryway past a small cafe and into an elevator up to the actual first floor of the hotel.

"This is interesting," I whispered to Auntie Lil. "I don't think I've ever had to take an elevator to get TO the check-in desk of a hotel."

"It's very common here," she answered.

We checked in and moved to another elevator to reach our room on the 24th floor—and it was luxurious. I dashed over to the floor-to-ceiling windows, then turned to Auntie Lil.

"Holy cow! This must be costing a fortune!"

"Not at all," she waved off my comment. "I do my research, dear, and of course I collect points."

"Well, you must have collected points for years to get this," I fell backward on the plump white comforter that covered one of the queen beds.

"Not to worry! I've told you before, this is a treat for both of us." She began to unpack her bags with efficiency.

I stared at the ceiling for a moment, then jumped up to unpack my own bags. We worked with an economy of movement, and I grinned at how the contents of our bags were very similar.

"Two peas in a pod. That's what we really are!" I referred back to her comment on the airplane.

"I'm going to jump in the shower before we take off for the rest of the day," I grabbed my toiletries and ducked into a bathroom that was nearly as large as the apartment I had recently vacated.

After my shower, I changed into an outfit of capris and a tank top covered by a stylish, fluttery, thin jacket cut on an asymmetrical bias. I decided to wait downstairs for Auntie Lil as she freshened up.

"I see. So if you live here, what are you doing in this hotel lobby? Just skulking around waiting to instruct American tourists on the local beverages?"

He threw his head back and laughed.

"Brilliant. No, I have a meeting with someone who is staying here. We have some documents to sign." He pointed to his smooth leather portfolio. "And what brings you to Singapore, Anna-plus-Alisa?"

"My aunt and I are vacationing. We'll be in Singapore for several days, then move on to China." His use of an expanded form of my name was charming.

"Are you having fun?"

"So far, we've checked into this lovely hotel and I've been enjoying this refreshing drink, so our experiences have been quite limited."

Jasper reached into the portfolio and retrieved a notepad and slim polished pen. He began a rapid scribbling motion while tossing out suggestions. He was obviously a man who was used to taking rapid and decisive action.

"First, get a multi-pass for the Duck & Hippo bus—make sure you get a map from them. Then go to the following stops: Little India … Kampong Glam … Little China … you won't want to miss the Peranakhan Museum. I think you need to walk a bit from the bus stop to get there, but the map will show you—"

"Jasper … Jasper … JASPER!"

His head shot up.

"I'm sorry, but you're throwing a lot of information my way. Ducks? Hippos? Glam?" I tilted my head in a question.

"Hmm? Oh, sorry. Let me slow down."

"Thank you. Oh, here comes my aunt. Hold for a moment so you can share the information with both of us."

Auntie Lil crossed the floor from the elevator, and her face was amused as she looked from one to the other of us.

"Annalise, who is your new friend?"

Jasper leapt to his feet. Manners. A good sign.

"Jasper Pennock, ma'am. I was having a delightful chat with your enchanting niece. To whom do I have the pleasure of speaking?"

"Lilliana Fontana." Auntie Lil extended her hand and sat next to me.

"What are you young people drinking? That looks very refreshing."

"It's called chia tea—wait, is that right?" I asked.

"Close enough. It's *teik chia*, Miss Fontana." Jasper explained the beverage to Auntie Lil as he motioned to the server to bring another round. She took a long draw from the slim glass and pronounced it perfect.

"Jasper was just making some notes for us for while we are here. He lives in Singapore."

"How kind!" Auntie Lil smiled.

"Not a problem, ma'am. I entertain visitors for my company quite often, so I have gotten a lot of feedback on what people like to see while they are here."

He began his list again, this time more slowly, and we peppered him with questions.

"Our taxi driver mentioned that we should eat chili crab. What do you think?" I said.

"Indeed! That is the delicacy of Singapore. I'll jot down the best restaurant for that. I presume you'll want to have that for dinner?"

Auntie Lil and I looked at one another and gave thumbs up. Finding great places to eat was always a goal of ours on vacation.

"Hmm." Jasper glanced at his watch. "I have a business dinner quite near there this evening in the same square surrounding the wharf Since you will be dining at this restaurant, would you ladies give me the honor of joining me for dessert afterward?"

"Oh, no—" I started to protest, but Auntie Lil cut me off.

"We would be delighted! Let's say we meet in the square outside the restaurant at about 9?"

What was she up to?

"Splendid!" Jasper stood. "I see the person I am to meet, so I need to take my leave of you now.

And with a quick handshake to each of us, he joined a group of men who had exited the elevator and were preparing to leave the building. Jasper's bright hair stood out among their dark heads. We could hear strains of an Asian language in the conversation as they exited, so our newfound friend obviously was not limited to speaking English.

I turned to Auntie Lil, but her mischievous smile stopped me from questioning.

CHAPTER THIRTEEN

"Now, Annalise, I know what you are thinking."

"Go ahead, tell me, because I don't think I'm even sure what I'm thinking." I leaned back on my chair and crossed my legs and arms simultaneously.

"Well, dear, there's a reason that Jasper was brought into our lives, so why not visit with him for a little while longer this evening?"

"You're not playing matchmaker, here, are you?"

"Nonsense."

I tilted my head and squinted.

"Well, in a way."

"Auntie!"

"Annalise, you haven't dated since that Dylan character, so I think you are out of practice. You were a bit reserved with that delightful Breccan in San Francisco—"

"That wasn't a date, Auntie Lil!" What on earth was she getting at?

"I realize that, dear, but you need to keep in practice."

What! Were these words coming from my self-sufficient aunt? I could see my mother worrying that I would never produce grandchildren ...

Then I remembered the story of the love of Auntie's life.

Oh.

She just wanted me to have what she never had. We might be in the 21st century, but she understood that even though her life journey didn't include a husband, she wanted to do everything she could to help me find one. How caring and sweet!

"I get it, Auntie Lil."

She bustled about, gathering her tote bag.

"Well, all you'll be getting is tired from sitting on that chair if we don't hustle out and take advantage of this beautiful day!" she said. "Let's get a move on."

We made our way out of the hotel and walked the few blocks to the nearest stop for the "Duck and Hippo" tour bus. The brightly painted tour line was a hop-on, hop-off loop around the city, and passengers received a set of headphones with a paid fare. Plugging the headphones into the jack next to our seat allowed us to find an English-speaking recording among the nine languages. As the bus reached designated stops, the recorded guide clued us in to what we were seeing.

The tops of the double-decker buses were open, which allowed a sunny view but could potentially be scorching on a high-digit day. Luckily this day was breezy and just sunny enough to make the ride very enjoyable.

We learned so much about the city history and architecture. We chose our stops for the day and decided to return to some of them the next day since we had purchased two-day tickets. We made sure to hop off at Little India as our first stop and enjoyed our stroll through the hurly-burly streets.

"This must be what it's like on some of the streets in the cities of India," I said.

"I suspect so," Auntie said. "Let's find the music shop that our taxi driver told us about."

We walked down busy streets toward the address, stopping along the way to marvel at the variety of shops and how the walkways, covered with overhangs to shield from the intense sun, were packed with what seemed to be not only tourists but also natives. Vivid colors and tantalizing smells mixed as we passed stores selling brightly colored materials for making saris and markets featuring glistening fruits and baskets spilling over with spices. Practically every jewelry shop displayed stacks of sparkling bracelets in the windows.

"When a woman becomes a bride, she wears stacks of bangles to indicate that she is married," said Auntie Lil. "The different colors and metals have different significance. I bet you feel a kinship to that tradition."

She lifted my arm, on which I wore a collection of gold bracelets—some antique family heirlooms and some gifts from her, Rory, and my parents, who know my love of bracelets.

"Well, you'll never lose me in a crowd." I jangled my arm and smiled.

After a few twists and turns and an impromptu stop to share an enticing vegetable Samosa from a street vendor, we found our destination and stepped through a slim door to the

Lucky Charm music store. The window to the side displayed only one stringed instrument, so we were not prepared for the plethora of instruments that filled the tiny, incense-scented shop.

"Yes, Missus?" queried a rotund man with bright white hair and mustache.

"Good afternoon. Our taxi driver sent us here. A Mr. Murukan?" Auntie Lil was quietly polite. She knew that as two women traveling alone in another culture, we might not always be as welcome as in our own environment back home.

The man's face split into a grin.

"Ah! Yes! Murukan! He is my cousin. Come ... come." He gestured us toward the back of the store where we found a small, well-worn settee.

"My name is Prasad, and this is my daughter Madhur." He indicated a young woman in her early twenties, dressed in the typical Indian garb. Her shalwar (leggings) were violet toned and kameez (tunic) was in a mustard print, trendy colors that were showing up on the runways, according to the fashion magazines back home.

"May I offer you a cup of tea or a glass of cola?" asked Madhur.

We knew that to refuse would be impolite, so we accepted the offer of tea.

"What brings you to our humble shop?" asked Prasad.

"With all respect, your cousin said that you might take a moment to show us one or two of your beautiful handmade instruments."

Auntie Lil was not only one of the most educated women I knew, but also the best at assimilating into another culture!

I knew some people from back home who would have been very ham-handed and demanding. Not my cultured aunt.

"Of course, of course!" Prasad responded. He sat comfortably on the floor and gestured to Madhur, and she brought him an instrument made from wood in warm honey tones.

"There are many variations of instruments in my homeland, but we specialize in those that are plucked, stringed instruments," he waved around the shop. "What would you say this is in my hands, young miss?"

"A sitar?" I hoped I was right.

"Correct! And probably the most recognizable in the Western world."

He began to play a lovely melody on it. Madhur returned with another instrument that looked almost like it, only larger and made from darker wood. She sat next to him compactly and, flipping her long black braid over one shoulder, leaned and began to harmonize with him.

"That, ladies, is the surbahar, which is essentially a bass sitar."

They played together for several mesmerizing moments, and when they finished, Auntie Lil and I applauded. Madhur and Prasad bowed their heads slightly.

"Thank you. Now let me tell you the history of these beautiful instruments."

He told their histories, turning them from side to side as he spoke. The story was fascinating.

"Would you like to try one, young miss?"

Would I!

"If that would be okay with you?" I could be cultured, too.

"Come, come." They gestured for me to sit on the floor, cross-legged as they were, and they set the sitar in my lap.

Prasad showed me how to hold my hands, and I tentatively struck a note. Buoyed by my success, I struck a few more. I looked up at Auntie Lil with a grin.

"Get a picture of this, Auntie Lil! No one will believe it!"

"I'm ahead of you, dear."

She had my phone out and took a few snaps.

"Your turn, now, Missus," indicated Madhur with a smile.

Auntie Lil moved to the floor and took possession of the surbahar. With a moment's lesson, she was plucking chords as well.

"Would you like a photo of both of you?" Prasad asked, grinning. He motioned to Madhur, and she took pictures of us with my phone.

We handed the beautifully designed and carved instruments back to Prasad and Madhur and returned to the settee.

"What else would you like to know?" he asked.

"Everything!" I said. "But wait, let me get my journal out, I want to take notes."

We passed a bit more time learning about his business, including the fact that he came from generations of instrument makers.

"Who will take over this shop from you?" I asked. "Madhur?"

Oops! I hoped I hadn't asked an improper question. There was probably some rule against women doing jobs meant for men here. My face must have shown my worry.

"No. My precious daughter is only helping me today because her brother has the day off. He is my apprentice. Madhur is premed at the university. Her talented hands will be used when she is a surgeon."

So much for preconceived notions, I smiled inwardly.

"My other siblings are younger, and some of them will also learn the craft," said Madhur.

"Well, this has been a wonderful learning experience, and you have been kind, but we shouldn't be taking so much of your time," Auntie Lil said and rose from her seat. I joined her.

"It has been our pleasure."

I waited for our host to attempt to make some sort of sale, because many of my friends had warned me that we would be walking into a hard sell whenever we stopped in a shop on our travels. So far, he'd made no effort to do this. And then, there it was.

"If you ladies are in the market for one of my instruments, I would be able to package it in such a way that I could ship it safely to your home," he began.

But then I was surprised.

"However, the decision to purchase one of these instruments is not one to be made lightly on the basis of a few moments over tea. Take my card, and remember the Lucky Charm if you are ever in the market for a purchase. We can discuss your exact needs, and you can purchase the instrument that is best for you."

"Thank you so much, Mr. Prasad. It would be an honor to own one of these fine instruments." Auntie Lil smiled and tucked his card in her bag.

We were ushered to the exit with many smiles and well wishes, and I waited until we were halfway up the street before I quizzed her.

"How did we get out of that store without a harder push to make a purchase?"

"Annalise, he is a true craftsman. We were lucky to have been asked to visit and treated as guests. I suspect that he makes his sales from wealthy clients the world over and doesn't need to push his wares on cheap tourists. He knows that when he gives out his business card, it will usually get into the right hands and he'll make a sale worth more than any penny-ante sale today. He wants his art to go to someone who will use it appropriately, not hang it in an overdecorated family room somewhere."

"Is that what he thought we'd do with it?"

"No, but he knew we weren't musicians," Auntie laughed. "Or at least that you weren't. Did you hear your, um, music?"

"Hey!"

Auntie Lil nudged my hip with hers, and we both giggled as we returned to the bus stop. After we got on board, we made plans to hop off at the next stop: the Kampong Glam.

CHAPTER FOURTEEN

Even though the Kampong Glam area was only a few blocks from Little India, it was as if we had traveled to another country. It was originally the home of the Malay aristocracy at the turn of the 19th century, but eventually became a multiethnic community with a heavy Arab population.

I shaded my eyes and took in the small shops painted in pinks, greens, and yellows. "These are gorgeous, Auntie Lil," I said.

"If we turn here," she said, consulting her map as we strolled, "we should see … aha … yes."

Towering in front of us was the Sultan Mosque. The onion dome glittered gold in the sunlight, and the windows on each side had the distinctive curves of Arabic design.

"Are we allowed in?" I asked.

"Ordinarily, yes, but I see that it is under repairs and closed today."

"Darn. I would like to have seen what that looked like inside."

We circled the formidable structure and took photos before moving on toward Muscat Street and then Arab Street where we encountered a row of vendors selling bales of textiles.

"Auntie Marta would be in her element here, wouldn't she," I said as I fingered the luxurious silks, batiks, and other materials.

"She would love the textiles, but as a quilter, she likes to stick with cottons."

"I don't know, she is a wizard with anything," I said, thinking of the wedding dress she had made for her daughter, my cousin Sandra, in vintage tulles and lace.

"Mmm," Auntie Lil said as she held a length of red batik against her. "How does this make me look?"

"Like a very edgy Mrs. Santa Claus with your white hair." I shook my head. "Too plain. You need pattern."

"You're right." She put it down.

"Do you think she'll make mine?"

"Your what, dear?"

"My wedding gown. Do you think Auntie Marta would make it?" I asked.

"Sure," she said over her shoulder. "What about this?"

She held a length of green print against her.

"Looks nice. Auntie Lil for someone who wants to matchmake me, you're not taking very much interest in my wedding gown." I hid my smile.

She stopped, burst into laughter, and hugged me.

And what about Kate Upton, who all the guys salivate over? She certainly isn't a size 0.

"If you've got it, flaunt it, I say," she said and stood with one hand behind her head and the other on her hip.

"Auntie! If Pop were here—"

"He'd throw a cloak over me and tell me to calm down." She waved her hand to dismiss that statement. "But that's your father."

I looked down at my own figure, not much different than hers. My recent depression-induced extra pounds notwithstanding, I never have felt anything other than curvy. Society puts artificial norms on us, though.

Heck, on the other end of the spectrum, even Rory has had doubts about her figure. Although she has always been slim, and you'd think that would be perfect, she went through periods of time when her self-esteem was damaged because the boys called her "giraffe" and "grasshopper."

"Why can't we be happy with the way we look as long as we're healthy, Auntie?" I mused.

"I'm not sure, love. The standards have changed throughout the ages, so the ideal for beauty has been a moving target. Do you realize that in the Renaissance, we'd be considered downright anorexic?"

I pinched my generous thigh and laughed.

"Well, I'd have to get THAT in writing!"

Auntie Lil propped her Jackie O sunglasses on her nose, then stood and gathered her bags in her brisk, efficient manner.

"In any case, Annalise, let's move along or we won't finish the rest of our touring today."

"Yes, ma'am!"

We moved to the bus stop, hopped on the familiar red bus, and exited at the stop nearest Chinatown, where we were once again transported to an entirely different culture.

"Isn't it amazing how all of these different areas have been able to maintain their roots and heritage in such close quarters?" I asked.

"This is one of the things that Singapore is known for," Auntie Lil said. "The island welcomes people from the separate cultures but doesn't force any to assimilate and merge into one central one."

"Hmm." I stopped to sit on a bench to add notes to my journal. Auntie Lil sat down next to me and waited patiently.

"I'll be done in a sec," I murmured, writing furiously, and then looked up. "Oh, sorry, Auntie. I don't mean to stop so often."

"No, dear, not to worry at all. I think it's important that you take down your thoughts as they come to you."

I stopped and leaned back.

"When we get back, do you think I'll look at the file on my iPad or toss my collection of random notes in a box somewhere, Auntie Lil?"

"Why would you say that?"

I sighed and thought for a moment.

"Well, they're just fleeting glimpses, not really tied together, you know? I don't have a real goal for them."

"I think your goal is to capture our journey. If you do that, you will have achieved it. Don't overthink these things, dear. You never know what will happen."

I flipped back through my notes. Maybe she was right. Overthinking had certainly never served me very well in the past. With a sense of determination, I added one more thing to the notes.

"What was that you just wrote?"

"'Stop overthinking!'" I said sheepishly.

"Good. Let's go."

We continued our walk through Chinatown at a leisurely pace. The open-air markets in this section of town were at once similar and quite different from the other ethnic areas we'd visited, and we stopped to enjoy the sights and sounds. I reminded Auntie Lil that as exciting as Chinatown was, it was twice as exciting to think that in a few days we would actually be in China.

At one point in our walk, she insisted on purchasing exquisite hand-painted fans from an elderly man in a shop that was no bigger than a phone booth. The fans were constructed of bamboo and cotton, and when unfolded, featured paintings of scenery so detailed they looked like photographs. We enjoyed choosing colors and designs that would match the personalities of the ladies in our lives. The artist didn't speak English, but through a series of hand gestures, he was spot-on in matching fans to our own personalities.

Leaving the shop, we were thrilled to have found such lovely works of art.

"That's exactly the kind of thing I like to find on vacation! Something unique," said Auntie Lil.

"I've not traveled very far out of Colorado, so I'll take your word for it," I said.

"Oh, but you will, you will! You have your whole life ahead of you."

I glanced at my watch and realized that we had strolled so long through Chinatown that it was time for dinner. We were one street over from the wharf, so we crossed there and walked to the Jumbo Seafood, which Jasper had recommended.

It was a very busy place. The outdoor tables were all full of happy diners. Inside, the restaurant was divided into one large room jam-packed with tables and several smaller rooms that each held one large community table.

Our hostess explained that a wait for two people wanting their own table would be 1 1/2 to 2 hours but that we could be seated immediately at a community table. We both nodded and said "community table!" in unison.

We wound our way through the tightly packed tables and were seated at a table for twelve in one of the smaller rooms.

"Well, Annalise, we're the first ones here. This should be an adventure!" Auntie Lil grabbed my hand under the table as we looked with anticipation to see who the next diners would be to join us.

We didn't have to wait long. A tall, blond couple entered and sat to Auntie Lil's right. They didn't look American, and in a few moments we discovered that they were from Germany.

"Are you here for the chili crab?" asked the woman, Elke, who spoke with a British accent.

"Definitely," answered Auntie Lil.

Elke's husband, Dieter, leaned across and explained that we were in for not only a culinary treat but also somewhat of a mess. He was proven correct when our server came and tied plastic bibs around our necks.

"Well, this will be fun!" I grinned.

Five more tablemates, a family visiting from Sweden, joined us. The parents, two teenage daughters, and a much younger son also ordered the specialty of the house. They were promptly kitted out with the bibs, which featured a drawing of a cheerfully smiling crab.

"The crab wouldn't be smiling if he knew what his fate was!" said the father, Max. We learned that his petite, dark-haired wife was French by birth and that they were in Singapore on their way to Hong Kong. They spoke English as well, so conversation was no problem.

Our group was chatting happily, anticipating who would complete our table, when our server entered with another couple. Imagine my surprise when it was our new friend Jasper, along with a stunning blonde!

"Hello, Anna-Plus-Alisa and Miss Fontana! I was hoping to run into you here before our dessert assignment. Please meet Diana."

Girlfriend? I looked at Auntie Lil.

Well, I wasn't expecting to be on a date with him, after all. He continued.

"My business dinner has been pushed to breakfast tomorrow, but I did invite one of the chaps who would be attending along with us. Here he is now—Mate, here we are!" Jasper looked out the door and waved another diner toward our room.

The table turned to watch a dark-haired, dark-eyed man walk in, squint, and survey the table. My heart caught a beat.

It was the man who ran me down in the bookstore at the airport in Denver!

CHAPTER FIFTEEN

This was the type of thing that only happened in the movies. Two people meet in a random situation in Act One, then mysteriously run into each other again in, what, Act Two? I wondered if he remembered me.

As he, Jasper, and the model-perfect Diana moved around the table, I wondered what seat he would take.

Yikes! He sat next to me! My heart started to beat hard.

I remembered the famous line from the movie *An Affair to Remember*: "All I could say was hello." I took a deep breath and turned toward him.

"Hello." I hoped my tone was sufficiently calm. I waited for his response. The first words out of his mouth would be so important.

"What? Yes … hello." He had turned toward me but had barely looked up from the menu, threw out those three words, then looked back at the menu.

That's it? I stared ahead for a moment, not knowing what to think. Did he not remember me? Did he remember me and purposely want to ignore me? Did—

Whoa, Annalise. There I was doing it again. Overthinking. I'd give him a moment to choose his meal, then try again. He closed the large menu, and I thought that was my chance.

"So, the chili crab is supposed to be the best here, I heard—" I began.

"Oh, I'm not having that." He cut me off.

Hmm. Not very polite.

Jasper leaned across our uncommunicative tablemate to me and added, "I suspect my friend is afraid to get his shirt dirty, Annalise."

"Oh, come on, we're all having it." I attempted to draw him out.

"Do you always follow the crowd?" he asked with a tone. Where was the attractive smile I had seen in the Denver bookstore? Was this man the sullen twin brother of that other one?

"Well, no." I pulled back myself. "But I don't choose to deny myself something just BECAUSE others are having it, either."

Jasper laughed heartily at that.

"She has you there, chap!"

Humph. Was rudeness going to be a theme? Well, I wasn't going to let that ruin my evening. I turned to Auntie Lil.

"What's up, buttercup?" she asked with a smile.

"The guy to my left? The only one without a bib at the table?" I said.

"Yes?"

"He's the fellow I ran into at the airport in Denver."

"Really!" Auntie leaned over to get a better look. I pulled her back.

"Not so obvious, Auntie!"

"Oh, don't be so worried. He's not looking this way now. Wait, now I see him. Well … he's very nice looking." She paused and attempted to be a bit more covert. "You could get lost in those eyes. I wonder what has made him so sad."

"Sad? You mean sullen, don't you?"

"I don't think so, dear." She shook her head. "He doesn't strike me as a mean person."

I gave him a sidewise glance as he was listening to Jasper and nodding. I guess he was smiling the first time I met him. Maybe I'd give conversation another shot.

"So …" I began.

He turned to me, unsmiling, but I continued. "What brings you to Singapore?"

"Business."

Did he think he had to pay per word in this conversation? I wasn't sure if I should follow up on that or wait for further discussion. I decided to follow up.

"What type of business?" I decided to smile, thinking that he might mirror my expression.

"High tech." Still no smile.

Oh forget it. No matter how nice looking this fellow was, he wasn't worth this much work. I turned to my other side and joined in the conversation that Auntie Lil, Dieter, and Elke were having about what group was truly the "Group of Death" in the upcoming World Cup.

"Annalise, solve this for us," said Auntie Lil.

"Seriously? You know that as much as I love watching soccer—"

"Fútbol" corrected Dieter with a grin.

"Futbol … with you, I am not as passionate about it. Sorry, Dieter, I'm an American football lover."

"What shall I do with her?" Auntie Lil shook her head. My aunt was so well rounded. Not only was she a woman of many talents, she also had many interests—opera, literature, basketball, even World Cup soccer.

As we moved from sports to movies, a fleet of servers entered with our dinners. For those who had ordered chili crab—i.e., everyone except the sulky man to my left—a deep cast-iron pot was set before each of us containing a formidable crab in a sizzling sauce accompanied by baskets of small, appetizing buns. To the side of our settings were a small hammer and other lethal-looking instruments that looked more suited for dentistry.

"What now?" I murmured to my aunt.

We both watched as the more experienced at the table attacked their crustaceans, cracking them open and retrieving the delicate meat within.

"Okay, here goes!" I said and attacked my own.

How delicious!

And how messy!

My hands—and I knew my cheeks and chin—were soon dripping with the delicious sauce.

"Did I steer you wrong?" asked Jasper, across his reserved friend, who was calmly enjoying some sort of noodle dish.

"Not at all," I said.

"Don't forget to dip the bread in the sauce," he urged.

I dipped. It was heavenly. I turned to Auntie Lil, who had already done the same and was signaling for the server to bring more bread.

"This is so good!" I said as I picked up a leg to crack it open. It was being stubborn, and I gave it a rather hard squeeze to extract the meat. I was successful, but it didn't land on my plate. By the gasps, I knew it landed exactly where I wouldn't have wanted it to land.

I cringed as I turned to my left and saw that Jasper's friend was decorated in not only my crabmeat, but also a large splotch of his wine, which had spilled onto his shirt when he tried to catch the crab flying toward him. While the colors merged to make a lovely design, I sensed that he was not interested in modern art on his tailored button-front shirt.

"Oops?" I said tentatively. "I guess that's why they give out bibs?"

The rest of the table laughed, but he was obviously not in the mood for a joke. He scraped his chair back, stood, and threw his napkin on his plate. Reaching in his wallet, he drew out some Singapore dollars to hand to Jasper.

"No, no, Mate, no worries," Jasper said. "This one shouldn't be on you."

When he realized what he'd said, he had difficulty holding back a smile. The rest of the table had trouble maintaining composure as well. Jasper's friend threw the money on his chair and walked to the door.

"I'll see you in the morning, Pennock."

And with that, he stormed away.

We were silent.

"What made him so crabby?" asked the youngest of the Swedish crew, not aware of what he'd said until the rest of the table burst into laughter. Everyone went back to talking.

"I'm so sorry, Jasper," I grimaced.

"Truly no worries. Mistakes happen."

"But he already seemed so …"

"Brooding? Grim? Gloomy?"

"Wow! I wasn't going to use any of those words, but okay."

Jasper took a deep breath.

"Annalise, he's had a long day today. You'll forgive him."

I sensed that there was something more, but Jasper wasn't sharing.

"Forgive me," Dieter broke in, "but that is who I think it is, right?"

"Who?" I looked from him to Jasper.

"That's Eli Chamberlain, isn't it?" asked the Swede. "I thought he looked familiar."

"Again, who?"

"He's the wunderkind from Graviton Gaming. You know, the Nuon gaming system."

Graviton Gaming? Oh! Right. The Nuon was the newest, hottest gaming system, outselling Nintendo, PlayStation, and all others. Every gamer I knew (specifically those in my own family) had salivated for one for Christmas, and those stylized, interlocking Gs were a fixture across the country—no, across the world.

So that was the inventor of the Nuon. I vaguely remembered his story. Something about being a prodigy of sorts at CalTech and turning down a job at Microsoft to start his own company. You'd think that working in high-tech marketing, I would know more about this, but I was not well versed in the gaming world.

"What's he doing here?" Dieter asked Jasper.

Jasper concentrated on his crab and attempted to avoid the question.

"I suspect our tablemate has gone off to change his shirt, compliments of Miss Fontana here."

Smooth. Neither confirm nor deny that the gentleman was Eli Chamberlain.

"Graviton!" said our youngest tablemate. "Is it true that they're working on a hover skateboard?"

"Well, I'd be the first to line up to ride one of those. Are you a skateboarder?" asked Auntie Lil, neatly deflecting the question and starting a different conversation.

I looked at Jasper, who kept his focus on his crab.

Hmm. I suspect that it would not be good to let it be known that Eli Chamberlain—if that was him—was seen being volatile in a restaurant for whatever reason. Well, not for me to dig any further. I turned back to my crab, a little more careful with my attempts to extract the meat.

After we were all done with our meals, and the carnage lay before us to prove it, the servers returned to clean away the plates and hand us all wonderfully scented, warm, damp towels to wipe our hands and faces. We paid for our meals and traded contact information, promising to keep in touch after returning to our home countries.

Auntie Lil, Jasper, the gorgeous Diana, and I left the bustling restaurant to stroll down the esplanade in search of the dessert spot that Jasper had in mind.

"I'm not sure that I can eat dessert," said Auntie Lil.

"Oh, you'll like this," said Diana, taking her by the arm and walking ahead of Jasper and me.

Jasper took my arm, and the four of us looked like a companionable family as we strolled among the other tourists.

"I'm really sorry about splattering your friend with my dinner," I began.

"Please, Annalise. He's probably forgotten about it already."

"He didn't look like he would forget about it."

"Seriously. He's a good chap. Today has been a long day for him. I encourage you to not think about it any further."

"Is that really Eli Chamberlain?" I asked.

We walked a few steps in silence.

"I'm going to tell you, but you must please not let it get any further. He wouldn't want a story about that incident in the tabloids. Yes, it was him."

"If he didn't want people to know he was out and about, then why was he in such a public place?" Really. Paparazzi are everywhere. Even high-tech geeks know that!

"He is generally not recognized since he rarely is photographed. I think his PR team would like him to be out and about more, but he keeps to himself quite a bit. As a Chinese American, he is even more anonymous when he travels in Asia."

He had a point. The only way that he would stick out is if there were some sort of incident … oh, right, like if someone spilled food and wine all over him. Like what I did.

"Now I feel worse!" I stopped and moaned.

"Come now. It's over. He'll be laughing about it."

I looked at him skeptically. He pushed me ahead.

"Well, maybe he won't exactly be laughing about it, but he'll get over it, and so should you! Look, we're at our dessert destination."

We had caught up with Diana and Auntie Lil. They were already in a line that snaked toward a tiny shop advertising "Japanese ice cream."

"What's Japanese ice cream?" I asked.

"Frozen deliciousness, according to Diana," said Auntie Lil.

"Exactly," said Diana. "Now, we're only 30 people back—"

"Only!" My eyebrows shot up.

"Oh yes! Sometimes there can be about 100 people in line," said Jasper.

"Wow! It must be good." I grinned.

"It is," nodded Diana, "so start thinking about what flavor you want. And think outside the box of chocolate and vanilla. They have lychee, curry, cactus, shrimp …"

We discussed the various unique flavors, and I didn't have time to worry about the inscrutable Eli Chamberlain.

CHAPTER SIXTEEN

Day Two in Singapore promised to be another sunny, hot one. Our hotel was two blocks from a lovely church, so we were able to walk to Sunday Mass with no problem. Afterward, we walked back to the open-air food court next to our hotel that promised typical Singaporean fare. We were looking forward to breakfast.

"This is quite different from cornflakes and milk, isn't it?" I said to Auntie Lil as we sat down at a small picnic table to enjoy fried rice, egg rolls, and a chicken dish.

"Mm-hmm," she answered as she simultaneously chewed and pulled out the list of activities she'd made. "We need to get a jump on our day if we want to see all the sights I have planned for today."

She pulled out a highlighter pen from seemingly nowhere and drew a route on the map.

"Let's hop on our trusty red bus and get over to the Singapore Flyer first. What do you think?"

My lack of answer caused her to pop her head up. She saw what I saw. Eli Chamberlain was striding purposefully toward our table.

"What do I say to him, Auntie?" I asked from the corner of my mouth.

"I think you start with 'good morning,' dear. 'Good evening' wouldn't do at all, don't you think?" she said with practicality.

I glared at her.

"I'm just trying to help." Her innocent face belied her smart-alecky tone.

"Good morning, ladies," he said.

Auntie Lil kicked me quietly.

"Good morning," we replied.

"That's a nice shirt," I said, trying to start a polite conversation.

His head tilted, and his lips began to turn up into a slight smile.

Oh. Right.

My face must have turned as red as the bottle of hot sauce on the picnic table in front of us.

"I mean …" I turned to Auntie Lil for assistance. She was not offering any. Traitor.

"Don't worry," he said as his smile turned a bit more sardonic. "I won't be sending you any cleaning bills from last night. As a matter of fact, that's why I came over when I saw you here, to tell you that you're forgiven."

"That I'm forgiven?"

"Yes. I realize that you couldn't help your behavior."

"My … behavior?"

My face was still red, but now it wasn't from embarrassment. It was more from a different emotion.

"You seem upset," he said, and his dark eyebrows bent into a V.

"No. I'm not upset. Confused is more like it."

"Confused?"

"Yes. I apologized last night for the mistake that caused the stain on your shirt, but today you imply that I was engaging in some sort of wild, reckless behavior."

Auntie Lil tugged at my sleeve, but I was already on a roll.

"So I'm confused as to why you feel that you had to ride over here on your high horse and lower yourself to give me some sort of royal pardon."

He pulled himself straighter, and any evidence of a smile disappeared. His ebony eyes flashed.

"So sorry to have disappointed you with my outreach of … friendship."

Auntie Lil once again attempted to break in, but I ignored her.

"You call that friendship!" I stood my full height, which was still a full head shorter than Eli's. "I don't need friends like you!"

"Fine!" he stared down at me for a moment, then turned to Auntie Lil.

"Good morning to you, Miss."

With that, he whirled about and strode off.

I plopped back down on the bench and crossed my arms.

"I guess that will show him," Auntie Lil said.

"What?" I whirled around to face her.

"Well, dear, just what did you accomplish?"

"I … he …"

Auntie Lil began to gather her materials and shouldered her tote bag.

"Annalise, I know what you were thinking, but would it have killed you to swallow your Fontana pride for just a minute?"

"You don't understand!"

"Oh, I understand only too well, sweetie. You just couldn't let it go. Even for someone you probably won't see again in an eon. Was it worth it?"

"Yes," I said petulantly.

She sat down next to me and put her arm around my shoulder, and waited.

"No," I finally admitted.

She patted my hand.

Finally we both laughed.

"What do you mean 'Fontana pride'? I am well acquainted with how Pop can be, but you always seem to keep your temper in check," I said as we both started moving toward the bus stop.

"Oh, Annalise, I could tell you stories," she said.

"Really?"

She shook her finger at me.

"That's for another day. Today is about sightseeing and sunshine."

I shaded my eyes and looked up to the sky, then turned away quickly as the huge golden orb caught my eyes.

"Definitely sunshine," I murmured as I stepped onto the bus.

We reached the Singapore Flyer, and again I shaded my eyes and looked up to the sky.

"Yikes! This is tall!"

"It's the largest Ferris wheel on the planet," said Auntie Lil. "Are you ready to ride it?"

"You bet!"

The queue for entry to one of the eight-person cabins on the wheel was not long, so we were soon aboard and ready to revolve for the next thirty minutes. A family with four exuberant children joined us. As we slowly circled, the children squealed in delight at the ability to see the sights surrounding the Flyer.

"This is awesome," I had to agree with the children as I leaned my head on the floor-to-ceiling glass. We were taller than most other structures in the area.

After a complete circuit, we exited the giant wheel, and I quickly found a bench to scribble my thoughts while Auntie continued the conversation she'd begun with our cabinmates. I snapped my iPad shut when she joined me.

"You are doing much better at journaling than I am," she said. "I notice that you keep your notes up to the minute."

"If I don't, I'll forget them," I said.

"I did notice that you didn't take notes after breakfast." She had a wry look on her face.

"You mean after that 'pleasant' encounter with our dinner companion?" I frowned.

"You are going to let that anger go, aren't you?" she sighed.

"If I don't, am I going to get another lecture on pride?"

"No, but you may get a nudge," she grinned.

I blew my bangs off my forehead. Nothing dies in the Fontana family. But I wasn't in the mood to hear a discussion about holding on to a grudge at that moment, no matter how kindly she would present it.

"Oh, look at the time. I promised to Skype Rory, and we have access to free WiFi here. I'd better get on that," I opened my iPad again and walked a few steps away.

"Hey, girlfriend!" her cheery face appeared on the screen.

"How are you so flippin' perky? What time is it?" I smiled back at her.

"I was expecting this call. Would you rather I didn't answer? I can hang up, you know," she teased.

"No, no."

"What's up? I can tell you have something on your mind … and you shouldn't because you are on an amazing trip."

I hesitated and turned to see that Auntie Lil had moved away from the bench and was admiring the plants near the exit. So I took a chance and embarked on the whole crab incident, including the follow-up this morning. Rory erupted in peals of laughter when I was done.

"It's not funny, Rory."

"It most certainly is. It sounds exactly like something that would happen to you—or to both of us, for that matter."

"Auntie Lil says I should just let it go."

"I hate to quote the most popular cartoon song of the decade, but she's right. Let it go. Why should you care what this stranger thinks? Wait … you would have been able to let it go if he had been just a random stranger. What made him so special?"

"Nothing, Rory." She was getting uncomfortably close to the truth.

"Aha! He wasn't just a stranger. He was a handsome stranger!"

Handsome? I sniffed. Since when have ebony eyes, charcoal hair that flops just so, and a blinding smile been considered handsome? Oh, only since forever.

"You're taking too long to answer, Annalise."

"His looks have nothing to do with his attitude."

"Tell that to everyone who's ever swooned over Mr. Darcy in *Pride and Prejudice*."

"Rory, are we going to spend this call discussing 19th-century literature or what?"

"You're right," she composed herself. "Tell me what you've been doing that doesn't have to do with flirting."

"I WASN'T—oh never mind." I ignored her impish grin. "Anyway—"

"I know, honey, please share the trip!"

I walked over to Auntie Lil, and together we shared highlights with her minus the crab incident.

"So cool! I wish I was there!" she said.

"So do I, but we'll take another trip."

"Rory, my love, we are happy to chat with you, but we need to go," said Auntie Lil.

"Absolutely!" said Rory. "Love you both! Have fun! Eat good foods! Skype me at our next appointed time! Bye-eeee!"

And she was gone.

Even from across the world, we could feel her energy.

"Well, Annalise," said Auntie Lil. "Onward?"

I put my iPad back in my bag.

"Onward."

The good thing about our circular journey on the red bus meant that we could visit the island at our own pace. The final stop that we didn't want to miss was a visit to the Marina Sands SkyPark on top of the Marina Sands building.

"There seems to be a theme to our sightseeing today, Auntie Lil. Everything is very tall," I commented as the minutes ticked away and the elevator climbed to the top.

"I never thought about it, but you are right," she said.

We exited the elevator into panoramic views and were speechless at how beautiful the SkyPark's lush greenery was 57 stories above the city. The wind whipped about us as we strolled arm in arm around the perimeter, mostly silent, stopping once in a while to point out the city's landmarks.

"Look! There's the Singapore Flyer!"

"It seems far below us now, doesn't it?" she said. "I think our hotel is in that direction. And over there is where our music shop is from yesterday."

"Auntie Lil, we've only been here a short time and already had so many adventures."

"Don't forget San Francisco," she pointed out.

"You're right. And we've just begun our journey."

She glanced at her watch.

"Speaking of which, we'd better get going or we'll miss our flight."

"Don't jinx it, dear," she laughed as we began our trip down the elevator.

The bus took us to our hotel, where we gathered our bags and managed to zip back to Changi Airport without incident.

"This plane won't be as big as the last one," Auntie Lil said. "So we won't see those amazing premium first-class seats this time."

"Darn it, Auntie Lil, I was expecting you to surprise me with one," I laughed.

"Oh, I'd be surprising myself!"

We boarded and got comfortable, but apparently a few passengers were missing, so we needed to wait.

"This flight is long enough without having to wait for people being late," complained a man a few rows up.

"Do you notice people who speak English seem to talk louder than people who speak other languages?" I whispered to Auntie Lil.

"Take that as a lesson," she whispered back.

I turned my head back to typing notes in my journal, and in a few moments I heard the English-speaker mutter "Finally."

Apparently the final latecomer arrived. I jerked my head up to see who could have delayed the trip and found myself staring directly into familiar ebony eyes hooded by serious, sooty eyebrows.

It seemed that Eli Chamberlain was flying to China on this night.

CHAPTER SEVENTEEN

I quickly ducked my head, and when I carefully peeked over the seat, his face was gone. His seat was farther up front. I leaned over my armrest into the aisle to see if I could see him, and was given a polite but firm tap by a flight attendant to lean back. We started to pull away from the gate almost immediately and were soon taxiing for takeoff.

"What on earth are you doing?" Auntie Lil asked. I had pulled my tablet back out as soon as we were given permission and was banging on the keyboard and mumbling.

"Nothing." I hunched over my tablet and kept typing furiously.

"Hmm." Auntie Lil was too sharp to be fooled. She leaned over my shoulder.

"Hey!" I nudged her. "I'm typing here."

"You're typing random characters. Unless you took a class in a language I've never heard of, or you're becoming a court reporter, you are flustered. What gives? What did you see?"

By this time we were in the air, so she could unbuckle, and she pushed herself up on her seat to get a better view of the front of the plane. She sat back down with a puzzled look.

"All I see are the backs of heads, most of which have black hair. What shook you like that?"

I took a deep breath.

"Remember how you said I should just forget about the incident at breakfast because I probably wouldn't see that person in an eon? Well, I guess they don't make eons like they used to."

"You're not making sense." Auntie Lil shook her head.

"Him. Eli Chamberlain. He's on the plane."

"No! How can you be sure?"

"He's the latecomer. I saw him board."

She leaned back and smiled.

"It's not funny, Auntie!"

"I beg to differ! It's very funny. Here you are, for all intents and purposes STUCK with the very person that you made a fool of yourself—"

"Hey! I thought you were on my side!"

"I am, dear, I am." She patted my knee. "But this plane isn't that large. Did he see you?"

"Unfortunately. When he boarded, my head shot up like a groundhog on February 2nd."

"How delightful!"

"I'm not sure I'd use that adjective."

"Well, Annalise, what are you going to do?"

A moment later, I yanked them out again.

"How did he even know we were on this flight?"

"He didn't. When he got on, he saw you staring straight at him."

"I wasn't staring at him! I looked up to see who the late-comer was and—oh, why am I bothering to explain?"

I jammed my earbuds back in my ears.

A moment later, I pulled them out.

"What about this morning?"

"What about it? He apologized, and you were the one who got snippy."

"What!"

She took off her glasses and folded them on her lap and turned to me.

"Dear, you are making so much of this. Yes, he had a few moments that were ... less than spectacular, let us say. But, all in all, he seems nice and we don't really know that much about him, yet."

"Yet? YET?"

"Now you're repeating the last word in my sentence twice?"

"Because you are indicating that we'll talk to him again."

"Who knows?" she shrugged.

"What did you do while I was gone from my seat?"

"Nothing."

"Why don't I believe you?" my eyes turned to slits.

"Oh, Annalise, calm down. All I did was chat with him for a moment. And you do have to admit, we're in an enclosed space for a finite amount of time, the end of which we will all exit the same path. It's highly likely that we'll run into each other again."

I was silent for a moment.

"You are incredibly logical, Auntie. It's annoying."

"And you are making more of this than is necessary. Do yourself—and me, by the way—a favor. Let this go, or even stroll up to his seat and make an apology." She replaced her reading glasses on her nose and returned to her book.

"I shall take that challenge to prove that I am a big person," I sniffed. I stood, straightened my outfit, fluffed out my perky bobbed hair, and walked purposefully toward the front of the plane.

Well, I walked as purposefully as one can in a giant flying tube that is jostling back and forth, but you get the picture.

I reached Eli Chamberlain's seat and was prepared to tap him on the shoulder, but he had on a large pair of Beats headphones with head leaned back and eyes closed.

I scooted back to my row.

"Well?" Auntie Lil said as I hastily buckled myself back into my seat.

"I think he was asleep. Bad form to wake someone up, don't you think?"

Auntie Lil didn't respond, but patted my knee and smiled. We both settled in to immerse ourselves in our respective books for the rest of the journey, pausing only when the flight attendant brought us our meal.

"This is really good," I commented as I scooped up the last of my kung pao chicken and rice. Fruit and a small piece of cake awaited for dessert. "We've certainly been getting well fed on every flight."

"Back in the old days, we used to get a full meal on every flight, no matter where we flew," said Auntie Lil.

"I know. I'm spoiled now. How will I ever go back to being satisfied with that tiny bag of pretzels and a cup of soda when I fly?"

"Have your mother pack a meatball hoagie?" Auntie Lil suggested.

"I don't know. I think I'd get mugged for it by my seatmate."

No sooner had we finished our food and enjoyed a delicious cup of jasmine tea than we were prepared for landing.

"Will we meet your group at the airport?" I asked as we organized our belongings.

"No, they'll be at the hotel."

"Do you think they're asleep by now?" I looked at my watch.

"I doubt it, but who knows? I only communicated with the organizer of this trip by email. I don't know any of them."

"This should be interesting."

"What's interesting is how you are avoiding looking toward the front of the plane."

"I'm sure I don't know what you mean," I sniffed.

"Well, I can see Eli Chamberlain from here, and I'm sure that we can catch up to him as we exit so that you can have the opportunity to set things right."

I peered over the seat in front of me and could see Eli chatting with the flight attendant as he was waiting to exit. He smiled as he turned toward me, and I ducked my head rather than catch his eye.

Darn! What was wrong with me? All I needed to do was make a cursory apology for my behavior, and I would probably not need to talk with him again. We were landing here in Xi'an to sightsee, and I'm sure that he was here to make some sort of high-tech business deal, so this would be a natural parting. Maybe I'd catch him as we exited the Jetway. How hard could that be?

Oh. Right.

I completely forgot about the fact that we would encounter all sorts of red tape going through customs and collecting luggage. By the time the people from the front of the plane had scurried through the airport, and the rest of us managed to deplane, I lost track of Eli Chamberlain in a sea of dark-haired people.

At least I tried.

Besides, I was in China! I was ready for sightseeing and culture.

CHAPTER EIGHTEEN

"Auntie Lil, I said it once and I'll say it again. You have great taste in hotels," I exclaimed as we moved through the oversized revolving doors and crossed the impeccably polished floor to check in to our Xi'an lodgings. The walls were decorated with impressive tapestries, and on every table stood a mammoth vase containing exotic flowers that coordinated perfectly with the colors of the brocade furniture.

"Don't give me credit on this one, dear. The organizer of the trip made the choice. We should be meeting her and the rest of the group in the morning for breakfast."

"Or sooner."

"What makes you think so?"

I took my hand off my wheeled suitcase and pointed to a boisterous group in the lounge off the main lobby.

"I don't mean to make a hasty judgment, but based on the, umm, demographic of that group, I think that's our tour."

We took in the men and women crowded around the bar and seated in the low, comfy-looking lounge chairs. I really didn't need the sleuthing skills of my favorite mystery writer to formulate my assessment. Gray or graying hair topped the women, as well as the men—well, the men who still had hair. They were all dressed in comfortable traveling clothes and the type of shoes that are mostly sold at mall stores specializing in walking attire.

Yep. If there was going to be a prize for youngest in the group, I wouldn't have to compete very strenuously.

A petite ball of energy who looked to be about Auntie Lil's age caught sight of us and bounded toward us.

"Lilliana Fontana?" she asked.

Auntie Lil nodded.

With scarf flying, the ball of energy flung her arms around Auntie Lil's neck.

"We're so glad you made it! After your email about your delay in San Francisco, well, we just didn't know if you might be delayed in Singapore. And this must be your niece. Annalise, is it? What a darling girl! Come on, let's get you checked in and get over with the group."

Whew! What a whirlwind.

She identified herself as Colette Ehlers and accompanied us to the check-in desk. She made sure our luggage was delivered to our room with dispatch.

"Now, I know you'll want to get upstairs, but come over to the lounge to say hello first."

Having no choice, we looked at each other, smiled, and shrugged as we moved over to meet our new best friends.

Colette clapped her hands to catch the attention of the group and announced, "Everyone, this is Lilliana and her niece, Annalise."

Dozens of smiling eyes turned toward us, and we heard a chorus of greetings—"Welcome!" "We're glad you're here!" "Now the group is complete!"

Our impromptu hostess continued her duties.

"Now, everyone, they've had a long flight from Singapore, so don't monopolize them tonight. Let them go upstairs to get to sleep."

One look around the room told me that these folks were not going to heed her advice. I was right.

"Annalise, what a beautiful name!" A pair of women whose facial features indicated they must be sisters pulled me toward the bar. I looked over to see Auntie Lil in what looked like a companionable discussion with a couple in matching outfits.

"Would you like a glass of wine, dear?" asked the taller of my newfound friends, calling over the bartender.

"Katherine, she's young. She probably would rather have a Cosmo," admonished the other.

"Actually, I'd be happy with a glass of iced tea," I smiled.

Katherine placed my order and turned back toward me, taking me in from head to toe with a sharp look.

"So, what brings you here with all of us fuddy-duddies? Vivienne and I had a bet that if you were traveling with your elderly aunt, you were being punished for some transgression."

"Kat!" reproved her sister with a gasp.

"Go on, Viv, deny that we said that," said Katherine in a matter-of-fact tone.

"YOU said that! I said nothing of the kind," Vivienne turned to me with a soft smile. "But, if you don't mind us asking—what brings you here, with us?"

I couldn't help but laugh. The Flynn sisters were mirrored halves. Katherine was sharp edges with a sharp, if honest, tone. Vivienne was all soft curves and managed to cushion her comments with a winning smile.

"I'm not being punished. Actually, this is a treat for me. Auntie Lil is giving me a great opportunity to travel with her."

"Hmm." Katherine trained her gaze on me and stepped back.

"No, really." I'm not sure why I felt the need to convince her.

"Pay no attention to her," Vivienne said, then pulled me toward her and whispered, "Katherine has the misguided notion that she is intuitive."

"Not misguided, Viv. This young lady has a story. Before our trip is over, I'll get to the bottom of this." She nodded briskly.

"Katherine!" scolded her sister.

I looked from one to the other. Quirky, to be sure. If these two were representative of the group, it should be an interesting week.

"Annalise, come and meet the Willems." Auntie Lil gestured me toward her and the couple she was chatting with.

I excused myself from the two sisters and took in the cozy couple. He was tall and dark-skinned, with a broad smile and a gleaming bald head. He looked like Chi McBride plus about twenty years. Her fair skin belied her Nordic heritage. She had obviously been a corn silk blonde in her day, but the tresses wound about her head in a braid were now mixed shades. Her eyeglasses were an updated cat-eye frame in clear plastic and surrounded deep-set eyes.

"Pleased to meet you." I reached out my hand for a shake.

"Oh, no, I'm a hugger," said the wife, who identified herself as Frida and embraced me before turning me over to her husband, who she called Bear.

"Bear?" I questioned.

"I got that nickname in college, and it just stuck," he said. "Much better than my given name, if you ask me."

Of course I had to ask him.

"My given name is Willie."

"Willie seems like a fine name."

"Say it all out loud."

Oh. Willie Willems. I'm sure the children in grade school had a field day with that when he was young! "Bear" it was, then.

"I was just telling Frida and Bear about our whirlwind tour of San Francisco. They lived near there when he taught at Berkeley."

"We loved our time in the city by the bay," nodded Frida.

"We had a lot of fun that day," I said.

"Your aunt said you met a nice young man while you were there," said Bear.

"Wow, Auntie Lil, you certainly packed a lot of information in a five-minute conversation." I elbowed her.

She just looked off to the side innocently while Bear and Frida smiled.

"We probably should be getting to bed, Auntie Lil. You must be tired. You'll excuse us."

But as I attempted to circle my aunt's shoulder and lead her out of the lounge, our effervescent hostess Colette and another couple joined us.

"Lilliana and Annalise, I know that you need to get to bed, but I do want you to meet Georgiann and Tom Perini. They're absolutely marvelous, and you have so much in common."

The Perinis could have been on a poster titled "Italian Grandparents." They were of similar height and weight and had matching Mediterranean features. Her haircut was so similar to my own mother's that, from the back, I might not have been able to tell them apart if Ma were there. I bet that at home, she had a well-worn apron hanging on the back of the kitchen door, and her meatballs and sauce were probably renowned in her neighborhood.

He was nattily dressed for this trip, but I'm sure that on a Saturday afternoon on his own turf, he would be puttering around a small garden in his favorite faded trousers and shirt, tying up tomato stakes or delicately caring for zucchini plants.

They greeted us each with a double-cheeked kiss, and I was immediately transported home.

"Annalise! What a beautiful girl. You and your mother here could be sisters!" said Tom with a clap of his hands.

"Oh, we're niece and aunt," I clarified.

"So, two more lovely single girls on the trip," smiled Georgiann. "We'll see if we can take care of that."

I smiled inwardly. She really WAS a lot like my mom!

"We're looking forward to visiting the terra-cotta soldiers." I thought moving the topic of conversation away from matchmaking was a good idea.

"Definitely. It was one of the reasons that Genio wanted us to sign up for this trip."

"Genio?"

"My brother," said Georgiann. "He is with us. Tom and I were going to go on another cruise to Alaska, but Genio-Eugene-said to branch out. He said that this would be more interesting. So far he has been right. There he is. Genio Cusamano, come meet the Fontana girls."

I turned to see an attractive man approach us from the corner of the room. His full head of hair was snowy white, and his eyes flashed under his matching snowy eyebrows. He was taller than his sister, but you could see the family resemblance in the broad smile and aquiline nose. I turned to Auntie Lil to comment on his movie star good looks but was struck by the look on her face.

"I apologize, but I really must take my leave," she said to the Perinis. "I think that the travel has caught up with me. Annalise, would you accompany me?"

She hooked her arm through mine, and I know that my face showed my confusion as I made our apologies. We moved through the lobby to the elevator, where Auntie Lil punched the button with a sense of urgency. Once we were safely within the small confines, she leaned on the back wall.

I turned to her and with tones that channeled my father, I said, "All right, Lilliana Aurora Fontana, what was THAT all about?"

CHAPTER NINETEEN

"I'm just tired, Annalise. There's nothing else to say." Auntie Lil delicately elbowed past me to jam her finger in the number of our floor and wouldn't meet my eyes.

"I have never known you to be tired in my entire life!"

"Well, I guess I'm allowed one then, right?"

We rode in silence for a floor or two.

"But, Auntie Lil—"

"Seriously, Annalise, I don't want to discuss this. Besides, aren't you supposed to be watching out for my health? What would your father say if he knew you weren't encouraging me to rest?"

Who was she kidding? She could run circles around me. There was no way she was run-down.

Oh. Unless she was. I mean. She did just have that heart scare. I glanced at her, worried.

Wait a minute.

"You're not fooling me, woman. That wasn't a health reaction, that was something else. You better come clean."

We reached our room, and Auntie Lil swiveled on her heel.

"I am politely asking you to drop it, Annalise."

Whoa. I had never heard that tone before.

"Okay, okay."

We entered our room, and Auntie Lil kept the conversation on anything but our hasty departure.

"This is quite a room, isn't it?"

"I'll say!"

The smooth, dark wood of the furniture lent a rich atmosphere that was accented by heavy, golden draperies and duvet covers in a matching gold. Our baggage had been placed neatly on fold-out stands and unzipped, ready for us to unpack. I strolled into the lavishly appointed bathroom and was impressed by the gold-flecked marble countertops and the basket full of high-end lotions and soaps.

"There are free bottles of water in here as well as out there," I yelled to Auntie Lil.

"Remember," she nodded as I walked back into the room, "make sure to only drink bottled water and use it for brushing teeth even though the water is safe for showers. There is a note about that on the counter out here."

I smiled, remembering my mother and her extensive research before I left.

"What time is it? I'm going to call Ma."

"She'll appreciate a call no matter what time it is. In the meantime, I think I will take a shower before I get into bed."

Auntie Lil pulled her pajamas and slippers from her bag and moved to the bathroom.

I dialed the home number and smiled when I heard my mother's warm tones.

"Annalisa, what's the matter?"

"Hello to you, too, Ma."

"Why are you calling?" Her tone was concerned.

I didn't want to go round and round with my mother about why she always assumed that something was wrong when we called. It just was her way. I took a deep breath.

"We were just thinking about you and wanted to call."

"That's nice!" She was genuinely pleased. "How is the trip? What have you done since San Francisco?"

I gave her a summary of our Singapore adventure—minus the embarrassment of my dinner faux pas, of course—and brought her up to speed on what we knew about our traveling group.

"They sound pleasant," she said. "Where is your aunt?"

"She's in the shower."

"Remind her not to open her mouth in the shower! And to only use the bottled water to brush her teeth!"

"I'll do that, Ma. We're both on top of the water restrictions." Oh, Ma. "Is Pop around?"

"He's at work, dear. What time is it there?"

"Bedtime. Well, Ma, I just wanted to touch base. Give him my love, and Nicky and Amanda."

"I will sweetheart. Take care of your aunt. Make sure you eat."

"You know I will, Ma. I love you."

"Love you."

I disconnected the phone. If only my mother were the kind of person I could have shared Auntie Lil's odd behavior with. I would have continued the conversation, but ...

The water in the shower was still running, so I punched in the number of the one person I knew I could share this conversation with.

"Editorial, this is Rory," came the voice of my best friend.

"Rory, it's me. Do you have a minute?"

. "Hey! What are you doing calling me at the office?"

"I'm glad to talk to you, too," I scrunched my face. Was no one happy to hear from me today?

"No, no, it's just a surprise," she laughed.

"I need to bounce something off you."

"Ooh. Sounds serious," she said. "Hold on, let me move into one of our meeting rooms and close the door. ... Okay. So what's up?"

Not trusting the decibel level of my own voice, I grabbed a key and slipped out of the room to the end of the hall.

"Okay, here's the thing." I described the incident in the lounge leading up to Auntie Lil admonishing me to "drop it."

"Hmm," said Rory.

"That's all you have? 'Hmm'? I could have gotten that from a stranger on the street who doesn't speak English."

"Ssh. I'm thinking."

"Well, you're thinking on my international dime, Rory." I paced.

"Do you want my thoughts or not?"

"Any day now."

"So here's what I think," she began. "Your aunt was tired."

That's it? I called all the way around the world for that? Before I could give a snarky reply, she continued.

"You guys have been going strong for how many days now? It just caught up with her. I think she just really got tired and was too embarrassed to admit it to you, because she had told your dad she would have been okay on this trip alone."

I pondered this.

"Annalise, are you still there? Remember, this is on your international dime."

"Cut the smart-aleck tone. I was just processing. I guess that could be it. But why would she be afraid to admit it to me? Does she think I'd double-cross her and tell on her to Pop?"

"No, but she might have had some sort of twinge in her heart and didn't want it to turn into something that you would make a major medical issue. Can you imagine that?"

"You're right, you're right."

"My suggestion is that you drop it for now and just keep watch to see if she shows any other signs."

"You're right, you're right."

"Of course."

I rolled my eyes even though she couldn't see them.

"So, other than that, what's happening?" she asked.

I wasn't prepared to present an entire trip report, so I managed to deflect.

"Oh, you know, we just checked in to this amazing hotel. We're starting out early on our tour here tomorrow morning. I'm actually out in the hallway so I don't have the whole schedule to quote to you, but it's going to be fun. I'm sure it won't be too strenuous, given the demographic of the group."

"Hey, don't underestimate them. They might run circles around you."

"At this moment, anyone could. I guess I shouldn't question Auntie Lil saying she's tired. I need some shut-eye myself." I stretched as I walked back toward the room.

"Well, make sure you rest … and eat good food," she teased.

"Thanks, 'Ma,' I'll be sure to do that," I joked.

"Send me pictures." I could see Rory bounce up ready to return to her day.

I punched the "off" button on my phone and paused a moment before entering the room.

"Where were you?" asked Auntie Lil sitting on her bed, luxuriously applying the sweet-smelling hand lotion provided in our basket of amenities.

"Chatting with Rory." I crossed to my bed. "I didn't want to disturb you if you were getting into bed."

"I see."

"I think I'll shower as well." I glanced at her out of the corner of my eye as I prepared to do so.

"I recommend it highly," she said as she snuggled under her covers, propped up with her book and reading glasses. It was as if nothing odd had occurred earlier.

When I returned from the shower, she was still engrossed in reading. I climbed into my own bed, armed with my iPad and prepared to write about our encounter with the tour group. Surrounding myself with pillows, I punched them to just the right height and propped my tablet on my knees. A moment later, I went to the wardrobe to retrieve the spare pillow to add it to my collection, then rearranged.

Without looking up from her book, Auntie Lil commented, "Everything all right over there?"

"Why do you ask?"

"I haven't heard that much pillow fluffing since I worked one summer at Bed, Bath, and Beyond."

"Ha, ha. You never worked at Bed, Bath, and Beyond, Auntie Lil."

"Well, you get my point. Are you settled?"

"All settled."

I attacked my project for a while, then paused with a sigh.

"What's up?" Auntie Lil asked.

"I don't know. I just went back to read some of what I had written."

"And?"

"It's all well and good that I'm writing it, but where is it going to end up? Am I really going to print it out and hand it to the family? And if I do, will they read it?"

Auntie Lil sighed and patted the space beside her.

"Bring your tablet over here. But leave the pillow fort behind."

I hopped over and settled in next to her, handing her my iPad.

"Well?" I asked after she'd flipped through a few screens.

"This is very well written, Annalise."

"You can be honest with me, Auntie. You don't have to be nice to me because I'm your niece."

"No, I'm serious, dear. You have a knack for making things come alive. The family will appreciate these."

"Thank you." I leaned my head on her shoulder.

After a moment, I had an idea.

"Do you think anyone outside the family would want to read it?" I asked.

"I think so. It's fresh and entertaining. Why do you ask?"

"Well, I was thinking maybe I could set up a blog. It's sort of a high-tech diary—"

"I know what a blog is, dear. I'm not your father."

We both smiled at my father's stubborn refusal to become fully engaged in the communication methods of this century.

"Well, what if I blogged about this trip rather than just keeping a diary and making people read about it all at once?"

Auntie Lil became excited.

"I think it's a great idea! You could include photos, couldn't you?"

"I hadn't thought about it, but pictures would be perfect."

"I love this idea, Annalise!" Auntie Lil hugged me tightly, and my iPad nearly fell to the floor.

I rescued it and flopped back on her bed laughing. Then I shot straight up. We were already in the middle of the trip! It was too late. I should have started in the planning stages. I slumped over.

"What's wrong, dear?" Auntie Lil asked.

I explained my concerns about missing the perfect starting time for the project.

"Nonsense." She waved her hand. "There is no reason why you can't start now. You have all of your notes from the beginning of the trip. You have all of our photos so far. The way I see it, you just need to set up a clean design and put the early writing in, then just keep up from now on."

She had a point. I wasn't designing a fancy website, just setting up a skeleton blog and feeding the content into it. Oh, wait …

I slumped over again.

"What now?" Auntie Lil asked.

"The firewall, Auntie Lil. I can't just send information out of China. The government doesn't allow that."

I moved back to my own bed. Oh well, it was a good idea while it lasted.

"What time is it in San Francisco, Annalise?"

"Planning on ordering some sourdough bread?" I asked.

"No. But it occurred to me that if we knew someone who could advise us on this ... situation, it would be handy, wouldn't it? Someone who was an expert on web design, for example, and who studied that at—"

"Gonzaga? I see what you're getting at, Auntie Lil, but I don't think that Breck Connolly would have the time or inclination to get involved with this little project." I shook my head.

"Well, why not?"

"Why not? Don't you think we took advantage of his hospitality enough the other day?"

"Oh, Annalise, I'm sure he wouldn't mind. Besides, all this means is that we'll just owe him a bigger favor." She reached for her own phone in her shoulder bag.

"This is a huge favor, Auntie Lil!" I protested.

"And one we'll be happy to repay when it comes time." With her reading glasses perched on her nose, she scrolled through her contacts to find his name and punched in the number.

"Breccan? Dearest, this is Auntie Lilliana Fontana. That's right, from the airport. Listen, I have the tiniest question to ask you. Do you have a moment?"

And she was off.

CHAPTER TWENTY

Everything looks great. I'll check in with you when I upload today's notes. I owe you so much.

I hit "Send" on my text, and with a whoosh my message shot off to Breck. His reply was nearly instantaneous.

No problem, pal. I was looking for a fun distraction to take my mind off a problem I'm trying to solve. Happy scribbling. Best to Auntie L.

I smiled at how Breck thought that designing an entire blog and figuring out how to make it work in China was a "distraction." And he did it in a few short hours. Oh well, we all have our skills and gifts.

Switching over to my brand-new blog, I scrolled back and forth with pride. Breck had come up with a simple design that I could easily maintain as well as a system to upload text and photos for the duration of the trip. He, Auntie Lil, and

I had come up with what I thought was the perfect title on the header—Travels with Gypsy, in honor of my father's nickname for me. I loved it all.

I sent the final link to my family and friends, put my technology away, stretched, and checked my watch. Yikes! I had been up almost all night working with my genius web friend. But I now had a government-approved blog set up and a method for uploading a daily diary. It pays to know people. Well, specifically, it pays to know Auntie Lil, I guess, because she always knew people.

Luckily I had showered last night, so all I had to do was fix my face and hair and get dressed. Auntie Lil had gone downstairs a few moments earlier to meet the group for breakfast, so I'd better not be too far behind.

The group moved back and forth from the breakfast buffet set up in a corner of the hotel's dining room laughing and talking. I found Auntie Lil sitting with the spirited Flynn sisters, along with a new gentleman. She waved me over.

"Annalise, dear, come and meet Father John."

Father John? This group traveled with their own priest? Well, I guess it would come in handy if anyone needed the last rites. Stop it, Annalise! That was a snarky thing to say. The real reason he was with them was so that they could celebrate Mass anywhere, since being in a country where churches were few and far between could cause a problem for a group of practicing Catholics. Father John stood to greet me, and I took in the fact that he was not wearing a clerical collar.

"Your aunt has told us all about you and your travel blog. What a wonderful idea!" Father John's green eyes twinkled, and his smile was friendly.

"She has? I just set it up!" I shot a look to my talkative aunt as he encourage me to sit.

"Well, we think it's a great idea," nodded Katherine. "Lil has given us all the link to share with our families back home. They'll love being able to have a minute-by-minute account of the trip."

Oh, great. No pressure, Auntie Lil.

"But you don't have any food! Come, walk with me to the buffet, dear." Auntie Lil stood and took my arm.

"Auntie Lil—" I began.

She cut me off. "Now I know what you're thinking."

"I bet you do! You just told a group of strangers about my project, and now they'll all be critiquing me in real time."

"Oh don't be ridiculous, Annalise. Think about it. You're doing them a favor by helping them send reports about their trip to their families. They won't be nearly as hard on you as you'll be on yourself, you know."

"Well, that's hard enough." I grabbed a plate and looked at the buffet. Wow. What a spread. A mix of American, European, and Asian dishes.

"I don't know where to start here! What did you have, Auntie?"

"I let Yan Mei make recommendations." She pointed to an attractive young Asian woman with black hair that fell straight down to the middle of her back. She was dressed in a stylishly cut, forest-green trouser outfit with some sort of badge draped around her neck.

"She's our tour guide," Auntie Lil continued, and she took my plate and filled it with the same items that she'd had.

As we returned to the table with my tantalizing breakfast, I heard Yan Mei speaking rapid-fire into her phone in what I assumed was Mandarin since that was the language of choice here. She snapped her phone shut and turned to us, and when she spoke, her English was impeccable. She sounded as if she'd studied abroad or come from the upper crust of England, as a matter of fact.

"Good morning, all!" Her smile was as perky as the rest of her demeanor. "Please enjoy your breakfasts. Remember that we will be leaving the hotel at 9:30 sharp to begin our day. Meet in front of the hotel where our bus will be parked. Ours is the only bus there, so you won't be confused. Later in the day, that won't be the case, so when you board, take note of what ours looks like."

With a smile, she gave us instructions on how to distinguish our bus from others.

"Do we have any questions?"

Several of the group asked about weather, footgear, and other typical concerns for a tour group. After sorting those out, Yan Mei smiled, checked her watch, and excused herself to finish morning preparations.

"She's really good, isn't she," I said to Auntie Lil.

"She's bright, personable, and seems knowledgeable. I think she'll be perfect," she answered, then headed back to our room to retrieve her travel bag for the day.

I resolved to get a few minutes with Yan Mei to interview her for my blog. Goodness! I had only been at this blog project for a nanosecond and I was already making plans for it. I chuckled to myself. My marketing background had kicked in full force, I guess.

"Are you going to be warm enough in what you're wearing?" That was our intrepid tour organizer Colette, taking in my outfit of matching charcoal tunic, leggings, and stylish black lace-up ankle boots.

"I have a couple of layers and scarves and my jacket ready to put on," I answered, patting my backpack. "Although the switch from dressing for 100 degrees in Singapore to 50 degrees here made for interesting packing."

"You'll want to have a hat and gloves as well," Katherine Flynn said, nodding briskly, as the sisters joined us.

"Kat," Vivienne broke in, "I'm sure Annalise was smart enough to pack for the weather."

"It never hurts to check, Viv," said Katherine.

They moved to the door, chattering back and forth in the same animated fashion. Traveling with those two for the next few days was going to be like being in my own episode of *I Love Lucy*.

Auntie Lil returned from her trip back to our room, and we were ready to go to the bus. As we crossed the lobby, the Perinis joined us.

"Oh there you are!" said Georgiann, wrapping her scarf tightly around her neck. "I wanted you to meet my brother last night, but you didn't have the opportunity. Genio! Genio, come meet the Fontanas."

Anyone else would have missed the sharp intake of breath from Auntie Lil, but I caught it. What was up with her? Was she getting ill? If she was, how would I be able to explain it to my father? I was supposed to be taking care of her, for goodness' sake!

But as Georgiann Perini's brother came forward, I realized that I didn't have to worry about Auntie Lil having another heart attack. Well, not the kind that put her in the hospital last month, anyway. Her reaction to the introduction to this handsome stranger was indeed a twinge of the heart, a romantic twinge!

"Pleased to meet you ladies," he said in a pleasing baritone voice, his snowy hair shining and his eyes flashing.

For perhaps the only time in my life, I saw my Auntie Lil speechless!

"We're pleased to meet you," I stepped in. "And pleased that you were able to convince your sister and her husband to take this trip. It's so nice to have them with us."

For the second time in as many days, I watched as Auntie Lil managed to pull herself together.

"Yes. Pleased to meet you. We're looking forward to the journey. Annalise, shall we board the bus?" She hooked her arm through mine, and we exited the giant revolving door to make our way to the tour bus. When we boarded, she hustled me into two available seats toward the middle of the bus.

"All right, lady, spill it." I turned to her.

"Spill what?"

"Look, you can fool strangers, but you can't fool me. What is the deal with you and the Silver Fox?"

"I don't know what you mean."

"C'mon Auntie Lil, you reacted to him like a preteen girl reacts to meeting a member of One Direction."

She didn't respond.

"Seriously, Auntie Lil. You have to tell me. Who is he? Former lover? Did you two smuggle drugs together?"

"Annalise!" she drew back, horrified.

"Well, if you don't tell me, I'm left with only my imagination."

"Well, nothing that dramatic, I can assure you," she shook her head and continued. "I just feel like I've seen a ghost, that's all."

"What do you mean?"

"Annalise, he's the exact image of Antonio, or what Antonio would have looked like if he had survived that fire and were alive today," she said quietly.

Auntie Lil's girlhood sweetheart! I took her hand, and we sat quietly for a moment.

"You don't think it is—" I began, but she cut me off.

"No, dear, we know he didn't survive, because, well—"

"You don't have to finish that sentence, Auntie Lil."

I looked up to see the Perinis and Genio enter the bus and take a seat toward the front. Good, I thought, because my formidable Auntie Lil needed time to compose herself. How difficult this would be for her.

She reached into her bag to find her hankie and dabbed her eyes.

"What are you going to do?" I asked.

"What do you mean?" she asked.

"Well, this has to be difficult. We're together on this trip. You'll see him for the next week."

"So?"

"So? Auntie Lil you have to confront this and work through these feelings."

"What is it with the younger generation and confrontation? All I have to do is keep myself together. And I certainly don't need to involve anyone else."

"You can't be serious, Auntie Lil. This will ruin your trip."

"Do you think I need to ruin his as well? And perhaps his family's? I don't know anything about him. What exactly do you propose that I do? Tell him he reminds me of a dead boyfriend? THAT is certainly not polite conversation over lunch."

"True, I guess it's not."

"There's nothing to be done. I'm sorry that I've had to involve you and cause you any discomfort."

"What? Now you sound like a stiff, unfeeling aunt out of a 19th-century novel. I'm your niece. You can tell me anything without worrying about my 'discomfort.'"

She smiled and patted my cheek.

"Well, maybe I didn't mean it in such a Jane Austen way, but I just don't want you worrying about me. How about this. How about we drop this conversation at least until, oh, we visit the Flying Goose Pagoda, hmm? Give us enough time to listen to that delightful Yan Mei do her duty as tour director for a while before we drag down the entire tone of the trip?"

She pointed to the front of the bus, where our guide had indicated to the driver to take off and was starting to distribute the itinerary for the day.

"Fine," I said warily, "but this discussion is not over."

"Oh, Annalise, you are so much like me. I have no doubt that you mean it."

CHAPTER TWENTY-ONE

I kept one eye trained on Yan Mei and another on Genio and another on Auntie Lil. Okay, that sounds like three eyes, but you know what I mean.

As we drove, Yan Mei gave us a cursory lesson in Mandarin, teaching us to say hello (ni hao), thank you (xie xie), and a few other very clipped phrases. Around the bus, I heard many variations of the phrases being practiced. She also gave us an excellent account of the history of Xi'an—once the capital city and home to emperors—and the entire Shaanxi Province.

We parked near the city center and walked through the gates. Yan Mei explained that the surrounding wall was the most complete city wall to have survived in China. We climbed to the top and prepared to walk around a portion of its eight-mile perimeter.

"This is amazing, isn't it?" said Frida Willems as she and Bear joined Auntie Lil and me. We paused at one of the ramparts to take a photo.

"Just a bit larger than the wall around my house," said Auntie Lil, who by this time was her usual sassy self.

We laughed with her.

"I can't imagine the time that went into constructing this," said Bear, leaning over the rampart.

"It is indeed a feat of architecture," said Genio as he and the Perinis joined us.

I could tell that Auntie Lil wanted to bolt, but I clutched her sleeve.

"Genio is a history buff," said his sister, "especially architecture in history."

"Really?" I said. "Auntie Lil is quite interested in history." He turned to her.

"Any particular period in history, Miss Fontana?"

"You can call me Lilliana, and my niece exaggerates my knowledge I think."

"I think you'll find she knows quite a bit about any historical period," I said. "She would be my Lifeline if I were ever on a game show and needed to phone a friend for a history question."

"How interesting!" he said. "Should we organize a Trivia contest for the group on one of our longer bus excursions?"

"What an idea! You two can chat about that while Georgiann and Tom and I continue ahead of you." I took the Perinis each by an arm and started to march ahead, purposefully avoiding my aunt's glare.

"Well, aren't you a clever one!" Georgiann smiled.

"Sorry?" I asked.

"Don't play coy, dear. I saw how you managed to get Genio and your aunt to pair up on this walk."

I didn't reply, but I'm sure my eyes gave me away.

"Annalise, my wife is a world-class matchmaker," said Tom. "She knows all the tricks and is just impressed that you were that smooth."

"Guilty as charged!" I laughed.

"To tell you the truth, you were just one step ahead of me," said Georgiann.

"You don't think Genio was upset, do you?"

"Dear, I know my brother. Last night after he saw your aunt, even from a distance, I could tell he was interested. But, tell me, she doesn't seem interested. She's not attached to someone back home, is she?"

Auntie Lil's story was not mine to share, so I tried to think of a diplomatic way to answer the question.

"No, no, nothing like that. I just think she was a bit tired. The day was long, and the flight wore both of us out."

"I see," Georgiann nodded.

"Georgie, you let nature take its course now," Tom wagged his finger at her. "The introduction has been made."

"Oh, I don't think we have to worry." Georgiann pulled us to the side of the wall, and as we waited for Auntie Lil and Genio to catch up, we could see that they were getting along fine. His eyes were flashing, and her smile was girlish as she looked up at him.

"I think we'll just watch what happens," I agreed and turned to take in the view of the park below. A group of twenty or so people were moving in a lyrical fashion practicing Tai Chi. I was mesmerized by the simple beauty of the act.

"I suppose they meet there every morning. What a quiet sense of purpose they have," I said.

The Perinis and I watched together for a moment without speaking. Then Georgiann turned to me.

"What about you, dear?" she asked.

"Me? I've not taken a Tai Chi class, but it looks very interesting."

"No, I'm not talking about that."

"Georgie!" interrupted her husband.

"Oh hush, Tommy. I'm sure Annalise doesn't mind a bit of casual questioning." She tightened her scarf against the brisk wind and shook her head at her husband.

He rolled his eyes in the manner of a man long accustomed to the habits of his inquisitive wife.

"Annalise, you might as well tell her why you aren't married yet because she'll not rest until she gets it out of you," he said with a weary smile.

"There's nothing to tell. I just haven't met Mr. Right yet," I shrugged, thinking of Dylan. I was so sure at one time that he was Mr. Right, but a little distance and time showed me that he was more Mr. Right-place-and-time than Mr. Right.

"Ah, but there was someone," Georgiann said. Give her credit, the woman was intuitive.

"There were a few. No one really special yet." I tried to evade the issue.

"Mm. I suspect this trip with us oldsters is not the place to shop around either."

"Well, I wasn't really considering this a husband-hunting tour! But you're right, not exactly many prospects." Why did a face with coal-black eyes under serious eyebrows and matching blue-black hair suddenly pop into my head?

"Well, we'll keep looking," Georgiann nodded purposefully.

"Georgie!" her husband exclaimed.

"It's fine, Tom," I assured him. "This gives me a feeling of being at home with my own mom."

I looked around. We had walked so far during our matchmaking discussion that we were in danger of not making it back to the designated meeting point.

"We'd better turn around. The others have already headed back to the bus, and I don't want to make us late for the rest of the day." I pointed to my watch.

"Goodness, you're right!" Georgiann turned and amped up the speed from our strolling pace. We reached the meeting point and found Genio and Auntie Lil seated on a bench, in a spirited discussion about Chinese dynasties. I stood in front of Auntie Lil for a moment before she noticed me.

"There you are!" she said. "I was wondering what had happened to you."

"Uh-huh." I looked from her to Genio.

She jumped up guiltily from the bench. She took my arm, and we began walking toward the bus.

"So Auntie Lil, how far did you get?"

"What?"

"Around the perimeter. How far did you get? Why? What did you think I asked?"

"Annalise. I know you think you are funny, but I assure you that you are not. I was simply having a conversation about architecture with a peer."

"Sure."

"Annalise." She stopped and turned to me. "You are incorrigible."

"Takes one to know one," I laughed and dashed toward the bus.

I was still smiling when I reached our seats and plopped myself down. I leaned over and had my head buried in my backpack, searching for gum, when my seatmate joined me.

"Sorry, Auntie, I didn't mean to be so impertinent. Gum?" I reached a piece up to her.

"Thanks, I believe I will" came a baritone voice that was definitely not my aunt's.

My head popped up so quickly that I banged it without ceremony on the rear of the seat in front of me.

"Ouch!" I said, turning to see the twinkling eyes of Father John where I should have seen those of my aunt. Did she send him back to reprimand me?

"I can see that you are confused," laughed the elderly priest. "I asked your aunt if I could trade seats for a bit. I'm not comfortable sitting so far toward the front."

I sat forward and leaned up to see where my aunt had landed. While she was too short for me to see her, I could easily deduce that she was in the window seat next to Genio. I leaned back. Georgiann Perini was really a master matchmaker if she could organize these benign chess moves.

"Father, I'm pretty sure you know it's a sin to lie. Come clean. Georgiann Perini encouraged you to trade, didn't she?"

"Hmm, now that you mention it, I believe it was Georgiann who suggested that this seat might be better."

I shook my head and smiled.

"Do you have a problem sharing a seat with an old man of the cloth?"

"I suspect that, other than my aunt, a priest would be the person my father would handpick to be my seatmate!"

"Sounds like your father cares about you very much."

"He does."

"Let me guess. It was your father who suggested that you accompany your aunt on this trip."

"How did you know?"

"Why else would a young woman want to be on a trip with people three times her age?" He gestured around the bus.

"Well, it was his idea, but more for Auntie Lil than for me. He wanted to make sure she had a companion for the trip in case anything went wrong."

Father John leaned his head back and laughed.

"Annalise, I barely know your aunt, but I can tell she is very self-sufficient."

"Ah, but you don't know my father," I shrugged.

"Oh, I think I do, I think I do."

I took in the lifework crags around his eyes and his general appearance. Yes, I'm sure he knows more than his share of protective fathers.

"So," he continued, "how about you? Are you having fun on this journey?"

I thought back to our layover in San Francisco and the adventures we had in Singapore and even the fun we were having so far in China.

"Definitely," I nodded.

"And this blog you've started? Is it fulfilling?"

"Well, I haven't been at it long enough, but so far so good. I like writing, I know that."

"Good, good," he nodded.

"Hey. My pop didn't get hold of you somehow to check on me?" I glanced at him sidewise.

"No, no dear," he patted my hand. "Just call it an occupational hazard, I guess."

I was about to ask him another question when the voice of Yan Mei came over the speaker. We had arrived at the Flying Wild Goose Pagoda, and she was giving us directions on how we would proceed with our visit.

Moments later, I waited at the entry gates and caught up with my aunt, who was exiting the nearby ladies room.

"Hello? May I introduce myself? I'm your niece?"

"What's your point, Annalise?" She arranged her jacket ostentatiously.

"Only that one minute I'm your best buddy, and the next you've swapped me out for a handsome stranger."

"First, it was you who micromanaged the situation so that Genio and I were left to walk together at the city wall. Second, I was just accommodating Father John's wishes to move to another seat, and third—"

She must have caught the smile on my face because she stopped her list.

"Go on, this is fascinating," I teased.

"Obviously, you are not listening," she sniffed.

"Come on, Auntie, I promise I'll be good and pay attention." I rearranged my face into a more serious look.

"No, I will not indulge you." Her tone became stiffer.

Oops, maybe I had gone too far. I opened my mouth to apologize when I caught her face soften and saw a smile spread across it. I looked over my shoulder, but I didn't need to in order to know who was walking toward us. Seeing the look on his face match hers, I knew that I was watching something special.

"Ah, here are the beautiful Fontanas!" He put his arm around both of our shoulders, but I knew there was only one Fontana girl in his line of sight. If he was trying to hide his feelings, he was totally unsuccessful.

"Genio, I was just telling Annalise that we were having a marvelous conversation about the history of this pagoda."

We were?

"Indeed," he nodded. He proceeded to comment on the story Yan Mei shared with us of the Buddhist monks who had lived there and who, at one point while praying for food, saw a wild goose fall dead from the sky. They ate the goose, but in honor of the gift of food, they became vegetarians and built the beautiful pagoda.

As the three of us walked along the grounds and into the pagoda, I watched my aunt and this charming man and marveled at how they looked so comfortable together. It dawned on me that the reason Auntie Lil had never found someone to share her life with was that she had never found someone who could stack up to her amazing intellect! This man certainly seemed like a candidate. Oh, I couldn't wait to chat with Rory about this amazing turn of events.

.

CHAPTER TWENTY-TWO

"Say that again," Rory said. "I think we have a bad connection or I've lost some of my hearing."

"You sound like a bad movie, Rory."

"Auntie Lil ... smitten like a kitten?"

"Yep. And it's not just one way either. This man seems to be totally into her as well."

I felt like Rory and I were back in junior high school, dishing the latest gossip. Somehow, even though she was sitting in New York and I was perched on a park bench in China, it was as if the years had melted away and we were plopped on my bed munching on chocolate chip cookies.

"Who would have thought?" she marveled.

"I know! The other day when we worried about her heart? Well, there was something going on with her heart, only not the way we feared."

"This is great. Right? I mean it's great, don't you think, Annalise?"

"I think so. I mean, she's only known him a day. What would our parents say—no, what would SHE say—if this were one of us?"

"Totally different. They would say we're too young to know what we're doing."

"Rory, I could make the argument that she's too OLD to know what she's doing. Older women get taken in by scoundrels all the time."

"Listen to you, Annalise. When is the last time anyone used the word *scoundrel* outside of a Harlequin Romance novel?" Rory laughed.

"Well, you know what I mean."

"I do know what you mean, and I think you need to cool your jets. Just because they sit together on a bus ride doesn't mean she's giving him the password to her bank account."

"You're right."

"Plus, she shares a hotel room with you. What is she going to do, bring him in there for some illicit activity? Who does he share his room with?"

"The priest."

"Ha! Even better. I don't think he'll be enticing her back there while the good father is … I don't know, praying or watching a religious movie."

"Really, Rory? Do you think there's a special channel in hotels just for priests that only show *The Ten Commandments* or *The Song of Bernadette*?" Sometimes Rory could be so obtuse.

"You know what I mean."

"I do. And you're right, I don't think we have to worry. Yet."

"We don't have to worry. Period," she emphasized, then added, "Just don't tell your dad."

"Do you think I'm insane? Pop would be on the next flight to China if he had to hijack the plane. No. This stays between Auntie Lil and me for now. Well, and you."

"And you know I don't have the desire to have your father grill me, so I'm not talking."

I turned and saw that our group was headed toward the bus.

"Hey, I have to leave. We're headed to the tombs of the terra-cotta warriors. Auntie thinks the reason I'm sitting by myself on this bench is that I need quiet to make an entry on my blog."

"Speaking of which, we all love it here."

"We? Who's 'we'?" I'm sure she could hear the panic in my voice.

"The folks in the office. You don't think I wouldn't share your scribbles with other people, do you?"

"It's just to keep the family and friends updated, Rory. Just how many people have seen it?"

"Annalise, what are you worried about? It's great. You've always been a good writer. You know, I think you may have found your calling."

"Oh sure, I'm just betting there is a ton of money in writing free blogs." I shook my head even though she couldn't see me.

"I don't know, Annalise, this could lead to something—" she began.

"Hey, stop distracting me, Rory. I need to go!"

"Keep me posted on the new romance!"

"Oh, I will. Bye!"

I walked back to the bus and joined the chatty Flynn sisters.

"Annalise, you are so industrious. So technological with your computer and your phone," said Katherine.

"She's got to keep up with that blot, Kat," said Vivienne.

"It's a blog," I corrected, hoping to be kind.

"Right, right," Vivienne nodded.

"We are going to give that information on how to connect to it to our family when we call them later, so they can read about our trip."

"Are you going to interview anyone?" Vivienne asked.

"I think you should interview the handsome young man," Katherine said crisply. "No one wants to read about us old skeletons."

Who was she considering a handsome young man? Everyone was far north of sixty. Well, maybe to her someone who WAS sixty seemed young.

I laughed to myself as we boarded the bus.

My laughter was short-lived when I glanced at the seat next to the one reserved for Yan Mei. Seated quietly listening to headphones, with his head buried in a tattered notebook, was someone I thought I would never see again.

Eli Chamberlain.

How I managed not to stumble as I dashed back to my seat was a miracle. I sat and crouched as low as possible. Peeking around into the aisle, I could see Auntie Lil and Genio moving into the same seats they had occupied on the last leg of the trip, which meant that Father John would come and join me.

There was probably no way I could get Auntie Lil's attention to get her to come back to her original seat.

Hey … how did she not see Eli, anyway? Was she THAT lost in Genio's gorgeous eyes? And if she did see Eli, did she not think I would need her to come back and sit with me?

I kept my head tucked, and when Father John arrived, he was overly boisterous in saying, "Annalise! What on earth are you doing? Hiding from the police?"

"Ssssh!" I pulled him down into the seat.

"What is the matter, child?" I could see that he was genuinely alarmed.

"Nothing," I whispered.

"Well, for nothing, you are being mighty mysterious."

"See that man in the very front seat? The one next to Yan Mei?"

"Yes?"

"Well, doesn't he seem suspicious?"

"He seems quite normal to me. What makes you think he's suspicious?"

It just wasn't in my genes to keep anything from a priest.

"I … kind of know him."

"Well, that's marvelous! Go up and say hello!" The cheerful priest stood up to make room for me to enter the aisle.

"Are you kidding me? That's the last thing I am going to do." I pulled him down unceremoniously and shushed him again.

"Well, if you know him, I'm sure that he'll be happy to talk to you, dear."

"Um, I wouldn't say that he'd be exactly happy to see me, Father." My face must have colored.

Father John lifted his head and looked up toward the front, then ducked down again to humor me.

"Well, could you do me a favor and tell me about it sitting straight up? I don't think my old bones can survive crouching like a character in a spy movie for too long. And our fellow passengers are beginning to look at us in an odd way."

He was right. People were trying unsuccessfully not to stare at us crouched over as if we were middle school students sneaking a cigarette.

Seated more comfortably, I embarked on the tale of the flying crabmeat in Singapore.

"It's not funny, Father!" I turned toward the window as he attempted to hide his grin.

"Really? You don't see the humor in it?"

I turned toward him.

"But … then … I tried to apologize and …"

Father John was having none of it. He just shook his head.

"I think you are focusing on how you feel. Did you think about how he felt? Maybe he's shy and didn't want the focus on him. Maybe he was trying to apologize to you and was confused that you were not accepting it."

Darn it. He reminded me so much of my own great uncle Sal—Father Sal.

"Is everyone on this trip so wise?"

"Yes. It was a requirement." He nodded soberly.

I laughed.

Peeking over the seat, I could see that Eli had removed his headphones and was in an animated conversation with Yan Mei.

Oh. That's how it was. Why else would he be on this random bus trip with so many senior citizens? He and our tour director were together. I got it. He was visiting with her on her job.

Well, why not? Look at how beautiful she was. Her skin was flawless, and her jet-black hair fell like a column down her back. And she was petite and slim. She was so tiny, you could put her in your pocket! Not like me. You couldn't use the adjective *petite* for me. Short, yes, but definitely not slim. In the Renaissance, I would have been ideal—voluptuous and full of curves. In today's times, I'm bordering on shopping in the "big girls" section.

Oh well. We're all attracted to different types. Some women prefer men who are blond with facial hair. Some prefer tall, some short. Personally, I've always liked dark hair and eyes.

Dark hair and eyes. Dark eyes under brooding brows staring back from the front of the bus. Oops. Any minute, they would catch mine. Duck down, Annalise!

"Now what, child?" asked Father John.

"I think he saw me!"

"And?"

"And … so he'll know I'm here."

"I hate to state the obvious, Annalise, but if we're all together on this tour, he'll figure that out quickly enough. What were you planning to do, wear sunglasses and a low-brimmed hat?"

I must have hesitated a moment too long.

"Annalise!" Father John shook his head.

"Of course not. Besides, he'll see Aunt Lil and know that I'm here."

At that exact moment, he had stood and was indeed leaning over the seat where she was and conversing with her. We soon pulled into a parking lot, and he straightened up to return to his own seat. Yan Mei's voice came over the loud-speaker to make announcements. Would he have continued up the aisle to talk with me if he hadn't been interrupted?

I leaned back and managed to let out the breath I had been holding. Of course he wouldn't have made an effort to come talk to me. He was being polite to Auntie Lil but went back to sit with his girlfriend.

Why did I even care?

"Annalise, you are deep in thought," observed Father John.

"Just trying to concentrate on the announcement." I managed to cover my feelings, I thought.

"Mm-hmm," said Father John, unconvinced, but apparently willing to avoid pushing me into further discussion.

We came to a stop, and our group began exiting, with the plan to meet in the courtyard of the small factory that manufactured replicas of the terra-cotta warriors we would be seeing soon. This particular stop was to be a mix of history lesson and an opportunity to purchase some replicas.

Father John and I hopped from the bus, and Auntie Lil greeted me with a hug. Genio was not in sight.

"Where's your buddy?" I asked.

"He's nearby. I told him I needed to visit with you."

Father John gave us a nod and moved on to join the others.

Silly me. I should have known my aunt hadn't thrown me over for a glorious head of hair and handsome mustache. I hugged her tightly.

"What's this? Did you think I had abandoned you?" she laughed and gently pushed my bangs from my eyes.

"No, but you saw our new bus companion, didn't you?"

"I see that Eli joined us. Delightful young man, Annalise. You'll need to say hello to him."

"What! We haven't exactly had a history of pleasant encounters, Auntie Lil."

And I'm sure his girlfriend would think I was just making a move on him.

"Nonsense. You can't ignore a person." She shook her head.

I suspect Auntie Lil had stars in her eyes from her recent conquest and wasn't able to see life as it was. I decided to give her a pass.

"Okay, okay. When I get the opportunity. But we better catch up to the group, don't you think?"

We met up with them as the factory tour guide was explaining the differences in the warriors we would be viewing at the site. It was fascinating to note that the hairstyle, facial hair, and even the front tilt of the shoe determined the rank of each warrior. Being able to get so close to these detailed replicas would make our trip to the excavation site more well rounded.

We moved into the factory showroom where we could purchase a replica from four inches to six feet in size, and Genio joined us.

"Are you purchasing anything?" he asked.

"Something small and desk-sized for my brother, Annalise's father," Auntie Lil said.

"Pop will love that," I nodded. "Probably a general, don't you think?"

"There are nice ones on that table." Genio led Auntie Lil one aisle over, and I remained, examining the horsemen.

"Did you see the life-size ones that you could order where you could have a replica of your own head on the top?" came a voice over my shoulder.

I nearly dropped the statue I had in my hands as I turned and looked up into the depths of Eli Chamberlain's ebony eyes.

CHAPTER TWENTY-THREE

"Whoah!" he caught the statue.

"That could have been expensive," I said but couldn't meet his eyes for some reason.

"It seems that when we meet, we always nearly just avoid a disaster." His face spread into a smile, and I was reminded not only of the flying chili crab but also the crashing book table display at the Denver airport.

"I guess so," I said.

"So, I spoke to your aunt earlier. Imagine my surprise to find that you ladies are part of this group. Particularly you."

"Why particularly me?"

"Well, you don't exactly fit the demographic of the bus," he gestured toward the rest of our tour companions.

"Technically, I'm here as my aunt's 'companion.'" Goodness. How did that make me sound? I turned to pick up another sculpture and became engrossed in it.

"That's sweet," he said.

"Sweet?"

"Yes, sweet. Not many people would take time out of their busy lives to accompany an elderly relative on a vacation."

Ha! If only he knew that were it not for this trip, the busiest part of my life would consist of helping my mother clean the attic. I looked up at him but saw a distant look on his face. Probably worried about the opening of the stock market or something.

"So what brings YOU on this bus, Eli?"

He cleared his throat and paused.

"Um. I just never had the opportunity to see the sights before, and Yan Mei said she was happy to let me tag along."

Oh. Right. Yan Mei.

"She seems … great." I hoped I sounded polite.

"She is. Do you know she speaks five languages?"

Of course she did.

"She's the most requested guide at the tour company."

Well, sure.

I was not in the mood to hear more accolades about the thin-as-a-model, picture-perfect, speaks-every-language, beloved-by-all Yan Mei.

"Um, I need to find Auntie Lil. I'll catch up and chat with you in a bit." My tone was sharp as I moved outside the shop.

There was what I needed: a tiny bench under a tree. I plopped down, pulled my tablet from my bag, and started banging on my keyboard.

I was lost in my writing and finally looked up when the chatter around me got louder. We were due to gather at the small restaurant near the entrance of the factory so that we could eat together. With a sigh, I closed my tablet and looked for Auntie Lil to join her. She was standing nearby, looking around, no doubt seeking me as well. When she spied me, she waved vigorously and a smile lit up her face. How could I feel down with this cheeky lady as my travelmate?

"Did you pick out something nice for Pop?" I asked as I crossed over toward her.

"Definitely. I found a very serious-looking general, just the size for the corner of his desk."

"That will work," I nodded. "Ready for lunch?"

"Genio is saving us seats."

The ground crunched under our feet as we took the last steps toward the small cafe.

"You're quiet, dear. Are you all right with lunching with Genio?" Auntie Lil asked.

"What? Oh. That's fine. I was just thinking about my next blog entry and was distracted." I didn't want her to worry about me.

Our group took up the entire cafe, and servers bustled around bringing the same dishes to all the tables while taking individual orders for drinks.

"This all looks good, doesn't it ladies?" Genio rose as we approached the seats he'd saved for us. His sister and brother-in-law were also seated at our round table.

"You bet! What are we having?" I rubbed my hands together.

Apparently the cafe catered to American tourists' tastes, so family-style bowls graced the center of each table and contained a chicken dish that resembled sweet and sour along with beef and broccoli and a vegetable stir-fry. We each had a spring roll and a cup of soup.

It was very tasty, but I couldn't deny that I was disappointed. I really wanted to eat more like the locals. Auntie Lil caught my eye and read my mind. Without a word, we both shrugged in unison, and I knew she agreed that we would try to find more authentic food for another meal. Our unspoken agreement brought amused looks to both our faces.

"Now what are you two giggling about?" asked Georgiann.

"Just thinking about how my father is going to react to his warrior figure," I said. I didn't want to insult anyone who didn't share our desire to be more adventurous in dining.

"I see," nodded Georgiann. She leaned over and whispered, "I thought perhaps you were talking about our new bus companion."

"Georgie!" said her exasperated husband.

"What? I saw Annalise talking to him. They are the youngest people on the trip." I could see where the dots were connecting in her head. Luckily, her brother stepped in to change the subject.

"Georgie, don't you think this beef and broccoli is better than the kind we get at the Lucky Panda back home?"

"Well of course it is, Genio. We're in China for Pete's sake!" With that she was off and running on the topic of food. I shot Genio a look of thanks.

While Georgiann was holding forth on the virtues of broccolini versus broccoli, I casually peered over my shoulder to the table near the entrance where Eli was eating with Yan Mei. I couldn't hear them, but I was pretty sure they were speaking in Mandarin. Well, I thought, they could be speaking in any of the five languages that were in her area of expertise.

Why was I so concerned anyway? It's not like I was attracted to him. Who cared about how nice he looked in his casual touring clothes with that scarf draped so jauntily around his neck? And who cared about how he flipped that forelock of hair out of his eyes with a quick shrug of his head just like the lead singer of a boy band? And who liked smiles that went all the way from someone's mouth to their eyes?

Me, I concluded mournfully.

I WAS attracted. And in the worst possible situation. Stuck with him, his girlfriend, and a busload of senior citizens in a country halfway around the world.

Welcome to the worst romance movie ever, I thought.

I picked at my delicious lunch, barely listening to the conversation around me, until I heard my name. It was Genio, on my right, asking me a question.

"I'm sorry, Genio, I must have drifted off for a moment. What did you say?"

"I was just asking what you do back home in Denver."

"Hmm. That's a complicated question. I'm sort of between jobs right now." I went on to explain my layoff and lengthy job hunt.

"It must be frustrating."

I appreciated the fact that he didn't immediately launch into well-worn platitudes like, "Oh I'm sure it will all work out" or "Keep your chin up." He just acknowledged my frustration.

"It is. Don't get me wrong, I'm not at the end of my rope or anything, but can I tell you something?"

"If you want to."

"I'm not even sure I want to get the same sort of job."

"I understand that," he nodded.

"You do?"

"Sure. That's what you trained for, but you've found parts of it that you like better than others. You probably would like to find a job that concentrates on them."

"Exactly!" How did he get that?

"There's nothing wrong with carving out your career to suit your strengths, Annalise."

"Doesn't that seem, oh, I don't know, selfish?" I knew my face scrunched up.

"Of course not. You chose a major in college when you were only about 17 years old. The fact that you completed a college degree is proof that you can commit to and complete a task, that's all. What you do with that collection of learning is up to you. You've gained more experience in, what about five years?"

I nodded.

"So now you're probably ready to commit to what your talents and gifts really equip you to do."

I thought about that for a moment.

"But I look at Auntie Lil who committed to her career for her whole life when she was younger than me. Or, my friend Rory—"

"But have you talked with them? Asked them about where they feel their gifts and talents are and when they discerned them? Everyone is different."

I thought about that for a moment. He was right. Rory had always wanted to do what she did. And Auntie Lil had never complained about her job because she genuinely loved it.

"What do you do, Genio?" I suddenly remembered that as the only representative of our family here, I should be quizzing him and his motives with Auntie Lil rather than concentrating on my own selfish problems.

"I'm retired. But before that I was an architect."

"Would I know any of your buildings in Chicago?" He must live in the same city as his sister.

"Actually, my work was more international."

Hmm. What's this ... international playboy? Just the type to break Auntie Lil's heart?

"Genio, I hear you over there downplaying your accomplishments," his sister broke in. "Annalise, you are sitting next to Retired Lieutenant Colonel Eugenio Cusamano of the Air Force. He was one of the major names in architecture and civil engineering in the Air Force in the 20th century."

I looked over at him, and he winked. I suddenly liked this humble man who preferred to be known as just Genio.

"No wonder you are such a good problem solver."

"Well, my sister likes to brag on me, but now that you know, let's just keep it to ourselves, okay?"

"Yes, sir." I looked across him to my aunt. Here I had been wondering whether he was good enough for her. I suspect his family should have been vetting us for him.

Changing subjects, I pulled out my guide and reviewed the information about the tombs of the terra-cotta soldiers, the next stop on the trip.

"It's hard to believe that this whole site was discovered because two farmers were digging a well," I said.

"They must have been pretty wise to realize that the random pieces they dug up were more than just pottery," agreed Auntie Lil.

We finished our lunch and returned to the bus. She joined me in our original seat for the short drive to the excavation site, and I managed to keep the conversation strictly about the scenery outside the windows. I couldn't wait to see the site, and was both pleased and a little sad when we were the last ones off the bus, sparing me the necessity of encountering Eli and Yan Mei.

The site certainly didn't disappoint! Dating back to the third century B.C., the thousands of warriors and hundreds of chariots and horses were constructed to protect the then emperor in the afterlife. Once the initial discovery was made in 1974, archaeologists and historians embarked on painstakingly reconstructing the thousands of terra-cotta figures while continuing to discover more of them in giant pits. Each of the separate pits we saw contained hundreds of the figures, and we walked around the site surrounded by a huge rail fence.

Auntie Lil and Genio moved a bit further down one section of the railing while I stopped, leaning over with my iPad to attempt to snag a photo. Then Eli Chamberlain moved next to me.

"Here," he said. "Let me take one with you in the foreground."

My heart beat a bit faster as I turned and leaned on the rail, facing him, and handed him my tablet.

"Hold on a second," he moved toward me and brushed my bangs from my face.

"There," he said. "We want to be able to see your eyes."

Was it my imagination, or did he linger just a bit when his fingers were on my forehead?

"Thanks," I stuttered.

He moved back to take the picture but paused with the tablet held to his side as he locked eyes with me. The moment was broken when a voice near us snapped us back to reality.

"There! I know—the young man can take a picture of all of us!" It was the distinctive, organizing voice of our group leader, Colette.

He quickly snapped the photo of me and handed me my iPad, turning to Colette and clearing his throat.

"I'd be honored, ma'am."

I pulled my iPad up to my face so that I could hide behind it while I pretended to take a picture. I could still smell the woodsy scent of his cologne where he had touched it. Oh no, that was too much.

Why was my timing so wrong? I walked around to the other side of the railing, leaving the sounds of the group being organized by Colette into the perfect shot. I took one tiny peek over my shoulder and saw that Eli was glancing my way.

Keep walking, Annalise!

CHAPTER TWENTY-FOUR

"We lost you? Where did you go?" Auntie Lil caught up to me in the museum at the end of excavation site visit.

"Oh, I guess I just got lost in the enormity of it all," I said, trying to cover.

Actually, it wasn't that far from the truth. I was amazed at the thousands of figures that were visible in the dig site.

"It is amazing," she agreed. "Shall we go up to the second floor?"

"Where is Genio?"

"He's already gone up with Georgiann and Tom. We'll catch up to them. The rest of the group is scattered about. Yan Mei has given us all time on our own until we need to be back at the bus."

"Back to the airport to fly to Beijing then?" I confirmed our schedule.

"Exactly."

We walked on in silence, only stopping occasionally to comment on displays as we saw them on the ramp up to the second floor.

Eventually, Auntie Lil could not hold it in any longer and pulled me to the side.

"All right, that's it. You need to explain yourself."

"What! I'm sure I don't know what you mean."

"Annalise, you haven't mentioned one word, not one syllable about your encounter with Eli Chamberlain. I have eyes. I saw you scamper away from him after he took your photo. Now tell Auntie Lil everything."

"What! There was no 'encounter' as you put it. He took my picture. That was it."

"I saw him look at you when you walked away."

"You need your glasses, lady," I shook my head. But, I wondered, what did she see? I couldn't ask her. That would just show that I was interested. Rats!

"Besides," I continued, "there's the little issue of Yan Mei. I'm pretty sure they're together."

"You don't know that!"

"Pretty sure, Auntie Lil."

She shook her head.

"You can shake your head all you want, but I'M not going to be swept away by some vacation fantasy."

Oops. I hoped I didn't insult her and her own vacation— what would you call it? It wasn't a fling. Flirtation?

"Annalise. What have I always told you? Life is a banquet, and most poor suckers are starving to death."

"Pretty sure you got that from watching Rosalind Russell in *Auntie Mame* too often," I pursed my lips.

"Whatever. I just think you are jumping to conclusions."

"I'M jumping to conclusions! Who's the one who is reading something from a random glance?" I really wanted to ask her what she saw, but darn it, if I asked, she would know that I was interested.

She put her hands on my shoulders and matched her hazel eyes to mine.

"Dear, please promise me that you won't just write this encounter off? I really think you owe it to yourself to open yourself up a bit."

I could have reminded her that not more than twenty-four hours ago, the shoe was on the other foot and that I was telling her she owed it to herself to talk with Genio. Not the time to get into that discussion, though, so I just nodded.

"Fine. I'll 'encounter' more."

"Good!" She nodded and pushed me ahead. "Now let's move on, or we'll be the last ones to the bus."

Well, I promised to "encounter," but I didn't promise to "engage."

However, I didn't even have an opportunity to encounter because the museum was quite large and we were both very inquisitive, so it was nearly an hour before we returned to the bus in the parking lot. And, indeed, we were the last ones to board.

I instinctively looked toward the seat where I knew that Eli would be sitting. Darn it! He had his headphones on with his nose buried in that tattered notebook and did not look up when I boarded. It may have been a bit obvious to hang out at the door, so I moved back to my seat. I could see that the seat next to Genio was open for Auntie Lil, so I knew that my seatmate would be the kindly Father John.

"Ah, there she is," smiled the priest as I approached, and he allowed me next to the window.

"Hi, Father. Did you enjoy the warriors and the museum?" I asked as I settled in for the hourlong ride to the airport.

"It was marvelous! And you?"

"I was amazed. I got some good shots to put in my blog." I reached into my bag to pull out my iPad and was greeted with a whiff of Eli's cologne when I opened it to show Father John my photos.

"These photos are really good," he said as I scrolled through them. "This one of you is particularly nice. You look utterly charming. Who took it?"

I looked at the snap that Eli took. I was forever captured in that moment after he had swept my bangs from my forehead. My face certainly showed my vulnerability.

"Eli took it."

"Ah. That explains it. A young woman always looks her best when she's enchanted by her dashing young man."

"Very poetic, Father, but I'm afraid it's also not accurate." I shook my head.

"No?"

"I'm afraid that if Eli is enchanting anyone, it would be Yan Mei." I swiped to the next photo.

"Hmm." He leaned up to get a better view of the front of the bus where the happy couple were seated and leaned back.

"Hmm what?"

"Nothing, child, just an old man's privilege to say 'hmm' now and again. It makes us sound wise and inscrutable."

I burst into laughter, and we resumed viewing the photos. Father John helped me choose a couple to post to the blog, and I finished typing my entry. I would be ready to upload it when we got to our hotel and had WiFi access.

When we reached the airport, we bustled around, going through the necessary preparations to check our baggage. It occurred to me that lunch had been a long time earlier in the day, when Yan Mei reminded us that we would be dining at a restaurant just before the security gate.

"Airport food?" I whispered to Auntie Lil.

She winked, a veteran of many organized tours. This was evidently not an uncommon procedure.

Imagine my surprise when we entered a very charming restaurant. It was set up in a buffet style, obviously catering to a quick-moving crowd. We paid our fee, then each chose from a wide variety of tempting items including a sushi bar, a Mongolian grill, and a made-to-order noodle station.

"How great is this!" I commented as I sat down at a table already occupied by Auntie Lil, Genio, the Perinis, and the Willems. The Flynn sisters at a nearby table had swept up Father John. I must not have been too subtle in glancing around the restaurant because Auntie Lil reached over to say, "He's not here."

"Who?" Really smooth Annalise.

"The person you don't want me to know you are looking for is not here. He didn't enter the restaurant."

"I'm sure I don't know what you are talking about. I was just admiring the decor," I sniffed.

Rats. He wasn't there. But Yan Mei was. Did that mean he wasn't coming with us for the rest of the journey? Oh, what difference did it make anyway? Sadly, I dug into my chow fun.

"How long is this flight?" asked Bear Willems.

"Two hours, love," his wife answered.

"Enough time to get in a nap," he commented.

"A nap before we get to the hotel to go to bed?" she laughed.

"It was a lot of walking today." He shook his head as he scooped more rice from a second plate onto his main plate. A very substantial man, he had a healthy appetite.

"I don't blame you, Bear," said Auntie Lil. "Tomorrow will be a long day as well. I think our lungs will be nearly worn out."

We all nodded. The air quality in Beijing was something we all had been warned about. My mother had packed a number of surgical masks for me to wear, of course.

"I guess we shouldn't expect to see much sunshine," Tom Perini shook his head.

His wife was unfamiliar with the pollution problem in Beijing, or most of China for that matter, so we passed the rest of our meal discussing that and other political topics in between replenishing our plates at the buffet.

Eventually, Yan Mei gathered us together for instructions on the next step of our journey.

"I can't go through security with you since I won't be accompanying you to Beijing, so I must say good-bye," she smiled graciously.

Well, that probably explained why her friend Eli wasn't there.

"When you land, you'll look for my colleague Lee," she continued. "He'll have a large sign with the company logo and your group name. He will guide you to baggage claim, then to the bus, and whisk you to your hotel, which will be your home for the remainder of your journey. It has been a pleasure to accompany you on your visit through Xi'an."

Her smile was bright and cheery, even though the next part of her task was to herd our group to the security entrance. I would imagine she breathed an inner sigh of relief once she saw the last of us go through. I pictured her and Eli sitting next to a cozy fire later, shoes kicked off with glasses of wine. My own feet dragged. I barely paid attention to Auntie Lil while we walked toward our gate.

"Come on, slowpoke. I wouldn't think you would be the last one in this group." Bear Willems encircled me with his comforting arm as his wife, Frida, looped her own arm through my other elbow.

"I ate too much, I guess," I lied.

"You remind me of our oldest daughter," said Frida. "She's more of a morning person. Is that it?"

That was an easy cover.

"I guess so." I hoped my smile was genuine. At that moment, my phone buzzed in my bag, and I realized I had an incoming text. I pulled it out and smiled. My brother. I waved the Willems on and stopped to read.

Ma wanted me to check with you "casually."

My fingers flew on my keyboard.

What time is it there?

Let's just say, Ma woke the birds and came over.

I laughed.

All fine here. It's all in my blog … read it!

We will … you know Ma.

This last was punctuated with a goofy face.

> No worries, Nick.
> SERIOUSLY. Go back to sleep.

As if. At least Ma is making breakfast!

> Yum! Enjoy! Love You!

Love You!

I slipped my phone back into my bag and, looking up, realized I had to dash to catch up to the group.

I was nearly breathless when I reached our gate and plopped down in a seat next to Auntie Lil.

"What was the holdup?" she asked.

"Ma—" I started.

Auntie Lil stopped me.

"Say no more," she laughed and turned to Genio. "Annalise's mother, my sister-in-law, is worried that we will succumb to some sort of tragedy on this journey. Tell about her potty preparations for you."

I recounted the tales of my mother and her uncommon concern for our toilet arrangements, much to the entertainment of not only Genio but everyone around us. I admit, I exaggerated just a bit.

"You are a natural storyteller, Annalise. Are you putting that in your blog?" Tom Perini chuckled.

"I hadn't thought about it."

"You should!" Auntie Lil turned to me, her eyes dancing.

"Don't you think it would hurt Ma's feelings?"

"I've known your mother a long time," she waved the thought off. "She'd love it and be proud of being mentioned."

Hmm. I didn't think about it before. The others moved on to tales of past travels while I pulled my iPad from my bag and started a file with the story. Come to think of it, there were other stories associated from before the trip that might be good as well.

I snapped my tablet shut long enough to board, ignoring everything but my thoughts, but the minute we were in our seats, I continued typing, pausing only when the flight attendants told us to turn off our technology. I returned to my task as soon as I could. Auntie Lil sensed my intensity and left me alone, concentrating on her reading material.

Before long, we landed in Beijing ready for the next phase of our journey. My heart raced a bit thinking of the sights we would see. Out of the plane, our group assembled to walk together to the exit. I glanced around at the familiar faces and gasped when I saw one I wasn't expecting.

Eli? Shouldn't he be back in Xi'an? How did I not see him board? Talk about a racing heart!

CHAPTER TWENTY-FIVE

His eye turned and caught mine at the same time. Was I mistaken, or did he wait for me to catch up?

"Miss Fontana," he gave a cursory bow of his head.

"Mr. Chamberlain," I mimicked. Pretty smooth, I thought. Maybe not.

Eek. The scrutinizing eyes of our entire tour group surrounded us, waiting to see what would happen next between us.

I turned to glare at Auntie Lil, but she shrugged, and I could read her thoughts. She hadn't shared my secret thoughts about Eli. So how did the others …?

Father John.

I know that he was only bound by the seal of the confessional for things discussed within it, but I thought that he would be respectful outside it for random embarrassing stories as well! I shot him a look but could tell that he too was not the culprit.

That could only mean … Oh no. Could EVERYONE read my emotions that easily? Was I no better than a teenager swooning over the lead singer of a boy band? Did that mean that Yan Mei could read me as well? Did she and her boyfriend Eli get a good chuckle over the silly girl with a crush?

I bowed my head, excused myself, and ducked into the nearby ladies room.

I was dabbing my face with a refreshing wipe (from one of several packages carefully packed by my mother) when Auntie Lil appeared beside me in the mirror.

"What's up, chickadee?"

As if she didn't know.

"Does everyone know?" I caught her eye in the mirror, afraid to look at her directly.

"These people have taken a liking to you, Annalise. They are interested in your well-being."

"They've known me for a day!"

"Well, at our age, we've learned not to hesitate."

I swung around to her, ready with a cutting remark, but she was calmly arranging her hair, preparing to freshen her lipstick.

Great. In planning this trip, I was worried about this elderly group moving too slowly. Now I can see that I should have worried about the opposite—at least in the emotions department.

"Do they just miss their soap operas from back home?" I mused.

Auntie Lil laughed.

"Oh, Annalise, trust me. Nothing is ever as bad as it seems. Now come on. The one thing we can't do is delay the group, for whatever reason."

She was right.

When we left the ladies room, the others were gone, obviously having traveled to baggage claim. We were the last to arrive, and our new tour guide was waiting patiently near our bags for the two of us. He had sent the others to the bus that was parked at the curb directly outside the doors. I felt a small pang of guilt for the delay.

We climbed into the bus after the driver loaded our luggage, and Auntie Lil hopped into a seat next to Genio, naturally. Expecting to join Father John, I hurried down the aisle to the only empty seat.

"Hello again."

Eli.

Of course.

I leaned my head out in the aisle, willing Auntie Lil to turn around. Somehow she did. My eyes were slits as I shook my head slowly from side to side. She smiled innocently. I turned back to my seatmate. Knowing that the entire bus was keyed in to my next move, I smiled and said hello.

"Father John asked me to sit with him, then decided he wanted to move for some reason," Eli said.

"Mm-hmm. For some reason." I chuckled inwardly.

We didn't have the opportunity to speak further because the bus pulled out and our tour guide began speaking. He was a slender young man with a serious face and dark, hipster-framed glasses. His personality belied his looks, however, and he warmly explained our next several days in China's capital city. He seemed younger than our last tour guide, and I mentioned that to Eli after the speech. I needed to talk about any random topic to remind myself that this handsome man beside me was off the market.

"Lee? I suspect he must be at least 21, 22 years old. Tour guides must have a college degree to work for this company," said Eli.

"I see."

He certainly knew a lot about this tour company. Well, I guess if you dated a tour guide, you'd learn these things.

"Ah." We returned to silence.

"Say, Eli, about Singapore ..." I began tentatively.

"You don't have to say anything. I owe you an apology."

"No, no! I owe YOU an apology because I was being bratty!"

"I was tense about some business matters. I'm sorry."

Our eyes met, and we laughed.

"Shall we just agree on a mutual apology?" he asked.

"Of course."

Whew. I was glad to get that out of the way!

Eli pulled his headphones from his bag, and I expected him to tune me out while tuning in to whatever he was listening to. I caught a snippet of the music and was surprised to hear that it wasn't rock, top 40, jazz, or even heavy metal. I caught a bit of a mournful female voice with a definite Asian influence.

"What are you listening to?" I asked, pointing to his ears in case he couldn't hear my question.

He removed his headphones and handed them to me. The music was haunting, and the voice was clear and bell-like. I listened for a moment.

"That's lovely," I said. "Who is it?"

"Her name is Tong Li. She's singing my mother's favorite song, 'Ode to the Red Plum Blossom.'"

How interesting! I didn't know very many young men who would listen to their parents' music unless the parents were in the room.

"What is the song about?" I asked.

"The lyrics are from an old poem. Loosely translated it means that the plum is beautiful and blossoms earliest, but she does not want to have her beauty compete with the spring and the other flowers. What she wants is just to be the herald of the spring. When all of the flowers have blossomed already, she will return among the flowers with a big smile."

I was mesmerized.

"That's beautiful! Did you grow up listening to this?"

He smiled a faraway smile. His face was relaxed, not anything like the tense businessman in Singapore.

"My mother's name is Plum Blossom, Mei Hua. My father found every recording of that song and bought them for her."

"How romantic! Does he like the music as well?"

"He was more of a blues fan, but more often than not, my mother got to pick what was on the stereo."

I thought about my own parents. I could imagine the same thing happening at my house. My father was definitely the head of the house, but he treated my mother like a queen. Very sweet.

"I take it your mother was from China?"

"What makes you sure of that?" he gave me a sidewise glance.

"Well, you speak the language so fluently, and her name … I … I didn't mean anything else." Rats. I hope I hadn't offended him.

"Yes. She was. Oh, don't worry, I'm not offended that you can tell I have Asian blood. Annalise, I can look in a mirror. I know that I don't exactly look like I was born in Sweden." He gave me that beautiful smile that I had first seen in the airport.

I decided to press my luck.

"But your name. Eli Chamberlain doesn't exactly scream out China."

"True. My father is not Chinese. He's of British heritage. And my real name is Yi Lai, which got mispronounced or messed up on those standardized forms, even though I was really careful in writing it."

I nodded. "I always ran out of blocks on the standardized forms at school and ended up being Annalis, with no 'e,' so people thought my name rhymed with *analyst* or something."

"Could have been worse," he observed wisely.

"Oh, trust me, sometimes it was."

"In any case, Yi Lai means 'justice cometh.'"

"That's awesome!" I turned toward him and accidentally brushed my knee against his. Oops. Pull back.

He looked at me quizzically.

"I won't bite, Annalise."

"What? Oh, I know. I just didn't want to take up too much room in the seat." Wow. That sounded mature.

"I don't see how you could. You're tiny."

I shot him a look. Seriously. I hadn't been called "tiny" since first grade.

"So. How did your parents meet?" I hoped I covered my gaffe.

"They met here in Beijing. He was a government attaché, and she was the pretty translator with the shy smile. After his tour of duty was over, he found that he couldn't go home and leave that smile. They married and moved back to San Francisco. He became a university professor, and she started working in a language school."

"Their story is romantic all the way around!" I exclaimed.

"Well. Yes, I guess so." I could tell that there was more to the story.

We rode in silence for a while.

"My father died when I was a boy," he said.

"I'm so sorry. And your mother?" The question was out of my mouth before I had the opportunity to pull the words back in.

His voice became quieter. "I had mom for a while longer. Through college and while I developed my business."

He straightened up, remembering his surroundings.

"I'm sorry, I don't know what's wrong. I generally do not burden people I barely know with this much information."

"It's okay. You don't need to say more. I was being too nosy."

I tried to move further toward my side of the seat.

He replaced his headphones, cleared his throat, and leaned back and closed his eyes.

We rode the rest of the way in an uncomfortable stillness, accompanied only by the chattering in the seats surrounding us and the swirling thoughts in my own head.

The minute we reached the hotel, I dashed from the bus and managed to avoid him as everyone collected their baggage and went through the check-in process at the hotel. We were on our own for breakfast, according to Lee, and with luck I wouldn't have to encounter Eli Chamberlain from now until we boarded the bus tomorrow for the next segment of our tour. I didn't even wait for Auntie Lil while I ducked around our group and scampered to the elevators to find our room.

When she arrived minutes later, she was more than a little curious.

"Well, for someone who is supposed to be my companion, you certainly are falling down on the job," she said as she entered our hotel room and found me banging away at my keyboard.

"What? Sorry, Auntie Lil. I have to upload this information to my blog since I have the hotel WiFi."

I felt her unspoken questions but managed to keep my head down. She began to unpack but made a comment.

"You'll have to finish eventually, dear. And I'm not going anywhere."

She was right, but with any luck I would be a bit calmer before the inquisition began.

"Oh, no. Can you imagine if it were Katherine Flynn sitting with him instead of me? Her brand of investigative questioning could wear anyone down!" I shook my head.

"There you go." Auntie Lil lifted my chin with her finger. "See? It could have been worse."

"You're right."

"Dearest, nothing looks good in the middle of the night. Now, get ready for bed. We have a long day tomorrow!"

She turned and crawled between her own covers, and we chatted about the next day's itinerary as I finished my bedtime preparations. Eventually, we both fell asleep, and before we knew it, morning had arrived!

This hotel had a breakfast buffet that was similar to the one we had in Xi'an, but Auntie Lil and I wanted to explore the neighborhood. So we ventured to a small coffee shop on the next street for our morning meal and strolled around the area before having to meet our group. It seemed that though we were comfortably settled in a four-star hotel, we were in an area that included five- six- and even seven-star accommodations.

"Wow! I can't imagine what the shampoo and soap are like in those rooms!" Auntie Lil commented. "Do you suppose you have your own butler in there?"

"I actually think you do have your own concierge," I said.

"Well, look at our hotel. We have a Lamborghini dealership on the first floor."

"Maybe in the seven-star hotel, you actually GET a Lamborghini when you check in," she giggled.

"What are you two ladies so amused about?" Genio Cusamano greeted us as we made our way through the revolving doors to the lobby to wait with our group for the bus.

"Oh, Auntie Lil and I were selecting our Lamborghinis." I pointed to the dealership across the lobby.

He played along.

"Hmm. I think the red one for you, Lilliana, and the jet-black one for you, Annalise."

"Done and done, Genio," laughed Auntie Lil. "And for you?"

"I'm more of a Ferrari man myself. You should ask your friend Eli Chamberlain for advice on choosing a fast car."

"What?" Why oh why was I jittery at the mention of his name in such a casual way.

"He has a sports car collection. Didn't you know that?" Genio looked puzzled.

"No, I wasn't aware." So the seemingly unassuming nerd had a flashy side. Who knew?

"It was in the article featuring him in *Business Today* magazine. I just thought …" Genio looked from me to Auntie Lil.

"Did you know that the Ferrari and the Fiat are manufactured by the same organization?" Auntie Lil switched subjects only slightly.

"Are you implying that I should tone my tastes down?" Genio caught her tone and dropped the subject of Eli Chamberlain and his taste in cars.

"Not at all," Auntie Lil shook her head. "Just pointing out a bit of trivia."

I left them to their automotive chitchat and pulled out my iPad. Since we were still in the hotel, I thought I could take advantage of WiFi and search for the *Business Today* article that Genio had mentioned, but I was unable to go beyond a certain point on the firewall. My technical guru Breck was able to give me a direct line to post my own blog, but I didn't have the unlimited access I was used to in the U.S. I pondered who I could ask to search for the article who would not bombard me with dozens of questions.

Sighing, I bypassed my normal partner in crime Rory and started typing.

Hey Breck,

Thanks again for all the work on my blog. Just checking to see if you have been following it and how it is showing up.

Say, are you familiar with Eli Chamberlain from Graviton Gaming? By chance have you read an article that may have appeared in Business Today? *Is there a way you can send me a link or a way I can find it on this side of the firewall?*

Hope all goes well. Don't eat too many hot fudge sundaes!

Annalise

I read and reread it. Just the right casual tone I hoped to achieve. I clicked the button to send and prepared to close my iPad. I was sure that he would be able to give me a few nuggets of info.

But just like that, I received a response. Was he sitting around waiting for an email on this topic?

Hey Gypsy Girl,

Your blog looks great. You are doing a fantastic job with it.

You're kidding about whether I am "familiar" with Eli Chamberlain, right?? Who DOESN'T own the Nuon gaming system? The article you are talking about isn't just in BT, it has been reprinted all over the web. I can't attach and copy it, but I've copied and pasted the words for you here. Pictures of Chamberlain that go with it are very James Bond. He is a multibillionaire. Just did a buyout of a rival company that manufactured their systems overseas and brought all manufacturing to US and creating tons of jobs in the Bay Area. Is there a feature on him in the airline magazine or something?

Give my best to Auntie.

B

I responded quickly:

Breck,

Thanks for info. Are you always awake and ready to answer my questions? We ran into Eli C., and I was just curious.

A

He shot back:

A,

You "ran into him"? Eli C. is a very valuable contact to have! If not for you, then for a certain web designer you know—hint hint. And, you know I keep odd hours, so email, call, text anytime.

B

B,

I'll keep that in mind.

Hugs,

A

I glanced around to see if we were ready to go, but since we weren't, I settled in to read the clip of the article he sent me.

Boy Wonder Saves Floundering Tech Company
Graviton Gaming Guru Does It Again

Eli Chamberlain, entrepreneur and technological whiz, is adding another building block to his tech kingdom with the purchase

---

of Crispchip Games, developers of the popular Five Feifdoms gaming system. Chamberlain says he plans to keep the FF system separate from the popular Nuon Gaming system.

"We feel that the FF is a perfect complement to the Nuon and adds an entry-level option for the beginning gamer," said Chamberlain.

Crispchip manufacturing will be moved to the Graviton manufacturing headquarters in the San Francisco area, adding approximately 2,000 design and manufacturing jobs to the area.

"Our goal is always to keep our manufacturing in the U.S.," said Chamberlain.

A native of the Bay Area, Chamberlain attended CalTech and began Graviton Gaming while still in college with the popular downloadable RealRespond game. From that game, Graviton developed others prior to the release of the dedicated Nuon system.

Chamberlain, a visible bachelor on the social scene, was most likely found with his mother on his arm as his escort to social events prior to her recent death from pancreatic cancer. He is a collector of Asian antiques and mid-century muscle cars. He is also a patron of the arts in the San Francisco area, sponsoring the popular SanFranBand (San Francisco Youth Band), which draws from schools around the area.

Wow. What a lot of information. When Jasper told us that Eli developed the Graviton system, I didn't put it together that he was so continental and well-rounded. I wonder if the reason he was so standoffish in Singapore was that he was in the middle of the negotiations for that deal? And having just lost his mother?

No wonder he was listening to her favorite music!

I closed my tablet and replaced it in my backpack. I only wished that I could have seen the photos with that article!

Leaning back in the comfy seat in the lobby, I knew I couldn't mull this information. I had to get myself back into tourist mode for Auntie Lil and the rest of the merry oldsters.

Our bus pulled up outside, and our spry tour guide Lee hopped off, entering the lobby with a wide grin and carrying a cardboard box.

"So, are we all here?" He glanced around to note that more of our group was joining us in various states of readiness, pulling on jackets, tying scarves, and settling bags for the trip.

"Looks like it." A voice that now had the ability to send a shiver down my neck neared me. Eli stood next to me, practically shoulder to shoulder.

"Good, good," said Lee. "I have gifts for you."

He opened the box and started distributing bright-green cotton bucket caps. What on earth?

"Please wear these so that we can keep track of one another on our journey." He plopped one on his own head.

The group laughed as they donned the hats, each person making his or her own fashion statement with a twist of the brim or a tilt of the cap.

"Wait," Eli said, turning me toward him. He had folded the brim of his hat around the sides and back, tilting it jauntily to resemble a fedora.

"You can't just plop your hat on your forehead like that. We won't see your eyes." He took my hat and folded the brim around, replacing it on the crown of my head, sailor fashion. Then he spun me to face the large mirror in the lobby.

Side by side, we looked like a pair from some bizarre musical on a cruise ship. I tilted my head and sported a cheesy grin.

"What? You don't like my fashion sense?" He grinned back and bumped my hips.

"Love it." I bumped back.

"Come on, let's find our seat." He took my arm to lead me to the bus, as naturally as if it were decided all along that we would be sitting together.

If Rory could only see me now!

CHAPTER TWENTY-SEVEN

Lee kept us occupied and amused with historical facts and stories as we wound our way through the city. I was pre-occupied with him and the sights, so I barely had time to talk much to my attractive seatmate. Soon we reached our desti-nation, and we all craned our necks to see the giant Tianan-men Square on one side and the entrance to the most iconic symbol of Beijing, the Forbidden City, on the other.

We unloaded the bus and clustered around Lee as he gave us directions for our day. We would be walking through the series of gates, starting with the Imperial Gate, and proceed-ing to the inner sanctum of the city.

As we entered the large area through the first gate, I was amused to see many groups of tourists in brightly colored caps similar to ours! They were all shades of the rainbow, some including patterns.

"This would be so funny from a sky view, wouldn't it?" Auntie Lil said, her own bright-green cap covering her forehead down low.

"Everyone, move over here to wait for Lee." The efficient Colette Ehlers rounded us up while Lee made final preparations.

"She is very businesslike," said Eli. "Is she always like this?"

"I don't know."

"Isn't she a friend of yours and your aunt's?"

"Not at all. We just met her the other evening. Auntie Lil found out about this trip in one of her magazines and booked us on it."

"Without knowing anyone?" He looked puzzled.

"Is that so odd?"

"It's just very brave."

"Well, what about you? You don't know anyone either. Oh, I forgot. You know Yan Mei." Stupid stupid.

"Of course I know her. And she was supposed to take this portion of the trip as well, but Lee is substituting for her. She had to take care of business back in Xi'an."

My heart sank a bit. *He is only still with us because she would have been with us.*

"I … I … need to speak with Auntie Lil." I moved quickly from him to my aunt, leaving him with what I was sure was a stumped look on his face.

I wasn't sure that I could stay away from him throughout the day, but I managed to do so because it turned out that he was in great demand for his translation skills. I concentrated on the wonders and sights as we moved slowly but surely throughout the 180 acres of splendor that was the collection of palaces in the Forbidden City. Wall after wall, gate after gate led to palace after palace, and each one was dazzling and beautiful.

Not being a student of Chinese history, I had to pay close attention as Lee explained the city's past along with the complex rules for living in the households of each successive emperor. Those households included hundreds of concubines.

"Hmm. You might figure that a man would need hundreds of women to take care of him," sniffed Katherine.

"Oh, Kat!" her sister shook her head.

As we moved closer to the center, we marveled at the different facts we heard, like there were 980 buildings in the entire Forbidden City with almost 10,000 rooms.

"My gosh! Who cleaned them all?" whispered Georgiann.

"Don't worry, Georgie, I'm sure they had staff back then," her husband wisely pointed out.

We moved slowly but surely through each successive gate, viewing each palace and building, taking photos along the way, until finally our little group of green-capped tourists was in the exact center of the city.

"This is beautiful!" Auntie Lil snapped photo after photo of the colorful trees and flowers in the Imperial Garden surrounding the Hall of Imperial Peace. The 12,000-square-foot area served as the most private retreat for the imperial family. "Oh! Annalise, please stand in the center of that tree!"

"It's actually two trees that have grown toward one another, Miss Fontana." Eli stepped toward us, finally shaking off my intricate dance of avoiding him on the walk.

"Really?" Auntie Lil was intrigued.

"Yes. The legend is that they are two lovers that were cursed to be rooted as trees, but even in their curse, they managed to find one another."

"That's lovely!" Auntie Lil smiled. "Annalise, step inside. Oh, and you step inside, too, just to show how large it is." She gestured to Eli.

I shot her a look.

"I'm sure he doesn't need to be in this picture, Auntie Lil."

"No! It's a fabulous idea!" Great. Colette Ehlers was now involved. We would never get out of it.

I stepped reluctantly into the opening between the two gnarled trees, and Eli stepped in beside me.

"No. You step behind her with your arms around her like this." Colette posed us. What was this? A prom picture?

As soon as we were posed—with my heart beating wildly, I might add—several cameras snapped, then others joined in. Others who weren't even from our green-hatted crew.

"Relax," Eli whispered in my ear. "You'll never see these people again. What's the problem?"

Was he kidding me?

I turned slightly, and we were nose to nose, his arms holding me tightly. I wanted to tell him exactly what the problem was, but for a moment, I was lost in the depths of his inky black eyes … and then his cheeky grin turned serious. The moment was broken with a guffaw.

"Hey, you kids, save something for the honeymoon suite!"

I broke out of his embrace and ran, scouting for cover. I found a nearby ladies room.

I knew I could only stay in there for so long, so after washing my hands a number of times, to the curious stare of the elderly attendant, I walked out.

I scanned the area for our crew but didn't see one green cap in sight. Surely they hadn't all left me behind? Had my own aunt abandoned me? I was one instant short of panic when I spied a familiar figure sitting on a bench behind a huge tree, twirling a green cap aimlessly in his hands. I took a deep breath and walked over to join him.

"Where did everyone go?" I asked timidly.

"They're in the outbuilding over there. I told your aunt that I would wait for you and we would meet them." Eli pointed to his left.

"Sorry I took so long."

"No problem."

He sat and I stood in uncomfortable silence.

"Shouldn't we go?" I turned to walk, but he pulled me down beside him on the bench.

"Are you still angry with me about Singapore?" he asked quietly.

I shook my head.

"Have I done something else to make you angry?"

My head shook again.

"Well, what is it then?"

I concentrated on the pebble I was kicking back and forth. How was I going to get out of this? How do you tell someone that you are attracted to him when you know they belong to someone else? Not exactly the conversation you want to start so that you can get the "oh we can be really good friends" speech. I hate that speech. Better to get it over with, though, so that we could get through the rest of this tour. I sat, took a deep breath, closed my eyes, and began.

"It's not that you've made me angry, Eli. It's just that I, um, have developed, um, feelings for you. I know that you probably think I'm silly and that you have women falling for you all the time. So now is your cue to give me that sympathetic look and tell me all about how you're already spoken for by Yan Mei and how you'll be happy to have me as a friend and all."

I stopped babbling, scrunched my eyes closed further as I turned toward him, bracing for the worst.

Nothing happened.

I opened one eye slightly to see that he was … gone?

With both eyes wide open, I swiveled back and forth.

What in the world?

I jumped up and looked around.

"Eli?"

Hey. I just laid my soul bare, and he didn't even have the decency to let me down moderately easily.

He popped from around the tree.

"Are you finished?"

"Am I finished? Am I FINISHED?" Now I WAS angry. "I just poured out my soul to you and you ask me if I am FIN-ISHED? What kind of cruel, mean-spirited—"

I grabbed his hat from his hand and punctuated my words with distinct swats.

"Hey, hey, hey—" He sheltered himself from the blows. "I wasn't trying to be mean. I was trying to avoid you hear me laughing."

"THAT'S WORSE!"

"No. Oh, I can see I'm making a hash of this. Please sit down and let me explain."

I looked him in the eye suspiciously but sat down at the very edge of the bench. I handed him his crumpled hat as he sat beside me.

"Annalise. I wasn't laughing at YOU, I was laughing at MYSELF."

"Not making this any better," I said.

"I was laughing because, well, you think I have women falling for me all the time."

Seriously?

"I've always been a geek, Annalise. The nerdy kid who studied science and computers and played video games. Not exactly the hot stuff that the girls chased."

"But you're a 'visible bachelor on the social scene,'" I clapped my hand over my mouth.

"I see you read the article in *Business Today*." He grinned. "That's my PR crew. They've been trying to change my image from a geeky mama's boy who collects antiques and cars to a man about town."

"But ... look at you!"

He shook his head and twirled his hat. Gosh, he needed his PR crew to work on getting him to believe in what he looked like.

"Sorry to burst your bubble. But, like I said, when you said those things, I couldn't believe you meant me, and I didn't want to hurt your feelings."

"So you left me here alone?" I pursed my lips.

"Well, I thought you had a lot more to say. You were kind of on a roll."

My annoyance began to rise again, then I remembered.

"What about Yan Mei?"

"What about her?"

"Well, you said that women don't chase you. Evidently she did, or you chased her."

He threw back his head and laughed.

"Yan Mei? She's my cousin! You thought she was—" He laughed again.

His cousin?

"But you seem so close!"

"We are. As COUSINS. Aren't you close to your relatives?"

"Well, sure, but she's from here, right? You can't be that close to someone from around the globe."

"She lived with us when she came to do her studies at Berkeley."

Oh.

Oh no. That made it worse. He wasn't going to give me The Speech because he was taken; he was just not interested in me at all. I blew out a sigh and braced myself.

"Annalise?"

There it was. The Serious Voice.

"Annalise. I was hoping you weren't angry, because I needed to tell you something."

"What?" I turned toward him.

"This."

He took my face between his hands and put his lips on mine, gently at first, then more insistent as his hands moved downward to pull me closer by encircling my waist. My arms moved on their own and entwined around his neck.

After a few moments, we broke apart, breathless.

"You sure know how to choose your words," I whispered looking up into those deep eyes framed with such serious eyebrows.

CHAPTER TWENTY-EIGHT

"I thought it was important that I got the phrasing just right." He brushed my bangs from my forehead and placed delicate kisses there as well.

"Do you know how lovely you are?" he whispered, holding me tightly.

My head was reeling. I didn't have a response. I closed my eyes and reached up for another delicious kiss and felt as if I could have stayed that way, entranced, forever, when the peaceful silence was brought to an end by the equivalent of a needle scratching across a record.

"Now I know they can't be too far from here."

Katherine Flynn.

Eli and I sprang apart. All we needed was for her sharp, feline eyes to spy us in an embrace.

"Kat, don't you think they're okay?" came the whispery voice of her sister, Vivienne.

"Nonsense, Vivienne. We're in a foreign country. Anything can happen."

"Her aunt doesn't seem worried," Vivienne mourned.

"Well, she's distracted by that Genio fellow. Probably doesn't know what day it is."

Hey! No one talks about my aunt like that. I sprung up, but Eli pulled me back down on the bench. Not a moment too soon because around the giant bush came Katherine.

"Here they are! Don't you two know you are delaying the tour?" She eyed us suspiciously.

"Goodness, what is the time? Totally my fault, ladies. You see, Annalise and I thought we spotted a red-billed blue magpie in this tree, and we were sitting quietly hoping to hear it sing. You are familiar with the magpies in Beijing, aren't you?"

Quick on his feet. Charming. A man of many facets was this Eli Chamberlain.

He stood and gallantly took one sister by each arm and led them toward the rest of the group. I shook my head and followed. The advantage of a life of introversion and study probably gave Eli a wealth of information. I was willing to bet that he didn't make up that bird at all.

After we reached the group, they all became curious about our avian pursuits.

"I didn't know you were so interested in bird-watching," Auntie Lil said with a wry smile.

"Just recently took up the hobby." I avoided her eye.

"Well, you should look up the Disheveled Canoodler. I'm sure the rest of the group would find that an interesting sight."

"What?" I glanced down and saw that I needed to adjust my jacket and sweater. I stuck my tongue out at her and turned to fix my appearance. As I did, I caught Eli's eye. He gave me a naughty wink, and I had to turn again before my face became red. This time I was face-to-face with Father John.

I just couldn't win.

Fortunately, Lee saved me from any line of inquisition.

"We will walk out of the Forbidden City through the back gate and travel to one of Beijing's *hutongs* for a special treat."

Eli was held captive by the Flynn sisters, who apparently were knowledgeable bird-watchers, so I walked along with my aunt and Genio.

"So, Annalise," Auntie Lil began in a tone that implied that questions were to follow.

"Stop it right there, Lilliana. I do not care to engage in whatever you are about to discuss."

"She's right, Lil." Thanks, Genio.

He continued, "She might want to practice her … bird-watching … a bit more before she's ready to discuss it." His snowy eyebrows raised and lowered as he grinned in mischief.

"Et tu, Genio?"

"Oh come on, Annalise. We're just teasing." Auntie Lil put her arm around my shoulders.

"You both think you're clever, do you? Well, how clever would you be if I dropped a note to Pop about your own little … situation?" I pulled my phone from my bag.

"Are you threatening to tell on me?" Auntie Lil laughed. "I think I can hold my own with my baby brother, dear."

"Ha! You're safe now, but picture him showing up at the airport after a few days of stewing on information that I could drop."

"I'd buy a new video camera just to shoot the excitement," Auntie Lil grinned.

I rolled my eyes.

We reached the corner of the hutong we were to visit. Originally, a hutong was an alley that joined courtyards near water wells; eventually, these alleys all joined together in a neighborhood that was also called a hutong.

As we reached the corner, we noted a string of pedicabs.

"Ladies and gentleman, these are your drivers who will drive you on a guided tour. At the end of the tour, you will have lunch with a family in the hutong. This is your surprise for today," said Lee.

Exclamations and chatter filled the air as we each claimed a driver and cab.

"Can you handle driving me around?" Bear asked as he helped his wife into a cab, then hefted his bulk into it.

"Many years of driving gives strong legs," smiled the driver as he slapped his thigh.

"Will the three of us fit?" I looked dubiously at a cab and at Auntie Lil and Genio.

"Not to worry, Miss. You go with young mister," said one driver as he coaxed Eli and me into his cab.

Eli grinned and said something to the driver in Mandarin. The driver responded with a thumbs-up.

"What did you just say?" I asked.

"Nothing. I just asked him to give us a smooth ride." His not-so-innocent eyes were not convincing.

I had a feeling that not understanding the language was putting me at a serious disadvantage.

As soon as we were all settled, we headed off in a long line. Eli secretly grabbed my hand and smiled as our driver began pointing out the sights on either side of the tiny alleyways we were driving through.

Eventually, we arrived in the center of the hutong, and the lead driver encouraged us all out of our cabs. He quickly assigned us to one of several small homes. Eli and I were crowded together around a table with Auntie Lil, Genio, the Perinis, and the Willems. The host, who told us to call him Mr. Yeo, greeted us in English, but asked Eli a question in Mandarin when he noticed his non-Caucasian features. They chattered for a moment, then Eli translated.

"They are serving traditional dishes, but not very spicy. He asked if I would like anything spicy, and I said I would see if you would as well."

We all immediately agreed, and Mr. Yeo clapped his hands and smiled.

"I am so happy! Many of our English-speaking guests are afraid of spice. We will make this very special for you!"

He bustled off, and we could hear a rush of Mandarin as cooking noises and smells began to emanate from the kitchen.

"I'm surprised," I said to Eli.

"Why?"

"Well, in Singapore, you didn't have the spicy chili crab."

"No, I didn't order the spicy chili crab. If you recall, though, I had it. I had it all over my shirt." He grinned.

"I meant, you didn't choose it. I thought you didn't like spicy."

"I'm just not fond of crab. I love all kinds of spicy things— food, people ..." Our eyes met, and I turned away. For a self-professed geek, he sure was a smooth talker.

Our host and his wife soon placed steaming, family-style plates of tempting entrees in the center of our table and small bowls of rice in front of each of us.

"Chopsticks?" he asked hopefully.

We all nodded. He explained the correct method of moving the rice from the bowl directly into our mouths and then described the entrees.

"Beef in chili oil, very spicy for young mister. Chicken with vegetables. *Jiaozi*—dumplings. Cabbage."

"We needn't have worried about authentic," Auntie Lil commented.

"Not today!" I agreed, slurping up a long slice of cabbage.

Conversation around the table centered on how delicious the food was. Many cups of delicious green tea accompanied our meal. Throughout, our hosts stood with smiling faces. A tiny elderly woman stepped out from the kitchen, wiping her hands on the towel wrapped around her waist.

I turned to her to give her a compliment, but the shake of her head let me know that she did not understand English. She turned to our host, who translated my comment and translated her whispered response.

"My mother is grateful that you enjoy your meal. She asks, do you cook for your young husband there?" He pointed to Eli.

"Oh, I don't … we're not married," I fumbled.

Mr. Yeo translated, and his mother smiled and made a comment.

"Mother apologizes but says you two look very well-matched."

I didn't know what to say, but Eli jumped in. A rush of Mandarin ensued, and the mother paused and smiled and placed her wrinkled hand on his cheek. She turned to me and gave me the same wordless gesture. With a bow, she exited the area and returned with a small, battered red tin. She urged it on me.

"What is this?" I was confused.

"That is Plum Blossom Tea, the traditional tea of five virtues," explained her son.

"Longevity, wealth, health, virtue, and the desire to die a natural death in old age," whispered Eli, his eyes glistening, and I remembered that his mother was named for the Plum Blossom.

"My mother is very wise, young miss. She says that this tea will be special to you."

All eyes were upon me. Not wanting to cause a scene, I opened the tin and took a deep breath. I encountered a fruity-floral scent, with a strong whiff of jasmine.

"Tell your mother I thank her very much."

She took my hands into her gnarled ones, bowed, and exited the room.

"How delightful!" exclaimed Georgiann. "What a nice souvenir."

I turned the tin over and over. Somehow I knew this was more than just a trinket that I was just given. I looked at Eli, but he just shook his head and smiled, speechless.

"I think that is very special, Annalise," Auntie Lil said, patting my hand. "What a charming story to add to your blog."

My blog. I had a lot to add to it today, but the most exciting thing that happened to me was something I certainly was not going to put out there for the whole world. I looked over at Eli and resisted the impulse to trace my finger on those delicious lips that were so recently planted on mine!

CHAPTER TWENTY-NINE

Our meal concluded simply with slices of fruit. Mr. Yeo and his wife escorted us out to our waiting pedicabs and, along with the remainder of our group leaving their host families, we prepared to depart the tiny neighborhood. There were many good-byes and photos.

I leaned back in our pedicab and propped my green hat forward on my head.

"I am ready for a nap!" I said to Eli.

"Would you rather walk off some of the meal?" he asked. I wondered if he was commenting on my less-than-model-perfect figure. I sat up, suddenly self-conscious.

He patted my ample thigh. Great. The widest part of a pear-shaped gal.

"I think Lee would be upset if we changed plans, don't you?" My tone was probably a bit sharper than I intended.

"Oh, I'm sure he'd cut us some slack," he grinned, missing the tone. "But I have to admit, I like being cozy in here, don't you?"

Cozy? Or wedged in? I tried to make myself as small as possible.

"Annalise, what is up with you?" he asked.

"Nothing. I'm just wondering what's up with you. Is your sense of perception off or something?"

"What?"

"Has it escaped you that I'm not exactly the thinnest girl on the planet?"

"Is that what's bothering you?"

"Well. Yes."

He grabbed my shoulders.

"You amaze me. You are so gorgeous, and you don't even know it. The first thing I noticed about you was your curves! You look like a real woman, Annalise. Don't you get that?"

I couldn't look him in the eye, and turned away. He took my chin and turned me toward him.

"No, don't turn those exquisite eyes away."

He kissed me and held me tightly.

"Do you know how difficult it was to not do that when we were standing in that tree in the Forbidden City? Or to do this?"

He ran his hands down my sides, and my body shivered. For a few moments, nothing existed but the interior of that pedicab.

Wait! We were in that pedicab! Anyone could see us. I broke away from him.

"Eli! The entire group can see us!"

He grinned and attempted to pull me back.

"I doubt it. I asked our driver to make sure we were the first cab in line on the way back. Our colleagues are behind us. If I'm not mistaken, pretty FAR behind us."

I peeked around the side of the cab. He was right. We were alone. When I was certain of that, I settled my back against his chest with a tentative amount of confidence.

"Eli?" I asked with his arms around me and his fingers entwined in mine.

"Mm," he kissed my temple, attempting to get back to where we were.

Though our tour group was not near us, I was not confident enough to resume where we left off.

"Eli ..."

"Yes," he continued, maddeningly moving his hands.

I could see that unless I took control, this situation was going to escalate.

"Hey!" I pushed him away, gently.

He got the message, straightened up, and sat with his hands folded in his lap and an innocent look on his face.

"You are impossible!"

"But irresistible, right?"

He smiled that gorgeous smile of his that had the infuriating way of stretching all the way up to his eyes. Darn it, yes, irresistible. Handsome, funny, and he always smelled so nice!

I leaned back and took his hand in mine.

"Eli, answer me this. How on earth did jet-setter you end up tagging along on this senior citizen bus tour?"

"Well, I could ask you the same thing, couldn't I?" He kissed my fingertips.

"That's not fair. You know that I'm here with my aunt. You're here by yourself. Who does that?"

His demeanor changed as a shadow passed over his face. Flirty Eli disappeared. After a few moments, he started speaking quietly.

"I told you that my father married when he was stationed here and brought his Chinese bride home, right?"

I nodded.

"Well, because my mother left, she renounced her rights and ability to return home. She knew what she was doing, but it always weighed heavily on her heart."

I sensed that he needed to complete the story without my interruption, so I remained quiet, my hand in his.

"After my father died, she wanted to return even more. Most of her family had died, but she still wanted to visit. I was just a boy, but I promised her that someday I would bring her here. I didn't know the implications of world politics at the time.

"Eventually, when I started my company, life became too busy. She kept up with news from China. When she learned more about the discovery of the terra-cotta soldiers, she dreamed of seeing them. Then, a distant cousin asked if his daughter, Yan Mei, could come visit. My mother welcomed her with open arms—anything to keep contact with her home country.

"She saw that China's borders were starting to open up, allowing for more people to visit. Even though it became possible for her to travel here, she became too ill to travel alone. I promised her that as soon as business slowed down we'd come together. She kept notes on everything she wanted to see."

His face clouded over as he reached in his pocket and pulled out the small, battered notebook I had seen him studying intently on the bus.

"I booked this trip on this tour line so that she would travel with Yan Mei, but she never wanted to come without me, and we kept canceling because business never slowed down. Eventually she was fighting cancer. I got her the best doctors I could afford, but … she lost the fight very quickly. On her deathbed, she made me promise to take the trip she couldn't take."

He clutched the notebook and put it back in his pocket.

"So, sure, I could go wherever and whenever I want. But this is the exact trip she wanted, so I felt I had to honor her, you know? Does it seem silly?"

He looked up at me. His eyebrows formed a deep V.

"I totally get it, Eli. Family is family."

"I just regret that she didn't get to come with me."

I sighed.

"But she is with you, don't you think?"

"That's a nice sentiment, Annalise, but you know as well as I do that I should have made the time to do it." He shook his head and slumped backward.

There wasn't anything to say. He needed to process his feelings.

"And the worst part … is you." He pulled his bright-green hat from his head and crumpled it between his fingers.

My heart fell.

"No, I don't mean that the way it sounded," he looked up suddenly and put his hand gently on my cheek. I saw you in Denver at the airport and thought I would never meet you again."

My heart jumped. He remembered! And more than that, I wasn't the only one that felt that "zing!" back in Denver.

He continued, "Then, we were random tablemates at a dinner in Singapore of all places. I missed my opportunity to talk with you because I was concentrating on a presentation I had to give the next day. After the crab incident, I felt silly for my reaction.

"Imagine my delight and surprise to find you on this trip. But imagine how hard it was to try and erase my earlier behavior. Yan Mei spent all of lunch at the terra-cotta warrior factory trying to help me build up my nerve."

I smiled inwardly. And here I'd thought they'd been engrossed in a lovers' discussion!

"Now, here we are. I'm on the trip that I wanted for my mother and I'm not thinking about her. I'm thinking about you. When I'm with you, I'm happy. I don't have the right to be happy."

How twisted is that logic? I wondered if this guy was actually Italian—his guilt was pitch-perfect.

"Eli, don't you think your mother would want you to be happy? I think she wanted you to take this trip because it would make YOU happy. I mean, take me out of the equation if you need to." I looked at his face and thought, Great, I bet he will take me out of the equation.

We rode in silence and reached the meeting point at the bus. We were the first cab there, and we alighted solemnly. Our driver looked from one to the other of us with a worried look on his face. Even though I didn't understand the language, I could tell that Eli was assuring him that the ride and tour were delightful as he gave him a handsome tip. We stood awkwardly waiting for the others, when a sleek black car pulled up beside us, and a tall man leapt out.

"Mr. Chamberlain, the office has been trying to reach you," he said.

Eli pulled his phone from his pocket.

"I had my phone off while I was eating. What was so important, Roger?"

The imposing man pulled him aside and whispered to him.

Eli punched numbers into his phone. Fun, relaxed Eli melted away, and I saw a glimmer of the man from Singapore.

"Daniel, it's me. Get Stephens now!" He strode over to me while he waited, shook his head from side to side grimly, and locked eyes. I backed away.

"Annalise … it's …" He grabbed my hand as he spoke, but apparently Stephens came on the line. "Stephens … talk to me."

And in a moment, he dropped my hand, was in the car, and whooshed down the road.

Dumbstruck, I looked around. The other pedicabs were rolling in, filled with laughing, green-hatted group members.

"Annalise, darling, wasn't that divine!" Georgiann Perini made a beeline toward me. "Where's that delightful Eli? Now don't tell me there isn't a bit of a spark there?"

Her knowing wink was almost too much to bear. I looked around for my aunt.

"More bird-watching?" Auntie Lil began teasing when I approached, then saw my face and stopped. "Annalise, dear, what's wrong?"

"Nothing, Auntie, nothing." I breathed heavily.

She knew better.

"Genio," my auntie said, "Annalise and I are going to get on the bus a bit early."

We climbed aboard and moved to the seat that had been mine and Eli's.

"Tell me what's going on, dear,"

I leaned my head on her shoulder and filled her in on the delicious high and devastating low of my trek across town. I finished with a long sigh.

Auntie Lil put her arm around me and squeezed me tight.

"Why do I have such bad luck, Auntie Lil?"

"I know everything seems bleak, sweetheart, but it's not."

We sat in silence for a moment, listening to the chattering voices outside the bus as our group took last-minute photos with the pedicab drivers. Finally, Auntie Lil lifted my chin toward her and looked me in the eye.

"Annalise, I know you are hurting, but you have a decision to make, don't you?"

I nodded numbly. There was no time for me to wallow in pity and bring the tone of this trip down. I needed to pull myself up and put my game face on.

Smoothing back my hair, I placed my green cap back on my head. The cap that had so recently seemed jaunty and bright now just felt garish and heavy. I rearranged myself and looked to Auntie Lil, who nodded to assure me that I was presentable. Just in time, too, because boisterous Bear Willems and his wife had boarded the bus and were laughing their way down the aisle.

"Nee high, ladies," he said. "Isn't my Chinese improving?"

"Bear, if you are trying to say 'hello,' it's *ni hao*. I think you should leave the speaking to me and keep us out of trouble." Frida shook her head and pushed him toward their seat.

"Earlier he tried to say 'thank you' and said something that translated to 'eat a lion.'"

Others boarded, raising the energy level.

"Lilliana! Yoo-hoo! Are you coming up here?" Georgiann motioned toward Auntie Lil while kneeling backward on her seat like a preteen on a cheerleading trip.

"I'm staying with Annalise for the trip to the hotel," Auntie Lil smiled.

"But isn't her friend—" Georgiann began, before Tom pulled her down to sit. She turned in the aisle to give a curious look.

"But, Tom—"

"For once, just sit without questions, Georgie!" we heard an exasperated Tom whisper loudly.

"Great." I shook my head.

"Keep your head up, Annalise." Auntie Lil patted my knee.

The Flynn sisters slowed down as they passed us wordlessly.

"Ladies," Auntie Lil nodded. "So nice to see you survived the cab ride. Did you mean to leave your top button undone, Katherine?"

I turned to the window and suppressed a giggle. Leave it to Auntie Lil to quash any comment before it began.

"Can I be of any assistance?" I turned to see Genio crouching in the aisle beside us. His kind face was a pleasant sight, and seeing Auntie Lil's eyes sparkle with him nearby brought a tug to my heart.

"No, Gen, we're just taking a little girl time between here and the hotel."

He looked from one to the other of us and nodded, understanding. He stood and said, "Father John and I will share the front seat, then. I'll check in with you before we leave for dinner?"

"Of course." Auntie Lil brushed his hand before he made his way back to the front.

"He really likes you," I said, forgetting my own emotional roller coaster for just a moment.

"Nonsense, we're just having a nice visit," she said, but her cheeks colored slightly.

Hmm. If that's her definition of a "nice visit," I'd hate to see how she defined "madly in love"!

CHAPTER THIRTY

"It's dinnertime, dear, are you ready?" Auntie Lil called to me from the bathroom of our hotel room as she finished fluffing her hair and touching up her makeup.

The remainder of our journey back from the hutong had included a visit to a jade emporium where much bargain shopping was done. After we returned to the hotel, everyone had some downtime before meeting for dinner.

Seated on my bed in my cozy pajamas, I continued typing on my iPad and shook my head wordlessly.

"Don't tell me you aren't going to eat!" She came out and sat next to me.

I leaned back against the headboard of my bed and sighed.

"Auntie Lil, I don't feel much like venturing very far this evening. Besides, you know I have to finish this blog entry."

"You're nearly done. And you need to eat."

"I just don't feel very social, that's all."

"You don't need to be social, you just need to come and eat. Besides, you are my companion, remember? You'd be falling down on the job." She poked my shoulder.

"Oh, really? I think we both know that someone else has taken my job as your companion."

She smiled a girlish smile.

"Let's get serious for a minute, Auntie. I know you say that you and Genio are just having a 'pleasant visit,' but anyone around you can see that it is more than that. What's going to happen at the end of this trip?"

It was her turn to sigh and lean back.

"I don't know, Annalise. Does anything have to happen?"

"Well, no, I guess not. But shouldn't it? Don't you want it to?" I was confused.

"Can't this be just a pleasant vacation interlude? A … fling?"

I burst out laughing.

"I don't think this qualifies as a 'fling,' Auntie Lil. If so, it's the most chaste fling on record."

"Don't be impertinent." She shook her head. "Why do you young people have to equate romance with the bedroom?"

"Why? Have you found other places to … you know …?" I waggled my eyebrows at her and was greeted with a smack of a pillow.

"Annalise. I refuse to continue this conversation with you if you drag it down that path."

"I know, I know. I just wanted to wind you up a little," I grinned.

"Your generation thinks it invented sex," she sniffed.

"Obviously not, or there wouldn't BE anyone in my generation." I was greeted with another smack with the pillow.

"Truce! Truce!" I cried.

She put the pillow on her lap and crossed her hands on it thoughtfully.

"Annalise, can I tell you something?"

"Of course."

"At first, I was attracted to Genio because he looked so much like Antonio."

"Big shock!" I looked over and saw that she was getting very serious. Uh-oh.

"Spending just this short amount of time with him, though, I can see that he is so different. Not that Antonio wasn't fabulous, but Genio is so sophisticated and witty and—"

She stopped and sighed.

I took a chance.

"Auntie Lil, do you feel like you're, oh I don't know, cheating on Antonio somehow?" It sounded odd even as I said it.

She stared straight ahead for a moment. "I couldn't put it in words, but that is a good way of describing it."

"But Auntie Lil! You can't be cheating on someone who has been dead for all those years! Especially since you weren't even married to begin with!"

She just shook her head and raised her hands, palms up.

"All these years and you never got serious with anyone. Was that the reason?"

"I don't know, Annalise. Maybe."

Geesh! Talk about loyalty. My aunt would win an Olympic medal in it, if it were an event.

"So, why now? Why Genio?"

She shrugged and grunted. My aunt, the queen of etiquette shrugging like a teenager.

My head spun, because when I was in situations like this, I usually got advice from … her. I reached into my brain for all the words of wisdom I had garnered from her and attempted to be wise beyond my own years.

"Maybe it's all for the best."

What? I knew that didn't make sense as it came out of my mouth. Too late.

"What's all for the best?" She looked at me quizzically.

"This. Genio. You."

"What?"

"Look, Auntie Lil, I don't think that you're the same person you would have been if Antonio would have survived and you two would have married. You probably—likely—would have had a blissfully happy life together. But because your life turned out the way it did, you are who you are. That's why you are in this exact place at this exact time. So I think you were meant to meet Genio in this exact moment. And, as far as these things go, I think that Antonio would be happy that you are happy."

Wow. Where did all that come from?

She stared at me for a moment, and I crossed my fingers inwardly.

"Oddly, Annalise, that makes sense."

Whew.

"I never thought about it much before, but hearing it out loud, awkward as it was, gave me something to think about."

"You're welcome?" Did I help or not?

"I was just a girl when I fell in love with Antonio. The life we built would have been the life we expected at that time. I can't compare what's happening now based on the thoughts and experiences of a seventeen-year-old."

Hey! I did help.

"So that's why this … thing … with Genio must just be an infatuation." She leapt from the bed.

No, no, no.

"Auntie, are you sure you heard what I said?"

"Quite sure, dear." She sounded more like herself. And with that, she gathered her things together.

"Come along, Annalise. We need to meet the others."

I banged my head softly on the headboard. At that moment, I heard the telltale beeps of Skype from my iPad. It was Rory.

"I have a call coming in, Auntie Lil. I'll just get room service and see you later?"

"Are you sure? We're walking down to the little tearoom down the street—you know, the one with the giant teapot out front that looks like it is constantly pouring tea into a big cup? We'll be there for a while. Finish your visit with Rory and come." Her eyes were pleading.

"I don't think so." I needed time alone.

Auntie Lil kissed my cheek as I connected my call.

"There you are!" Rory's impatient face appeared.

"My fault, Rory," Auntie Lil smiled into the screen. "I was saying good-bye and encouraging Annalise to come to dinner after your call."

"Oh … go!" Rory said.

"NOO!" I insisted. "You, stay on the line. And you, go join your dinner partners."

Auntie Lil blew us both kisses, and as soon as the door to the hotel room clicked shut, I grabbed my head in my hands and said, "Arrgh!"

"Bad day at the office?" Rory teased.

"You just don't know." I rearranged myself on the bed, laying stomach-down with my head propped in my hands.

"Spill it!" she encouraged.

"It's Auntie Lil."

"She's not sick, is she?" Rory's voice raised in concern.

"No, no. But remember the crush I told you about?"

"Tall, distinguished, yes. What's up? They didn't get married, did they?"

I rolled my eyes.

"What? It could happen, Annalise. They're not getting any younger."

"And they're not getting any less traditional, either, you clod. I know that she's a little old for the big white meringue dress and veil, but she'd still want a church wedding with the family."

"You have a priest with you. It could happen." Leave it to Rory to push a point.

"Finished?"

"Yes." She batted her eyes prettily.

"Okay." I blew out a breath and recounted my talk with Auntie Lil.

"She actually asked you for advice?"

"THAT'S what you took away from the story?"

"Yes." She swiveled in her desk chair.

"Are you KIDDING ME?" I sat straight up.

"Well, yes." She stopped swiveling. "Oh, relax, I didn't mean to insult you."

"What would you have said if you wanted to insult me?"

"Calm down. Sheesh. What I meant was that she must be really churning inside if she came to you—to anyone. Don't you get it? Your aunt is the most solid person we know, right? Always in control? For her to get rattled enough to open up so much, she must really have feelings."

"Right, right, right."

"And the fact that she took such pains to brush it off is the exact opposite of how she feels."

"I already figured that out."

"Yes. But do you know how HE feels?"

"Oh."

"She is just hiding her feelings so that she doesn't get hurt again. If we knew how he felt, then maybe—"

"He could let her know, and she could either open up more or confirm her feelings to call this off." I nodded.

"Exactly."

"Rory. I think you're on to something."

"That means you need to talk to him."

"What! I barely know him."

"Well, how else are we going to know?"

"You realize you're asking me to pull my father's 'Just what are your intentions?' routine with a man old enough to be my grandfather—and a decorated war hero at that."

"Well, you should have it down pat, having heard your father and brother do it often enough."

She had a point. It's a wonder that any of my potential boyfriends ever came back for another date after one round of 'If you hurt Annalise, I have a shotgun and a shovel and no one will miss you, boy' at my house.

"What are you thinking, Annalise?"

"I'm wondering how I can casually pull this off."

"I have confidence in you."

"That makes one of us."

"You'll be great. I have another question for you. How are things with you and your own tall, dark, and mysterious stranger?"

"Conversation over, Rory." I had a sudden stab in my heart.

"Oh no! You don't get off that easily. I notice that he has appeared more frequently in pictures in your blog."

"What? No. Everyone is in the pictures." Really? Was I that obvious?

"You forget I've known you for a long time, sister."

I remained silent.

"I can wait." She tapped her fingers on her desk. Finally, I broke.

"There WAS something there."

"Aha! I knew it. Wait … what do you mean 'was'?"

Why couldn't I just have broken the connection after telling Auntie Lil's story? What a pair the Fontana girls made!

I told Rory about the day and the beautiful things that Eli had said to me and how it was capped off by his unceremonious departure. It hurt worse because she wasn't there in person.

"Wait …" She opened another window on her computer and started tapping on the keyboard. "Let me see if there's any news on Graviton Gaming." Her eyes scanned. After a few moments, she shook her head.

"Nothing in the news, Annalise."

"Maybe your intrepid sources haven't caught up yet." But I knew someone who might have better sources. No. I wasn't going to bother Breck about this. I already dragged him into my silly romantic escapades once in the last 24 hours.

"There is this recent article in *Business Today*, Annalise. Should I send it to you?"

"I've seen it."

"What? I thought you were behind a firewall."

"My new friend Breck sent a copy of the text."

"Hmm. This is a good story." Trust Rory to go into editor mode. "Wow! Your Eli is hot!"

"He's not 'my' anything, Rory."

"Whatever. Gorgeous in a suit and in casual clothes. And this one picture, shirtless in board shorts on the beach."

"What!"

"Ha! There isn't a beach photo, but I bet he looks really good on the beach."

"I never thought about it." My face turned crimson.

Rory stopped teasing.

"Look, Annalise. A person just doesn't express feelings like he did and then forget about that person. Don't overthink him having to leave."

"I wish I had your optimism. I think I just have to do my best to stay upbeat for the rest of this trip and remember my job."

"You know that your 'job' as Auntie Lil's companion was just a courtesy."

"I know, but I also know that I wasn't supposed to come here boyfriend-hunting."

"Hmm."

"Don't 'hmm' me, Rory. Look, I need to go catch Auntie Lil and Genio if I'm going to do Operation Shovel and Shotgun tonight." I jumped up from the bed.

"Loving the name," Rory laughed. "Report back to me! And listen. Take care of YOURSELF!"

"If you insist."

We blew each other a kiss and cut off the conversation. I posted my blog, then raced around getting dressed so I could scoot down the street and ambush my aunt and her unsuspecting beau.

CHAPTER THIRTY-ONE

I made a mad dash to the charming little tearoom three blocks from our hotel. I entered it and scanned the room, immediately finding the small group of tourists who were my temporary family. I politely allowed the hostess to guide me to the table.

"Annalise! I'm so glad you decided to join us!" Auntie Lil jumped up to give me a hug. The others scooted around to make room for me, and the hostess brought me a table setting.

"If I'm too late, I'll just have some soup." I caught my breath.

"Nonsense! We've ordered plenty, and it hasn't arrived," Genio smiled at me from beside my aunt. I was comfortably settled at the cozy table that also included Father John, the Perinis, and the Flynn sisters.

"Where are the others?" I looked around.

"Scattered around the neighborhood. I think that our group is well represented at quite a few restaurants in the area," said Father John.

"I believe a couple of people even went to McDonald's." Katherine Flynn's tone clearly indicated that she disapproved.

"Oh Kat, sometimes people just want a taste of home," Vivienne said, smiling at the rest of us to apologize for her sister's judgmental tone.

"Actually, I understand they serve different cuisine at the Golden Arches here," said Genio.

"Really?" asked his sister.

"Oh yes."

I caught the twinkle in his eye and knew that a tall tale was coming.

"The Big Mac isn't made of beef. It's called the Big Mock and is made of octopus. And the fries are tofu."

"You're kidding!" Vivienne's eyes widened.

"I think I read that the chicken nuggets are made from chicken feet," Auntie Lil said, jumping in on the story.

"Well, all the more reason not to go there!" Katherine nodded her head vigorously.

"Genio, stop pulling these ladies' legs," Georgiann Perini said, catching on to her brother's antics. "Goodness, Lil, you are just like him! You are both terrible!"

I could hold my laughter no longer. But as I looked from Genio to Auntie Lil, I saw something more than shared high jinks. Oh, Auntie, your words earlier in the hotel room couldn't hide how much you've fallen for this man so soon!

The delicious meal arrived, and our waitstaff placed bowl after bowl on the huge lazy Susan in the center of the table. Conversation switched from the day's activities, including the many jade bargains, to the anticipation of walking on the Great Wall the next day.

"Are you ready for the wall?" Father John asked from beside me.

"I'm so excited," I replied. "I have wanted to see the Great Wall ever since I was a little girl and read about it in history books."

"I hope the weather and the air quality hold out," he said.

"We haven't had one sunny day, have we?" I mused.

"Think about the fact that the people here rarely have a sunny day!"

I thought about living in Denver where it was persistently sunny. These few days in China, where industrial pollution shielded the sun, made me a bit homesick. I had taken more than a few photos of people going about their daily lives wearing surgical masks to keep poor air out of their lungs.

"My mother packed masks for Auntie Lil and me, and I didn't really take her seriously," I confided to Father John.

"Well, we seldom see the wisdom of our parents until later, don't we?" he smiled.

I smiled back. It was my father who convinced me that this trip would do me good and help clear my head from my job and romance woes. I hoped that his wisdom would kick in soon. I was sure it would.

"Annalise, where is your friend Eli?" Leave it to Katherine Flynn to stick a pin in my feelings of goodwill.

"Mr. Chamberlain is friends with all of us, you know. And I believe he had to attend to business back home," I said.

"Hmm. You seemed pretty chummy to me. I noticed—" Katherine began.

"Annalise," cut in Genio, "I'm stepping out to take a photo of that amusing giant teapot. You are the best photographer here. Would you come and help me?"

He rose from his chair and stood behind mine to assist me.

"Gen! We were waiting for the special dessert of the house!" his sister insisted.

"We'll be back in a minute, Georgie. Just make sure to save us some," Genio said, leading me out by the elbow.

Outside, I poked him on the shoulder.

"Your story would have held up better if one of us had brought out a camera, Genio."

"Well, I think we will be fine. There is a three-tiered tray of desserts arriving at the table as we speak, and all conversation will surround that, don't you think?"

I moved to a small table in the restaurant garden and sat down in a chair. Genio joined me.

"Katherine Flynn is … inquisitive, don't you think?" I said.

"To put it mildly."

We sat in silence for a few moments watching the traffic. Quite a few bicycles passed with an interesting blanket contraption that covered the handlebars and the riders' laps. Riders slipped their hands through the "glove" area on the handlebars to keep them warm during their ride.

"That's a neat idea," I commented on the bike handwarmers.

"When the primary mode of transportation is a bicycle, someone was bound to discover a way to stay warm on cold days."

I nodded.

A few moments passed while I tried to come up with a way to bring up my concerns about him and Auntie Lil. Without realizing it, Katherine had given me the perfect opportunity, and I didn't want to waste it.

"Annalise." "Genio."

We laughed as we both spoke at the same time.

"Ladies first," he said, dipping his head in a nod.

"I know this may seem odd, but I need to ask you what your intentions are with my aunt." Well. How much more awkward could that have been?

"My intentions?" He looked at me wide-eyed.

"Yes. I'm the only family she has with her right now, and it's my responsibility to protect her." Oh, great.

"Am I to understand that you are giving me the 'potential suitor' talk?" His lips curled into the barest hint of a smile.

"You are making fun of me!"

"No. But I have to admit it's refreshing to hear that 'intentions' question at my age."

My eyes narrowed into slits.

"It may seem funny to you, but Auntie Lil is very special to me, to my whole family. I won't stand by and have her affections toyed with."

"Annalise!" My aunt's voice came from behind me. I swiveled around.

"Auntie Lil," I gulped.

"Child, what are you doing?" She strode over.

"Apparently your delightful niece has mistaken me for some sort of playboy," Genio grinned.

"I didn't say that!" I turned back to him. "All I wanted to know was whether you considered this time together somewhat serious or just a vacation fling. I don't want my aunt to get hurt."

"Annalise, where did you get the idea that this was your business or your responsibility?" Auntie Lil shook her head.

I looked at the situation from outside and realized how ridiculous it must sound to her. Darn that Rory for putting ideas in my head!

"She was just being caring, Lil. I think it's sweet," Genio said.

Great, one was angry and the other condescending?

"Look, after our discussion earlier, I just wanted to make sure you weren't making the wrong decision based on incomplete information, Auntie Lil. You know … what we talked about …" I didn't want to say anything about Antonio because that was her story to share.

"What incomplete information?" Genio asked.

I looked from one to the other. If I said anything more, was I really going to muck this up? I had to take the chance.

"If you are just passing time with her, then she's not going to take a chance …" I couldn't complete the sentence.

Genio took her hands in his.

"Lilliana, if you think I'm 'just passing time,' then you are mistaken. Can't you tell? I've never met anyone like you, and the thought of letting you go after this trip … well, I don't think that I can bear it."

My aunt looked up into his eyes. "I … I … was hoping that I wasn't wrong about what I, what we, were feeling, but I didn't want to get my hopes up. I've only had one love in my life, and that was so many years ago. It was hard to believe that love could come again."

He took her into his arms and they kissed.

I deduced correctly that it was time for my exit, so I backed away. Unfortunately, I backed into one of the cafe chairs, and it made a loud scraping noise. They moved apart but just slightly.

"Don't mind me," I smiled sheepishly. "I'll be going back in for dessert now."

"Annalise, wait. Don't you want to know what I was going to talk to you about?" Genio asked, keeping his arms around my aunt.

Rats. I couldn't imagine what he would have to say. The only thing I could think of was that he was going to grill me on Eli, since we had come out here right after Katherine Flynn made her comments.

"No rush. We can talk later. Dessert's calling." I tried to leave.

He reached out for my hand and clasped it.

"Coincidentally, I was going to ask you if you thought your aunt might be interested in getting serious. That's why you shocked me with your 'intentions' question," he said.

"What!"

I burst out laughing. I was worried that he was about to cast her aside, and he was worried that she was about to cast him aside.

"Hey," I stopped laughing. "Do you realize that if I hadn't said anything, you two might have dragged on, not expressing your feelings?"

"Yes, yes, you can take all the credit," drawled my aunt.

"You realize what this means, though, don't you?" I said.

"That I'm the luckiest man alive," Genio hugged my aunt and kissed her cheek.

"No. That you two have to tell Pop. Now if you want to hear the 'intentions' talk, there's the scary one."

"Don't be silly, Annalise. I'm a grown woman and years older than your father. He doesn't frighten me, and he shouldn't frighten you, Genio." Auntie Lil tossed her head back.

"We'll see," I shrugged.

Genio winked at me and said, "We'll use you as our advocate, Annalise. I'm sure you can explain it all to your father with as much delicacy as you did here tonight."

"Hey!" I looked at him prepared to fight, but could see that he was kidding. Hmm. He would fit into the family just fine.

We returned to the dining room to find that many of the desserts were gone, but Georgiann had thoughtfully set aside at least one of each type for the three of us. We devoured the stacks of *nian gao, aiwowo, wan dou wuong, tanghulu,* and lovely cream cakes.

"So, my friends, shall we attempt the walk back to the hotel, or should we find someone to roll us back there?" asked Father John, patting his stomach.

"Even if we could find such a 'roller,' I think we need the walk, don't you?" I said, leaning back on my chair.

Chairs scraped as we stood to make our way out the door for a leisurely stroll back. Our day was to begin early, so we all said our goodnights at the elevator and parted company.

When we reached our room, I gave Auntie Lil a sidewise glance as she prattled on about what sweaters to layer in the morning for the best warmth.

"That's what you're concerned about? Sweater layers?"

"What do you mean, Annalise?"

"Auntie Lil! A man just professed his love for you! You didn't even kiss goodnight! You just went to your separate rooms as if … as if …"

At that moment, there was a slight rap on our door.

I looked at Auntie Lil and leapt over my bed to beat her to answer it. I peeked through the security hole and then slid the door open only slightly.

"Why hello, Genio," I grinned through the slight opening before I was shoved aside by my aunt.

"You are incorrigible, Annalise! I'm so sure that he's out there!"

She shook her head just before his arm reached through to pull her to the hallway. I pressed my eye to the peephole in time to see them entwined in an embrace, but then they quickly moved out of sight into what I knew was the dim alcove at the end of the hall.

"Hubba hubba!" I whispered to myself.

CHAPTER THIRTY-TWO

"So?" I grinned at my aunt the next morning.

"So what?" she answered innocently.

"I think you know what."

It wasn't as if she had been out all night. Her moral code would have preempted that. But she looked like a woman who had been well-kissed when she tapped on our door for me to let her in after her rendezvous! I resisted the urge to grill her after opening the door and allowed her to prepare for bed. But now, I wasted no time in questioning her.

"Have you seen my olive-green scarf?" she asked, digging through her large suitcase.

"Have you seen your face in the mirror?" I pushed.

She sat down and sighed.

"You're not going to be civilized about this, are you?"

"Of course not! Would you?"

I knelt in front of her, taking her hands into mine.

"Are you happy, Auntie?" I searched her face.

"I believe so, sweetheart," she said. Her answer dropped decades from her countenance.

"Oh, Auntie, then I'm happy for you." I leaned my head on her knee, and we stayed like that without speaking for several moments.

"What will this mean?" I whispered as her hand patted my head lovingly, as she had done so often in my life.

"We both have lives that are established, dear."

I held my breath. Surely she and Genio hadn't had a "this could never be" type of discussion in the hallway last night?

"But, on the other hand, we're not getting any younger."

Yes, yes, get to the point.

I held my breath and looked up at her.

"How do you feel about being maid of honor at a very small wedding?"

I jumped up and squealed!

"Auntie! I would be delighted!" I danced around the room humming "Here Comes the Bride" while she laughed merrily. Eventually I fell into her lap, making both of us fall backward onto the bed.

"Annalise! Please don't cause me to break a hip! I don't want to stand before the priest on crutches."

I rolled over and sat beside her, keeping her hand clutched in mine.

"You are pretty sneaky, you know?" I said. "How did you not burst into the room last night with that little bit of information?"

"I wanted you to get a good night's sleep before we traveled today," she said.

"Why yes, that was so much more important." I nudged her foot with mine and then shot straight up.

She reacted in a predictable way.

"Annalise, I need you to keep this to yourself. Genio and I don't need anyone else to know about this just yet."

"But Auntie! This group! How will you keep this information from them?"

"We just will, that's all. I'm only telling you because I know you can keep it to yourself."

"Seriously? You two are not going to tell Georgiann? She'll be crushed." I shook my head.

"Genio knows his sister. He'll tell her in his own time. Meanwhile, zip your lip, okay?" She stood to continue preparing for the day of sightseeing.

"Okay," I reluctantly stood to finish packing my day bag. This was huge! I wanted to tell someone!

"What about—" I started.

"We will tell your father when we get home." She took my shoulders anticipating my question.

"WHEN WE GET HOME! THAT'S DAYS FROM NOW!"

"Such drama, child. Where do you get it?"

"Uh … from my father—and from you, I might add. Remember, you're my godmother?" Family lore was that babies took on the characteristics of whoever held them when the priest baptized them.

Auntie Lil just crossed her arms and shook her head.

"Fine. But you realize what a burden you place on me." I twisted my mouth grimly and went back to my preparations.

"Yes, yes, this is all about you, after all." She smiled as she tossed me my neon green cap and donned her own.

I arranged my hat in the mirror and felt a pang. Was it just yesterday that I had a playful day with Eli as we wore these silly green hats? Better yet, did it even happen at all? Staid, stoic Eli Chamberlain of the tense eyebrows? Was that him with me in the pedicab, his jet eyes flashing and dark hair flopping boyishly? And what was that enchanting scent that I would forever associate with him?

I sighed.

"Annalise, are you okay?" Auntie Lil turned from applying her signature lip color.

"Just wonderful, bride-to-be!" I pulled myself together. I didn't want Auntie Lil to have to worry about my silly crush.

We knew the weather on the Great Wall would be damp, so we added rain gear to our bags and descended to the breakfast buffet room. My fears of overdressing were set aside when I saw some of our colleagues and noted their decidedly more puffy state.

"Are you girls going to be warm enough?" asked Colette when she saw us. Our intrepid tour organizer's dubious tone indicated that she clearly did not think we would be.

"Thin layers, Colette. That's what we're going for. And we're carbo-loading right now. Don't you know that's the way to go?" Auntie Lil said and steered us away, leaving Colette with a curious look.

We deposited our belongings at a table.

"Carbo-loading? What are we, getting ready to run a marathon?" I shook my head as we moved to the buffet.

"Colette is delightful," said Auntie Lil, "but sometimes it's fun to give her something to think about."

"Right, right."

We wove our way back to our seats at the precise moment that Genio and the Perinis were depositing their gear at our table.

"Good morning Georgiann and Tom. Genio." Auntie Lil was overly polite.

"Oh my gosh!" Georgiann exclaimed. "When will the wedding be?"

Auntie Lil and I gaped at her. How …?

"Georgie, what are you talking about?" Genio whispered and looked around the room.

"You can't fool me, Eugenio. You've proposed to this lovely woman." She grabbed him in a bear hug.

"Georgie—" her brother began to caution her.

"Genio, you know better than to try to disagree with your sister," Tom shook his head in amusement. "She's the Engagement Whisperer. She can smell a proposal a mile away."

"At the moment, do you think you can convince her to lower her voice to an actual whisper?" Genio asked, then laughed when he realized what he said. His sister was not capable of that volume. He hugged her and kissed her cheek.

"Yes, Georgie, I've asked Lilliana to marry me."

Georgiann clapped and squealed, then stopped abruptly.

"And you said yes?" she addressed Auntie Lil.

"Yes, I said yes," Auntie Lil acknowledged.

"I knew it, I knew it!" Georgiann squeezed her, then turned to me.

"Welcome to the family, dear girl!"

"Thank you." I could barely breathe in her clasp.

Others in our group had noticed the commotion and gathered around us.

"What's this?" Father John asked.

"These two are engaged!" Georgiann exclaimed.

"Well, that explains your late-night stroll for a refreshing beverage last night! Seems you found something a bit more refreshing," Father John winked at Genio.

"Here, here, what is going on?"

Oh no. The deflating tones of Katherine Flynn. If she brought the mood down, why I would—

"An engagement, that's what. Lil and Genio," Father John said.

"Well, what took you so long? Anyone could see you'd be a fool to let her slip out of your hands." We watched in amazement as Katherine gave Genio a handshake and Auntie Lil a perfunctory hug.

Vivienne followed her sister's lead but with much broader hugs and kisses.

"Oh, Kat, isn't it grand?" she breathed.

"Yes, yes. It's delightful. But engagement or no, we need to eat and get on that bus to stay on schedule." There was the Katherine we knew. However, as she walked back to her table, I spied a whisper of a smile on her face.

We continued to chatter and buzz about the big news, but also managed to enjoy our breakfasts and make it to the bus waiting in front of the hotel on time. Green caps perched jauntily on heads, we began our day.

"Good morning!" Lee smiled as we boarded. "Today you will see the amazing Great Wall of China, and I have some other exciting views for you."

We had grown accustomed to Lee and his use of superlatives, his favorites being *amazing* and *exciting*. Our day had barely begun, and I was already exhausted just from his descriptions! To give him credit, though, he did come through with extraordinary sights and information on the hourlong journey to the Great Wall.

At our destination, we retrieved tickets to ride the popular cable car to the middle section of the wall, which was constructed in 1504. Although it is possible to walk along massive lengths of the wall, we were going to concentrate on that small area.

As we exited the cable car and climbed the rocky steps to the wall itself, I had to pinch myself inwardly. Here I was! Standing on the Great Wall of China!

"Wow" was all I could say.

"Wow is right." Auntie Lil put her arms around me, and we stood that way for several minutes, taking in the beauty and awe. Lee had given us the history and background on the way over, so we were free to walk on our own before meeting back as a group.

I felt like a fifth wheel with Auntie Lil and Genio, so I headed out on my own. The wall is a treacherous walk, sometimes reaching 45 percent in tilt, so I moved slowly, glad for my sturdy hiking boots. Occasionally I stopped to take a photo across the valley, or what I could see of the valley through the haze.

"Whew! Can you imagine building this, brick by brick, mile by mile?" I commented as Auntie Lil and Genio caught up with me. I just shook my head. I started to move again, but Auntie Lil caught my arm.

"Walk with us, dear," she said, her green scarf wrapped tightly around her face and neck. Since we were about 3,400 feet above sea level, the whipping wind made us both glad that we had layered tightly.

"I don't want to be in the way," I said.

"In the way? Don't be silly!" Then she caught the look on my face. "Oh, Annalise, you will never be in the way anytime in my life."

"Of course not," agreed Genio, his own face ruddy from the wind.

"Besides, you are officially my companion until I say you are relieved of your duties," she laughed.

We took off together, and I was glad to walk with Genio, whose knowledge of architecture added to the experience. His sister and brother-in-law joined us, as well as the Willems and Father John, and our usual subset of the tour group was complete.

"Omigosh, do you see those girls walking in high heels?" I pointed.

"I would have two sprained ankles in an instant! This is a desperately uneven surface," Auntie Lil noted.

"Ma would be proud of us—form over fashion," I laughed.

After an hour at the wall, we all descended at various times via the cable car to meet at the bus.

"Wasn't that amazing?" Lee grinned.

Indeed.

We warmed up quickly on the bus ride back to the city, laughing and chatting about our experiences.

The remainder of the day consisted of a visit to the grounds of the Summer Palace, with a walk around the man-made lake, then back to the city, and finishing with a visit to the Quing Hao market—five stories of vendors selling everything from knockoff handbags and electronics to spices and teas. We returned to the hotel after dinner, tired, and dispersed to our various rooms for a good night's sleep. I could hardly believe that our journey was nearing the end. Only one day more!

CHAPTER THIRTY-THREE

"Did you know that giant pandas are actually flesh-eaters?"

"Good morning to you, too, Ma." Did I actually spit out my toothpaste, rinse like a madwoman, and dash out of the bathroom to answer my phone and get this dubious fact?

"I'm just saying," she continued, "most people think they only eat bamboo, but they really prefer to eat flesh."

"Why are you telling me this?" I rolled my eyes, glad that she could not see me through the phone.

"Aren't you going to the zoo to see them this morning?"

"Yes. But I'm not climbing into their cage or pit or wherever they stay, so I think I'm safe from them chomping on me. Besides, where did you get this fact?"

"I was just watching a special on the National Geographic channel and thought you might want to know."

I took a deep breath.

"Ma, I appreciate your concern, but I'm pretty sure I'll be safe from the danger." I smiled, thinking of the chubby black-and-white pandas we would encounter from behind a screen at the zoo.

"Did you also know—" she began.

"No. But I think I'd rather let the guide surprise me." I stopped her.

"Suit yourself," she chided, then switched to another topic. "How is your aunt?"

"Why?" I felt suspicious.

"What do you mean 'why'? We sent you to keep her company. I would think that it's not out of the question to ask how she's doing. You're very touchy, Annalise."

Of course it wasn't out of the question. And there was no way that Ma could know about Auntie Lil's recent activities. But this was Ma, and she has this extraordinary sixth sense about things.

"She's great, Ma. We're both great." Maybe I was a bit too cheerful.

"Let me talk to her."

"NOOO." Auntie Lil had gone for an early morning walk and breakfast at the nearby coffee shop with Genio.

"No? Annalise, why would I not be able to talk to your aunt?"

"Shower. She's in the shower."

"Hmm. Okay. But you have her call me as soon as she's out." Ma was determined. I had to deter her. Well, nothing to do but throw myself under the bus.

"Ma, do you not trust me? Why do you think that you need to check in with her yourself? If you think that I'm not doing a good job, well, then—" I tried to muster an indignant rather than panicked tone.

"Calm down," Ma interrupted, with a tinge of hurt in her own voice. "I trust you. I just wanted to check in with her, that's all. I would never think that you aren't a capable person."

"Oh, Ma. I'm sorry. Look, I'll have her call you." I was sure I could dash down to the cafe.

"No, dear. I guess I'll just leave you gals alone. Have a nice day. We'll see you at the airport."

Guilt, guilt, guilt!

"I'll have her call you."

"Whatever works for you. I love you."

"I love you, too."

I knew I'd better have Auntie Lil call her, no matter what the time difference was when she returned from breakfast. I hadn't wanted to hurt my mother, but she'd understand once the news was all out.

I sat that way for a moment and was startled when it rang again. I glanced to see the number and breathed a sigh of relief to see it was Rory.

"I'm so glad it's you," I said.

"Well, you always should be." I pictured her cheeky grin.

"So much is going on."

"Considering you didn't let me know what happened with Auntie Lil and the handsome Genio, you do owe me some information, so—"

"Oh! Right! Well …"

I brought her up to speed, including my conversation with my mother.

"Wowsers!" she said, regressing to one of our junior high terms. "Just like that! They are getting married?"

"Yep."

"Well, relax. I think I would have done the same thing with your mom on that conversation."

"Really?"

"Oh, yes. Would you really have wanted to tell her the news? You'd be throwing a grenade and coming back to the rubble in a day. Nope. I say let Auntie Lil drop that little bomb."

I ignored her metaphors.

"Rory, when are you coming home to Denver?"

"I can be there when you get home, if you want. Do you need something?"

"Just thought it would be nice to visit."

This trip with Auntie Lil was a nice break from reality, but once I got home, I had to get back to making decisions about things like my career. When I left, we had paused the discussion of my moving in with Rory. We needed to open that discussion again.

"Sure, sweetie, I think that would be great. Besides, I would want to get there as quickly as possible to pick up the souvenir that I know you carefully chose for me." That's what I loved about Rory. She always knew how to brighten my mood.

We finished our conversation quickly when I realized how much time I had spent on the phone. I was still in my pajamas and needed to get dressed and meet the rest of the group downstairs in just moments.

As I strolled into the breakfast room, Georgiann Perini yoo-hooed me over to her table. I was happy to join her, her husband, and the Willems. Bear and I then walked over to the buffet.

"Well, Annalise, are you ready for our final day?" Bear asked.

"I can't believe how much we've seen and done in the time we've been here," I replied. "Have you and Frida had a good time?"

"Wonderful!" He put his arm around my shoulders in a hug worthy of his name. "And we're so glad you joined us to give this group a little bit of young blood."

"What are you talking about? It was a challenge keeping up with you!"

"Well, gal, Frida and I have been on several of these group tours, but this surely has been our favorite. You are a breath of fresh air."

"That's so nice of you." I was glad that he didn't bring up the subject of Eli. Maybe Auntie or Genio had warned him against it.

"I think what is the best is your reporting in your blog. You writing to let everyone back home know what we're doing has made it easy for us."

"Oh, it was just some fun scribbling, Bear."

"What was fun?" Frida asked as we returned to the table.

"I was telling Annalise how good her reporting is on her blog about our journey."

"Indeed," said Frida. "Our family said that they really appreciated it and liked hearing about it as we go rather than waiting until we get back."

"I'm glad they like it, but seriously, I just thought it would be something fun for my own family."

"Do you not know how many followers you have?" Frida asked.

"Not really," I shrugged.

"Dear, if you look at the bottom of your blog, you can see how many visits you have. You have reached the thousands."

"What!" I stared at her. Breck told me there was a counter, but I hadn't paid attention to it.

"Oh, definitely. We didn't have just our family read it. Our children sent out the link to everyone in our parish. That's about 3,000 people."

"Our son did the same thing with his parish. That's about 4,000," added Tom Perini.

"You're kidding me! I just thought I was writing for a couple dozen people in our families!" Suddenly I felt very exposed.

"Hardly," chuckled Bear. "You have quite the audience. People like your reporting. Have you ever thought about writing as a career?"

"Well, I always wrote a lot in my marketing job, but I never thought about concentrating on it." Who does? Actually, everyone thinks they can be a writer, but very few people can do it.

"Hmm. You might consider it. If you need a reference, you can use me," said Frida.

"Thank you very much." Were references from random travel groups held in high value?

"Oh and us as well!" Georgiann agreed.

"Thank you all!"

We finished our breakfasts in enough time to don our sprightly green caps and join Lee at the bus to begin our day of touring. Auntie Lil and Genio walked up from their morning stroll just in time to hop on the bus. She scanned the seats to find me comfortably next to Father John and blew me a kiss. I smiled back at her as Genio gently ushered her into their seat and joined her. If there was ever any doubt that this was a match, just a few minutes of watching them together would dash it.

I walked up to her to tell her to check in with Ma.

"She said not to worry about it, but—" I began.

"She's probably sitting by the phone. I know, I know." Auntie Lil drew her phone out of her bag and gave Ma a quick call.

"Good morning, friends!" said Lee in his upbeat manner. "Are we ready for our exciting day?"

I moved back to my seat as the group gave a resounding "Hurrah!" and we were off.

"So, Annalise, I see that I have the pleasure of being your seatmate once again, now that our friend Mr. Chamberlain has departed," Father John smiled.

"Oh, Father, you know I would choose you as my escort any day."

I hoped he wouldn't push the conversation further. Unfortunately, he did.

"Has he contacted you?"

My silence answered his question, and he took my hand in both of his.

"Well, dear, I wouldn't worry too much about that. It's not exactly like he just went to the next town and was easily available, or—"

"I appreciate that you are trying to make me feel better, but I think I just need to chalk this up to experience, Father."

Yep. Just one more experience. I kept my head down, hoping not to cry.

"Annalise, look at me," Father John said, and I turned to him. He continued in his pastorly way, "You are a beautiful, intelligent young woman. Not only that, you are kind and compassionate. I know it's difficult, but don't dwell on this. Remember that our prayers are not answered in our time or in the way we expect."

His words were consoling. I blinked and nodded—then giggled when I realized his cap was askew, making him look decidedly goofy in contrast to the wise words that had come from his mouth. I reached up and straightened his hat, and we laughed together.

"My friends, we are at the zoo!" exclaimed Lee. He gave us directions for the first stop that day.

"I kind of think we've been a traveling zoo all along, don't you?" Father John whispered.

"Indeed!" I laughed.

CHAPTER THIRTY-FOUR

"What was I thinking when I bought all of this?"

It was morning, and I looked at my purchases from the trip that were spread out on the bed, and wondered how I was going to squish them into my luggage.

"Hmm." Auntie Lil reviewed her own stash. "It seems that we both have accumulated a bit of loot. Although, I'd say the, ahem, 'small' stuffed panda you bought at the zoo yesterday wins the prize for largest."

"What?" I grabbed the fluffy toy and hugged it. "It's for Nicky and Amanda's baby. You know how much Amanda loves pandas."

"Yes, but did you have to get a life-sized one?" she teased.

"Exaggeration is not a good look on you." I threw the panda at her.

"Stop it! You don't want to wear the toy out before it gets home." She tossed it back.

I flopped into the cozy armchair near the bed, clinging the panda to me.

"I can't believe we're getting on a plane in a little while to go home! Didn't we just get here?"

"Time has flown by, I'll admit," Auntie Lil nodded.

The previous day had been a whirlwind of activity, from the zoo visit, the walk through the Botanical Gardens, and a breathtaking martial arts exhibition at the "Legends of Kung Fu" show that night. This morning, we would be driving past some of the buildings constructed for the Olympics, then straight to the airport.

"Auntie Lil," I shot straight up. "We're flying to Denver today, and everyone else is flying to Chicago."

"Yes, dear," she continued arranging and rearranging items in her suitcase.

"Well, that means we say good-bye to … everyone … as soon as we go to the airport."

"What are you getting at? Oh. I see." She stopped packing and came over to sit on the edge of the bed facing me. "Annalise, darling, Genio and I have already made plans."

"And?"

"And, we'll execute those plans when we return."

"Execute? Wow, that sounds romantic." I pulled a face and leaned back.

"Annalise, what do you want me to say? That I've changed my ticket? That's not practical, is it? He can't change his either. No. We'll go to our own homes, and we'll move along from there."

"But what if—" I started, but she hushed me.

"There isn't a what-if. We've planned to get married, and we will. Goodness, Annalise, what gives you the idea that things change so quickly?" She stood to go back to her packing, then returned and sat. "I get it. You're worried because you've seen changes in your life and you think that will happen to me, right?"

"Well … yes." I wasn't exactly the most optimistic person after my own recent life changes.

"Don't worry, dear. Everything will be fine."

"But, what if—"

"No what-ifs, Annalise," she emphasized as she took my face in her hands. "We will remain positive. Deal?"

I looked at her and realized that anything I said was only going to be mean to her. I swallowed my doubts.

"Deal."

We resumed packing and reminiscing, and my nagging worries were pushed to the back of my head.

"What are you doing under there?" Auntie Lil's voice called out as I was scouting beneath the bed.

"I can't find the little red tin of tea that the grandmother gave me at lunch in the hutong," I said.

"Are you sure you didn't already pack it?"

"Positive."

I reemerged, unpacked my bag, and searched through it again.

"Gone." I sat mournfully.

"Maybe it's in your backpack?"

"I already dumped that out. Oh no! I think I left it in the pedicab."

Great. That was one of the only memories I had of Eli, and I lost it. I sat for a few minutes.

Then I remembered the giant bag of memorabilia that Rory had scoured from my room when we did the Dylan purge. No. Better that I didn't clutter up my luggage with physical memories. It was bad enough that I had to try and scour my mind.

"Annalise? Are you okay?" Auntie Lil emerged from the bathroom with her toiletries.

"I'm just fine." I hopped up and said with more enthusiasm than I felt.

Eventually, the luggage was packed and zipped, and we were dressed and ready to join our friends.

The mood on the bus was less festive than in the past days since everyone was not only tired from the journey but also anticipating long plane rides home. Lee and our bus driver tried to make our remaining time meaningful, and we snapped many final photos. More photos were taken at the airport, including with Lee, and I was certain that the young man would look forward to going home to relax before taking on a new group of travelers.

"Here we go again," I commented to Auntie Lil as we began the long process of checking in and the trudge through TSA on the way to our gate. Since our flight was boarding at a gate near the rest of the group, we were spared having to say any good-byes until we were closer to boarding.

Auntie Lil and I moved along with Genio, Tom, and Georgiann. I smiled and thought about the fact that we were gaining not only the wonderful Genio when he and Auntie Lil got married, but also these two as well as an entire clan in Chicago. Life was going to get interesting. I couldn't wait for Ma and Georgiann to meet and compare meatball recipes.

Once we navigated TSA and check-in, we took our time walking to our gates, clustering together for last-minute chatter and trading addresses. The Chicago crew boarded first, and Auntie Lil and I stood to wave them onto the plane.

"Come along Vivienne," Katherine hustled her sister toward the gate, not looking back. In a rare burst of independence, Vivienne dashed toward us for two quick hugs.

The Willems embraced us and collected their belongings. Bear towered over his doll-like wife as they made their way toward the plane.

"Thank you for adding so much sparkle to this trip," Father John kissed each of us on the cheek and made his way.

The Perinis gave many hugs and kisses and admonishments to visit and call before Georgiann directed Tom on exactly how to carry their belongings. He rolled his eyes but secretly winked toward us.

Colette counted each as they boarded and stopped short before admonishing Genio. She just smiled and left him with us.

He was the last to board, of course, leaving Auntie Lil with a swoon-worthy kiss. I was close enough to hear their good-byes.

"Until then, my love," he whispered.

"Until then," she acknowledged.

My heart beat quickly as she turned to me, eyes glistening. It occurred to me that she had said good-bye one other time to the love of her life and never saw him again. What must be going through her mind now? She walked to the window, leaned her head on it, and waited for the plane to take off.

Once the jet had gone, I needed to distract my aunt until it was time for us to board.

"Hey, let's go to duty-free. What do you think?" I said brightly.

She wiped the tears from her eyes.

"Seriously, Annalise? Do you think you have room to pack one more thing to take home?"

"Probably not, but let's just go in and pretend we're high rollers looking for lavish goods. What do you think?"

"Why not? Maybe we'll run into someone famous."

As she said that, my heart dropped. The last time I ran into someone at an airport, it was a handsome stranger with jet-black hair and a smile that went all the way up to his ebony eyes. No. Shake it off. I couldn't keep Auntie's spirits up if I started wallowing in my own pity!

"Doubt it, Auntie. They have people who shop for them."

"Well, I'll be your people and you be my people," she smiled as we moved arm in arm to the duty-free shop.

We oohed over the high-end products at the shop, then separated to peruse the more commonplace items such as the candies. I rambled and soon reached the back of the shop, and was jolted when I caught a whiff of a very familiar scent. I whirled around to see a young woman with a sampler bottle.

"Do you like this?" she asked. "It's MAN by Jimmy Choo. Very distinctive."

"Um, yes. Very nice." I was shaken. My mind fell back to a pleasant ride in a pedicab with someone who was distinctive.

"Perhaps you have a special young man you would like to give a gift to?"

I stared at the marketing card accompanying the scent. Kit Harington of *Game of Thrones* fame was the spokesman, and his piercing gaze connected with me from the card.

"You know nothing, Jon Snow." I whispered the phrase most associated with the striking actor's character.

"Pardon me?" the sales clerk asked, smiling.

"I … um … yes, it's very nice, but I don't have anyone to bring it to as a surprise."

No one. And now when I watch Kit Harington in the drama, will I only think of that other nice-smelling man? Life can be so random. I spun to abandon the sales clerk and seek Auntie Lil. She was near the checkout.

"Did you find anything, love?" she asked.

"Oh, you know. I wouldn't have room to pack it if I did." I hoped I had covered.

"Well, I'm buying these lovely chocolates, then we can go to the gate."

"Perfect."

Breathe.

Everything will be normal when we get home.

I hoped.

CHAPTER THIRTY-FIVE

I would have thought that the fourteen hours of flying time would have been interminable, but both Auntie Lil and I slept as if we were drugged. Even the hour we spent checking through Vancouver changing planes did not drag—aided by a stop at the Tim Hortons doughnut counter.

We ascended the escalators at the airport in Denver to be met by our family brandishing welcoming signs and flowers.

"My baby!" exclaimed my mother as she crushed me to her.

"It's good to see you, Ma, but you are going to squoosh me," I protested mildly.

She ignored my protests and covered my cheeks with kisses, then moved on to Auntie Lil. I'm sure that passersby imagined we had been gone for years rather than days.

"Let's get your bags," my father said after giving me his own crushing hug. "Your mother and Amanda have dinner ready at home. Do you need something to tide you over for the drive?"

And people wonder why my curves are plentiful.

After retrieving our bags and getting us sorted into the two vehicles that had come to take us home, we were off. Auntie Lil was spending the night with us after what I knew was going to be a lavish Italian dinner because—as my mother put it—we "hadn't had a decent bowl of pasta in days."

"So. Tell me everything. No. Wait until we're home. Amanda is there making sure dinner is ready. No, I can't wait." My mother was as skittish as a twelve-year-old. I was in the car with her and my brother, and Auntie Lil was in the other car with my father. I would have felt safer together with my aunt. Less chance of spilling something on accident.

"It was all beautiful, Ma. We have tons of pictures."

"Yes, yes, I saw all the pictures and read your reports, but I want to hear everything from you." She turned around and waited eagerly.

"Well. Um." I was truly stumped. There was a lot to tell, and some of it wasn't mine to tell.

Thank goodness for Nicky. He caught my eye in the rearview mirror and could tell that I was hedging for a reason.

"Geesh, Ma. Let the girl get used to the time zone and the altitude, why don't you? Besides, do you really want to hear things twice?" He winked at me.

"Nicholas! I want to hear everything!" She paused and turned back to me. "But, if you want to wait, I suppose we can."

"Ma, I promise to go into scads of detail." *Maybe not.*

"You can ask all the questions you want." *But I might not answer them.*

"Let's just wait until Auntie is around, okay? Besides, why don't YOU fill me in on what's been going on here at home?"

That did the trick. Once I had Ma giving the latest news and views during my absence, I was set until we arrived home.

We pulled into the driveway of our comfortable brick home just moments ahead of Pop and Auntie Lil. When he careened into the driveway, I knew something was up. Ma and Nicky went into the house with my bags, but I cautiously waited for my father and aunt to leave their car.

Blam! My father's door slammed shut. He walked to the trunk and yanked out Auntie's luggage, then stomped up the steps of the front porch.

"Auntie Lil? What gives?" I walked over to her door as she stepped out quietly.

"Well, dear. You know how I always tell you that unwelcome news doesn't get any better with time?"

"Don't tell me that you told Pop about Genio?"

"I'm afraid I did."

"And?"

"And he's not too thrilled about having to walk me down the aisle, I guess," she said as shouldered her carry-on.

"I don't think it's that, Auntie Lil. I think it's more that he isn't thrilled about the whirlwind aspect of it."

"Well, he'll have to get thrilled, won't he? I'm not changing my mind. Remember, I'm the older sister?"

We walked up the stairs and into what I knew wasn't going to be a nice, quiet family dinner.

I was right. Their "discussion" began immediately after we said the blessing—frankly, I'm surprised my father held off that long—continued through bread, cold cuts, salad, and pasta and was full force during dessert. Requests for Ma's famous lemon torte were punctuated with many spoon wavings and rolling of eyes.

During it all, I managed to avoid being a star witness, despite the pleadings of both sides.

"Tell him, Annalise. Tell him what a wonderful man Genio is."

"Annalise, tell your aunt how vacations give you a distorted view."

I didn't want to cause the vein on the side of my father's head to erupt. On the other hand, he kept bringing up such good, practical points that I was worried I would be disloyal to Auntie Lil if I agreed with him.

"Enough!"

It was Ma who brought the 12-round bout to a close.

"Frank, your sister is old enough to make her own decisions."

Auntie Lil looked at him smugly.

"Lilliana, we need to meet this man, don't you think?"

My father one-upped the smug quotient.

"Annalise, do you think we should meet him?" All eyes turned to me.

I cleared my throat. Never was there a more important sentence to utter.

"I think that you all would like Genio if you met him. I think that you should reserve judgment until then."

I mentally crossed my fingers.

"It's settled. Invite him, Lilliana. We will have no more discussion until then. Now, who wants more lemon torte?"

My mother. The supreme negotiator.

We all looked at one another, afraid to add anything to the discussion, when the front door opened and in flew the scarlet-haired whirlwind that was Rory.

"Hi everyone! Did I miss anything?"

Having Rory there cut the tension somewhat. After we finished eating, she insisted on modeling the body-hugging emerald-green cheongsam that I had brought back for her. She was also the prime commentator on the gifts that Auntie and I had distributed to the others. Eventually, Auntie Lil and I begged to be allowed to go to bed, and even my mother recognized that jet lag and time change overrode her desire to hear any other travel stories.

"Lilliana, I made up the spare room for you. The other sisters are coming tomorrow, then we can take you home—unless you want to stay with us for a while. Rory, you are welcome to stay with us tonight if you like. Do you want me to call your mother?"

"I'll visit with Annalise for a while, but I'll go back over to Mom's. Thanks, Mama Fontana."

Rory and I glanced at each other. Leave it to my mother to feel that she still needed to call Rory's mother to assure her that her daughter was safe with us.

She and I climbed the stairs together and fell onto my bed, prepared for a good gossip, when Nicky ducked his head into my bedroom.

"So, Annalise, the trip was good, then?"

"Yes, Nick. Weren't you downstairs when Auntie and I went over all of that?" I covered my eyes with my forearm.

"It must have been good based on this picture." He came over and scooched between us, nearly knocking Rory off the bed and holding his phone in his outstretched hand inches from my nose.

"Hey!" I sat up. As I did, I came face-to-face with a photo of a couple framed by a leafy bush.

Entwined in an embrace.

I gulped.

It was Eli and me, in the garden of the Forbidden City. You couldn't tell it was him because of the tilt of his head and the shadow of his cap, but you could definitely make out my face.

"Nicky! Where did you get this picture?" I jumped up and snatched the phone from his hand.

"I take it that I'm not wrong then? This is you?"

Rory pulled me back down and leaned over my shoulder.

"Annalise, is this you with the brooding mystery man that you told me about?" She looked at Nicky and clapped her hand over her mouth.

"Too late, Rory. You can't cover for her because I can read her like a book. That is very definitely Annalise. What I want to know is, who is the guy who looks like he wants to devour you alive?"

I punched my brother in the shoulder in a well-worn move from childhood.

"Stop it, Nicky."

I kept staring at the photo while a myriad of emotions washed over me. First, my heart pounded and my face flushed at the thought of the two of them looking at this photo of me in such a vulnerable moment. Another set of emotions hit as my heart fell, thinking about the conversations Eli and I had had during the trip and how our time together was broken off so suddenly.

"I'm waiting," Nicky moved to the stool at my makeup table and began to swivel back and forth.

Rory put her arm around my shoulder. I cleared my throat and told my brother an abbreviated story of the ill-fated romance, all the while keeping an eye to the door to make sure my father or mother didn't barge in on us.

"And you haven't heard from him?" Nicky asked when I finished.

"Nope."

"What a jerk." My loyal brother.

"That's not fair. I don't think. Oh, I don't know." I stumbled for the right words. "But you still haven't told me where you got this picture."

"You know Lorna who works in my office? She is always trolling the web for bizarre top-ten lists. Apparently, someone posted this in a top-ten kisses list or something like that. She showed me because she thought it looked like you."

"Oh no!" I imagined this going viral with Lorna's celebrity-obsessed friends.

"Don't worry. I managed to convince her that it wasn't you because of the short hair."

Trust my brother to come up with a lawyer-like defense.

"But I knew it was you. And, sis, I knew that if Pop saw the picture ..." He didn't finish the sentence.

"It would make his conversation with Auntie Lil seem positively tame by comparison," Rory finished for him.

"Right. So ... you think you won't see this fellow again?"

"I doubt it, Nick. He doesn't know where I live or a lot of other details about me, so I guess we're just strangers."

He returned to sit on my other side. The three of us kicked the bed with our heels in silent unison.

"Please keep this to yourself," I finally said to him.

"Well, I can. But you know as well as I do that if a picture is on the web, it's out there for anyone to see."

"I know, I know."

"And if Pop sees it before he knows anything about it, his head will explode."

"I know, I know."

Finally, he stood up to leave.

"Well, I left Amanda downstairs to cover while I could talk to you alone. Sorry to blindside you, kid, but I figured you'd want to know."

"No, I appreciate it. You know, I really suspect that Pop won't see it since he is not on the web and he and Lorna don't exactly travel in the same circles."

The three of us laughed at the idea of my conservative father being buddies with the bubbly Lorna. Nicky hugged me and left to collect his very pregnant wife to go to their own home.

I flopped face-first on my bed and screamed into my pillow.

"Very articulate," Rory commented.

I sat up and brushed my hair back.

"My head is spinning, Rory."

"I think you are just jet-lagging, Annalise. You need a good night's sleep and then get yourself back into a groove, and you'll be okay."

"That's just it. I don't want to go back to my sad little groove. No job, living here. Wasn't this where we were less than a month ago?"

"Not exactly."

"What do you mean 'not exactly'?"

"Well … actually, you could have a job if you wanted it."

"What?" She could be so maddeningly cryptic sometimes.

"So, remember I told you I shared your blog with my editor?"

"And a lot of other people, apparently."

"She thinks you have a flair for that type of writing. She is willing to offer you some freelance work, based on a final interview of course."

"What! Just based on my random scribbles?"

"Well, that … and some other writing I gave her."

"What other writing?" I eyed her suspiciously.

"After your layoff, you had me review your portfolio for job interviews, remember? I just pulled out your resume and the pertinent writing items."

"What!"

"What's the problem? You were thinking of moving to Manhattan anyway."

"But—"

"Come on. I know you like to do things on your own, but can't you just take a moment and accept this tiny bit of help from YOUR BEST FRIEND?"

I sat with my legs and arms crossed. It was true that I had a history of being fiercely independent. But if I learned anything from my months of job hunting, it was that we are all better when we help each other.

"Did you schedule the interview for me, too?" Knowing Rory, she had already picked out my outfit.

"Well, no, but I did tell her that you would be available next week." That cheeky grin had never changed from grade school.

I pounded her with one of my many pillows. We were shrieking like schoolgirls when my mother appeared in the doorway.

"I thought you were sleepy, Annalise? Shouldn't you get to bed?" Her tone was gentler than her words.

"I am. She started it …"

Rory leapt to her feet, hugged my mother, and blew me a kiss.

"See you girls tomorrow!" And she was off.

"That girl has always had more energy than either of her brothers! I pity the young man who tries to keep up with her!" Ma sat down beside me.

"I know what you mean."

"Annalise, tell me the truth. Do you think your Auntie Lil is making the right decision with this Genio person?"

"Oh, Ma, only she knows. But he is kind, and he seems genuine. You'll see when you meet him. And his family seems a lot like ours." I hoped that would help.

"Well, we'll find out soon enough. Your aunt called and invited him for the weekend. We'll see how your father deals with that."

"First of all, I'd recommend not calling him 'this Genio person.' Not a good way to introduce our family to his."

"Annalise, do you question my social skills?"

"Oh, no, not yours. But there are all the aunts."

"Ah, yes."

"Ma, how did you deal with meeting all of them?"

"Lots of prayer and healthy slugs of your grandfather's wine."

I burst into laughter. My mother was the perfect mix of piety and practicality!

"Get to sleep now, baby girl. We have a lot of sauce and meatballs to make tomorrow." She kissed my forehead and left the room humming.

CHAPTER THIRTY-SIX

"Annalise!" Georgiann enveloped me in a mighty hug and kissed me on both cheeks as soon as she spied me at the airport. Tom and Genio were slightly behind her, no less happy but a bit more reserved. She stepped aside to allow Genio to greet his intended before sweeping Auntie Lil into a hug as well.

"Hello, dear girl." Genio took both of my hands in his and kissed my cheek as well. Tom followed with a hug.

It was hard to believe that it had only been days since we'd last seen these delightful people. It was harder to believe that they were in Denver to meet my family. I was happy that Tom and Georgiann had accompanied Genio on this trip.

We chattered together on the way to baggage claim.

"Now, I know you must think that we are moving in, but of course Georgie felt she had to pack half of Chicago to come here," Tom said, shaking his head.

"Hush, Tommy! I wouldn't dream of coming to meet the family without a few trinkets." She waved him off.

Auntie Lil and Genio were a few steps behind us, and we allowed them their space.

"So, Annalise, how are you doing?" Georgiann whispered conspiratorially.

"I'm great, Georgiann. Just getting over jet lag, as I'm sure you are." I didn't know what she was getting at, but I knew I didn't want to find out.

We managed to snag all the luggage, move to the car in the parking lot, and get on our way without a hitch.

"It's just beautiful here in Denver!" Georgiann exclaimed.

"We have more than 300 days of sunshine a year," I said in my best tour guide voice.

"Quite a difference from our smog-filled days in Beijing, eh?" Tom commented.

We reminisced about the weather and other topics from our trip, hardly believing that it had been such a short time ago. Soon we were pulling into the driveway of my parents' house.

"Get ready for the onslaught," I muttered.

"Annalise! Be positive!" Auntie Lil chided.

"Sure. Say that now. But do you see what I see?"

No sooner was the engine turned off than dozens of Fontanas appeared as if from everywhere: the front door, the backyard, the garage. Did I even see one of cousins climb out of the chimney? No, impossible.

"Here we go." I prayed a quick prayer.

As if it were the Red Sea, the humanity parted and allowed my father to walk across the porch, down the stairs, and onto the driveway. Genio opened his door and assisted Auntie Lil out of the car.

"Frank, this is my fiancé, Genio," she said confidently. "Genio, this is my younger brother, Frank."

Yep. Auntie Lil set the stage.

Pop and Genio shook hands.

"Genio, come walk with me." Pop invited him around back, and we knew they were going to the far corner of the yard to the small gazebo with the small bench. So that's where the most important talk of Auntie Lil's life would take place.

The residual silence was broken by my mother descending the stairs, wiping her hands on her apron.

"Annalise? Introduce me to these nice people and let's get them something to drink."

She ushered Auntie Lil, Georgiann, and Tom to the chairs on the front porch. She then directed some of the older cousins to unload luggage from the car to the guest rooms.

Whew. Life was back to its boisterous normal.

As I fetched iced tea from the kitchen, I heard some of the aunties whispering about Genio.

"He's very handsome!"

"Who could trust a man that nice looking?"

"Well, Lil isn't getting any younger."

I shook my head and tried to ignore them as best I could.

Returning to the porch, I heard Georgiann's distinctive voice.

"We just love Lilliana! And your Annalise ... well, who couldn't love her? Just a shame about that young man."

Wooops.

"Hey, Georgiann, tell Ma about the food in China. She'll love to hear about that."

"Oh, yes, it was delicious." Georgiann was off on another topic, but my mother's eye caught mine, and I knew that the topic of "that young man" would come up later.

After what seemed like an eternity, my young cousin Tony came running up the stairs.

"Uncle Frankie wants Auntie Lil," he announced breathlessly and dashed back to whatever game he was playing with the other cousins.

"Well … I've been summoned." Auntie Lil set her tea glass down delicately, rose, and smoothed her hair. She tilted her head toward us and left for the backyard.

"Your flowers are lovely," Tom said, looking for a topic to discuss.

"Thank you. I have always liked to have color in the yard. Do you have flowers in your yard at home?" Ma asked.

We proceeded to discuss the merits of hydrangeas versus petunias that would have bored even the most ardent gardener.

Finally, my father appeared around the corner.

We all held our breath.

"Nicky!" he summoned my brother.

What in the world?

"Yes, Pop?"

"Call the Knights' hall. We need to reserve it. If my sister is getting married, we have to have a nice reception."

I jumped up and ran to hug him.

"Pop! You are the best."

"Your Auntie Lil is a smart woman. She's found a good man. I'm happy for her. Now introduce me to these fine people." He turned to Georgiann and Tom and sat with them, calling for a glass of tea for himself.

I walked around to the backyard to find my aunt. She and Genio were still in the gazebo, sitting quietly. They motioned me over.

"I'm so happy!" I kissed both of them.

"So, are you still interested in being maid of honor?" Auntie Lil grinned.

"You bet! How soon?"

"As I told you, we're not getting any younger, so as soon as we can."

"I'll clear my busy calendar," I said. I had the least busy calendar of anyone.

"I better get back to help Ma get the food out. I think the natives are getting restless." I turned to leave, but Genio caught my arm.

"Thank you, Annalise."

"For what?"

"For coming to China with your aunt."

"What? She would have come anyway!"

"Probably. But without you, I'm not sure she would have had the courage to take a chance on me … on us. You are really the reason we're together."

"Oh, don't be silly." My face turned red.

"You were her inspiration to be brave. Just remember that. Remember how brave you really are yourself."

I looked at him. He was sincere.

"Thank you. I appreciate that!"

I walked across the lawn. Me? Brave? Who knew?

CHAPTER THIRTY-SEVEN

I thought this maid of honor thing was going to be a piece of cake. Literally. I thought I was going to help Auntie Lil pick out a dress, flowers, and cake.

I didn't know that I was going to be the right-hand man, er, woman and have to answer every question that every single person had for the wedding. The brief period before the wedding was a whirlwind of activity—and this was for a simple wedding. I couldn't imagine what it would be like to plan a lavish wedding for a spoiled, dreamy-eyed young bride.

Not to mention that in between planning, I had to negotiate the interview with Rory's editor, who agreed to take some articles from me on spec. I wasn't going to be making a lot of money from these efforts, but I had finally figured out that writing was what I loved to do. I would continue my blog, turning from travel topics to more general topics. I still had a number of followers, and the number was growing. In addition, I was signing up advertisers. Thanks to Breck, I was becoming a whiz at social media. It was incredible to think that a chance encounter with his sister on an airplane would lead to a semi-business relationship with him. I wouldn't make a decision about moving to Manhattan until after the wedding, but since I could write my articles from anywhere, I knew I could live anywhere.

Brave. Maybe I was brave. I remembered Genio's words.

The wedding day arrived, and everything went off without a hitch. Auntie Lil wore a gorgeous cream silk suit with a matching birdcage headpiece, and she looked like she'd stepped off the runway at Paris. For me, we found a swing dress in a shade called Persian that defied anyone to call it green or blue. The handy thing about having a priest in the family is that when he celebrates a wedding, he makes it even more personal. Uncle Sal—Father Sal—was joined by Father John from our trip, so that made it twice as lovely.

When it was finally time for the reception, I thought my duties were done, but there were still a myriad of questions that I was answering throughout the afternoon. I was in the kitchen of the Knights' hall, scouting down more cocktail sauce for the shrimp, when my cousin Tony flew through the double doors.

"Annalise, somebody needs you!"

"Of course they do. Tell them to get in line."

Tony flew back through the doors in the way only a pre-teen can.

Moments later, he banged through the doors again.

"He says it's really important!"

"What could it be? No swizzle sticks? Tell him I'll be right there!" I blew my bangs out of my eyes.

The doors slammed open again, and I yelled without turning.

"Tony! I'll be there—oh!"

My gawky cousin didn't wear Jimmy Choo cologne. I only knew one person who did.

I swung around to find Eli Chamberlain standing quietly.

"What are you doing here?"

"I came to see you."

"What? Here? But how did you find me?"

"Did you think I couldn't?"

"Well, no. I suppose that if a wealthy tech guru wanted to track anyone down they could. But why?"

"Why?"

"Yes, why?"

"Surely you're joking."

"No. I mean, we had a pleasant afternoon, but then you disappeared. Why would you track me down?"

"A PLEASANT AFTERNOON?" His eyebrows met in a deep V.

"What did you expect me to think? I didn't hear from you. I thought I was just a diversion."

"A DIVERSION?"

"Are you just going to repeat everything I say?"

He moved toward me as the doors swung open again. In my reaction, I managed to squirt the cocktail sauce from my hands directly onto his shirt. He looked at me in disbelief, casting about for a towel.

"Sis? Did you find the sauce?" an impatient Nicky asked.

"In a minute!" I pointed him toward the hall.

As he turned to leave, he saw Eli. He paused and pointed as if to say "Who's this guy?" I was frozen in place. Eli looked up from attempting to clean his shirt, and Nicky caught him full-face. My brother's eyes widened, and his mouth opened.

"I said I'll be out in a minute." I shoved Nicky through the doors.

"My brother," I explained.

Eli nodded.

"Again with splattering me with sauce?" he asked, cocking his head.

I didn't have a good response, so I just said the first thing that came to my mouth: "So, you were just about to explain to me how you toyed with my emotions, then dropped me like a hot potato."

Wow, where did that come from?

Eli pushed the adorable flop of bangs from his forehead and breathed out patiently, "I was called away on a BUSINESS emergency, dealing with a merger."

Oh right, the Crispchip purchase.

"At that point, I didn't have CONTACT INFORMATION for you."

Oh. Right.

"As soon as I could, I went to my cousin at the tour agency, who couldn't give me your information because you didn't book through her. Then I went to your blog, went to your contact information—which, by the way, you don't answer— and got an answer from your tech support, who made me jump through hoops for privacy's sake. You never answered my emails in the last day or so. Finally, I came here to your hometown, only to have to track you down at your aunt's wedding. She, by the way, was DELIGHTED to see me."

My tech support? Oh. Breck. Hey, why didn't he tell me?

"Hold on." I dug through my tiny maid of honor clutch bag for my phone and searched for emails. The last few days were really hectic. There, buried between the many wedding correspondence notes, were the emails from Eli. Not to mention one from Breck telling me to expect them.

I looked up at Eli.

"Sorry?"

He looked at me, unbelieving.

"Sorry? Sorry? That's what you have to say? You are the most exasperating—"

He took two steps and pulled me to him. Placing his hands on either side of my face, he gave me a spine-tingling kiss. I dropped my phone and purse, and reached up to twist my arms tightly around his neck. We stayed locked in that kiss for many minutes. Soon his hands moved down my sides to hold my waist and finally my hips. We were backed up against the counter in the kitchen, and I finally pushed him gently back.

"What? You don't like me anymore?" he whispered as he moved his hand to the nape of my neck.

I reached up to trace his lips with my thumb and stared into the depths of his ebony eyes.

"Oh, no, not that at all," I whispered back, and he commenced another delicious kiss. I had to push back again.

"It's just that my father and my whole family are just on the other side of that wall, and I'm not sure I would want to be you if they came through the door at this moment."

He held me tighter as he kissed my neck.

"What's going on here?" Funny how my father's voice could fill a room. We sprang apart.

"Pop!" My eyes darted from him to Eli and back again. "This is Eli."

"Mm-hmm. And what is all over you, besides this Eli?" His unblinking hazel eyes bored into mine.

I looked down at my dress. The cocktail sauce that I had found and then spilled on Eli was, um, now on me as well.

"I was testing the cocktail sauce?"

My father stood patiently despite my impertinent answer. Finally, Eli moved toward him to shake his hand.

"Hello, sir. I'm Eli Chamberlain. I can appreciate your curiosity. If this were my daughter—"

"But she's not." My father cut him off.

Eli started again.

"It's not what you think."

"Tell me what I think. Then tell me what it is."

I closed my eyes. I knew that no matter how high-powered Eli Chamberlain was, he was no match for Frank Fontana.

Or was he?

"Annalise, can you give your father and me a minute?"

I was wide-eyed as he ushered me through the back door.

I paced outside, the gravel in the parking lot crunching under my feet. I knew a lot of girls my age would think this was ridiculous, but my family was my family, and whether anyone else considered it old-fashioned was not pertinent. Even Auntie Lil couldn't escape it at her age.

After what seemed like hours, they called me back in.

"Annalise, it seems as if you have quite a persistent admirer. He explained to me what hoops he jumped through to find you." My father's tone was even, so I didn't know where he was going with that.

"He tells me that you might have feelings for him as well?"

"Yes?" That was wimpy. I cleared my throat. "Yes." That sounded better.

"I like him. He's solid." My father's tone was certain.

Whew.

"Get yourselves cleaned up and come join the party. You don't want to miss any more of your aunt's wedding reception."

He kissed me on the cheek.

"Of course, you don't have to rush out there, Gypsy. You can take a few more minutes." He winked and left. An old softy after all!

I turned to Eli.

"I don't think we'll be able to get this mess cleaned up, do you?"

He pulled me toward him.

"So … let's just see if we can make it messier?" He smiled.

I laughed as the door banged open again. What now?

Nicky had returned with two Knights of Columbus Fun Run T-shirts.

"Pop says you might need these," he laughed as he tossed one to each of us, along with a pair of sweatpants for me.

"Thanks. Nicky, this is—"

"Eli Chamberlain. I know." He shook Eli's hand. "Sis, do you think you could have mentioned that your mystery man was the CEO of Graviton Gaming?"

"It didn't seem relevant."

"To you. But I guarantee you that there are a slew of cousins out there who are going to be very excited to meet the man who invented the Nuon gaming system."

"I'll try to live up to their expectations," Eli said as he swapped out his cocktail-sauced shirt for the T-shirt.

"Ha!" I ducked into the pantry and changed. When I returned, Nicky was gone.

"I have something for you." Eli held out his hand.

The battered canister of tea.

"I thought I lost it," I whispered.

"I had it in my pocket when we got out of the pedicab. I didn't think our visit would be cut short before I could hand it back to you."

I opened it and breathed in the fragrance of the plum blossoms, remembering how his father had found every recording of the song honoring the flower because of his love for his bride.

"So ..."

"So ..."

"So this is real?" he asked, clasping both of my hands in his.

"Seems like it. But, Eli, what would you have done if I'd turned you away?"

"But you weren't going to, were you?"

"What makes you so sure I still won't?" I tilted my head.

He took my face in his hands and looked into my eyes.

"Because I went all the way to China and back to find you. I'm sure not letting you go now."

OTHER BOOKS
BY BARBARA OLIVERIO

Love on the Back Burner: A Tasty Romantic Comedy

Readers' Favorite Award™-Winning *Love on the Back Burner* spins the story of sassy Alexandria D'Agostino. She is youngest in a tight-knit Italian-American family with a successful marketing career and a passion for cooking, yet her romantic life is less than 4-star. For years, she has tried cooking her way into men's hearts by flaunting her old world culinary skills, but now, she's changing the menu. She dishes up childhood favorites to a succession of first dates (recipes included). The book features an engaging cast of characters including a rock-star-turned- priest brother, a no-nonsense Italian immigrant grandmother, and a crew of friends who are always up for a good meal. With a dollop of persistence and a dash of laughter, will Alexandria discover the recipe for happiness—and perhaps love?

Love on the Lido Deck:
A Nautical Romantic Comedy

Sharp-witted, always-organized Keira Graham has traded in her high tech career as a systems analyst for the whirlwind world of event planning. As she builds up her fledging business, she learns that her widowed mother has news of her own—a serious gentleman caller! Is Keira ready for mom's new romance?

When she gets a game-changing opportunity to organize a major event on a luxury Caribbean cruise, Keira turns to best pal chef Alexandria D'Agostino to help recruit famous chefs who will offer classes for foodies looking for fun in the sun as they gain cooking know-how. The cruise becomes a rollicking adventure for Keira, her sassy assistant Juliet, the entire D'Agostino clan, Keira's mother and other surprise guests. And has Keira meet her match in charismatic Cruise Director Brennan McCallister, who could have something more than keeping everything shipshape on his mind?

Filled with wit, charm, and a few recipes along the way, *Love on the Lido Deck* brings characters to life with laugh-out-loud situations, crisp dialog and sweet romance on the high seas.

Available on Amazon, BarnesandNoble.com, iTunes/iBookstore and wherever fine books are sold

ABOUT THE AUTHOR

Award-Winning author Barbara Oliverio applies her writing skills to both fiction and non-fiction and is a public speaker and retreat facilitator. She and her husband have well-worn passports with many stamps. This is her third novel.

For bulk sales or author appearance, contact
Barbara@scolapastapress.com
www.scolapastapress.com

Like: facebook.com/AuthorBarbaraOliverio
Follow: twitter.com/@BOliverioAuthor